PLANE JUSTICE

H.C. Hannah

ISBN: 9781548065300

Team One, this is for you. You know who you are...

CHAPTER ONE

August 2000

There was a solemn hush in the courtroom as the sealed note containing the verdict was passed from the jury foreman to Judge Halliday. The judge carefully unfolded the single sheet of paper, adjusted his glasses and took a moment to examine the words written in front of him. He handed the note to the court clerk, who in turn handed it back to the foreman of the jury. The judge leaned closer to the microphone.

'Please read your verdict to the court.'

The foreman of the jury spoke slowly and deliberately.

'On both counts of murder, we, the jury, find Graymond Sharkey guilty as charged.'

The convicted man stood next to his lawyer, a faraway, dazed expression on his face. It was almost emotionless; a look that even the most experienced criminal psychologist would find difficult to read. It showed neither innocence nor guilt. His lawyer, in a dark, pinstriped suit straight out of Savile Row, nodded once, gravely, perhaps resignedly, with little show of surprise. He glanced at his client who did not respond, and then at the jury with another nod, this time of thanks, acknowledgment, to a group of twelve loyal citizens who had fulfilled their duty of upholding justice, unanimously agreeing on a fitting verdict for a guilty defendant in an open and shut murder case.

The elderly lady in the second row of the spectators' gallery dabbed her eyes with a tissue and brought a hand up to her mouth to suppress a sob. Her cheeks were red and blotchy in the harsh, fluorescent light of the courtroom. The elderly man sitting next to her gently patted her arm. The girl with the long, dark hair tied back in a ponytail placed her pencil on her notebook and frowned slightly, with a puzzled expression. She had occupied the same seat in the back row for the duration of the trial, reeling off copious pages of shorthand in the manner of a rookie journalist, desperate for a breakthrough story. For a brief moment, her eyes met the eyes of a young man in his twenties, seated on the other side of the courtroom. He wore a navy baseball cap, pulled down low, obscuring much of his face. He instantly looked away, but the memory of that fleeting moment would remain with the young journalist for a long time. There was no doubt about it; it was the look of sheer and utter relief.

CHAPTER TWO

October 2016

Graymond Sharkey scrawled an illegible signature on the release papers. He was a free man. Theoretically, he was released on licence, which would remain in force for the rest of his life, but the release licence contained no conditions and, as far as Graymond Sharkey was concerned, a life outside prison walls meant freedom. He slid the documents across the counter to an unsmiling desk clerk and picked up a small suitcase. Stepping onto the street outside, he looked around, slightly disorientated. It was a warm October day. The hazy light of the late afternoon sun splashed golden rays across the leaf-strewn pavement. The noise of a siren overlaid the sound of early rush hour traffic. Commuters and tourists hurried past Graymond, ignoring him, as he stood motionless and bewildered. His newfound liberty had not yet sunk in. Seventeen years in prison had felt like a lifetime — it had been a life sentence, after all — but now it felt as though it had been no time at all. And he was finally free, just an ordinary member of society with the rest of his life to live as he chose.

Graymond stepped forward decisively and hailed a cab.

'Liverpool Street Station,' he muttered through the passenger window, before opening the rear door and sliding into a seat, placing his suitcase between his knees. The driver nodded and pulled away from the kerb into the stream of traffic. Graymond gazed out of the window as they passed familiar buildings and iconic landmarks of the City. Most of these places were just as they had been seventeen years ago, although a considerable amount of new construction work appeared to be taking place. He saw the cab driver glance at him in the rear view mirror.

'How's your day?'

'Fine,' Graymond replied shortly. He wasn't in the mood for talking.

'You here in the City for business?'

'No.'

'Pleasure?'

'Neither,' Graymond said through gritted teeth.

'Visiting friends? Family?'

Graymond scowled.

'I don't have any of those,' he said sharply, 'and I'm not here for a chat.'

The cab driver looked back at him with a mixture of interest and pity.

'We've all got somebody,' he said, ignoring Graymond's allusion to riding in silence.

'Well, I haven't,' Graymond snapped, 'not any more. And I said I don't want to chat.'

'No problem sir,' the cab driver replied. They sped through the streets of London, the cab driver minding his own business and Graymond staring out of the window with interest but little emotion. Suddenly, the voice from the front spoke again.

'If you don't mind me asking you sir, how is it that you don't have anybody?'

Graymond scowled and hesitated for a moment. He hadn't rehearsed any conversations like this with the prison counsellor, and was ill-prepared with answers to such questions. In addition, he had said he didn't want to chat; weren't London cab drivers supposed to button it up if the passenger didn't want to speak? What was this driver's problem? Graymond decided if a polite request wouldn't work, he'd frighten the cabbie into silence.

'Why don't I have anyone? Death and betrayal,' he replied coldly and slightly dramatically.

Reggie the cab driver had many unusual conversations with his passengers. In fact, he thrived on challenging discussions, particularly with controversial topics such as politics, religion, philosophy, fate and destiny. He was always ready to engage with a comment, but at this moment he wasn't sure he had one. Perhaps it would be better to leave this unpleasant man to his own sour thoughts after all. There was silence for a moment, before Graymond spoke again.

'I was released from prison today.' He paused. 'I was inside for seventeen years. A life sentence. They've let me out on licence for good behaviour or something.'

'What were you in for?' If Reggie was alarmed by Graymond's statement, his voice never gave it away.

'Murder.'

'Okay.' Reggie wasn't shocked. He glanced nonchalantly away from the rear view, as if he drove murderers around the City every day of his life. The scare tactics hadn't appeared to work, but suddenly Graymond felt the urge to continue.

'I'm not guilty though. Never was. I'm an innocent man.'

'Right,' Reggie was nodding. No disagreement here, sir.

'I might have been guilty of theft,' Graymond's gaze shifted from the window to the front of the cab. 'But I sure as hell didn't murder anyone.'

'Who did then?' Reggie spoke before he had time to check himself.

'I don't know,' Graymond replied pensively. 'But I'm going to find out.'

'Seventeen years is a long time,' Reggie volunteered. 'Things change. People change.'

'But the truth doesn't.' Graymond spoke with a determined expression. 'The truth never changes.'

Liverpool Street Station was suddenly ahead of them.

'Here we are then sir,' Reggie said, slowing the cab to a stop at the side of the kerb. Graymond leaned forward and slid Reggie some cash. He added a modest tip, although he wasn't sure what the going rate was these days and the driver hadn't exactly acceded to his request for some quiet anyway. In fact, he was lucky to have received any tip at all, Graymond thought curtly.

'Thank you sir,' Reggie pressed one of the rubber buttons on his meter. As Graymond climbed out of the cab, pulling his suitcase behind him, Reggie wound down his window.

'I hope you find it.'

'What?'

'The truth.'

'I will,' Graymond replied, before he disappeared anonymously into the crowd in front of the station entrance. The truth was something Graymond had dreamed about every night for the last seventeen years of his life. And now it was time for the truth to finally be discovered. Except Graymond had work to do. He wasn't exactly certain of what the truth was. Sure, he'd been there that fateful night. It was a night that he'd tried so hard to leave behind, and then so hard to recall in order to piece together the events as they had occurred. But he only had half the jigsaw puzzle. He wasn't sure who had the other half, or even what the picture looked like on the other half. The only thing Graymond knew for sure was that a murderer had gone free that night, while Graymond had paid the awful price for a crime he hadn't committed.

****

11:45 p.m.
August 14, 1999

Jimmy the pilot executed a well-practiced glide approach onto the dimly lit runway of Blackdeane Airfield. The Cessna 172 Skyhawk aircraft kissed the tarmac and slowed to a running pace in order to vacate the runway onto taxiway Delta, its white strobe lights intermittently glowing and fading. It was a perfect landing, but then it had to be; aboard the utility aircraft was over two hundred million dollars' worth of stolen artwork from stately homes across Europe, carefully packaged and stashed in large duffel bags. The glide approach, without any engine power, was for noise reduction purposes, not that there were many houses within earshot. The airfield was located in a remote part of the Essex countryside, but due to the nature of the flight that evening, Jimmy and his accomplices didn't need any complaints or uninvited intruders.

'Am I cleared to taxi to the apron?' Jimmy's voice crackled over the speaker in the air traffic control tower.

'All clear. Come on over,' Rory, the headset-clad air traffic controller replied, staring through the darkness at the faint strobes of the Cessna on the

far end of the runway, like sequins sparkling on a backdrop of indigo velvet. The night was warm and humid, and Rory downed the last of his Evian as he glanced across at the third member of the trio, who was also the brains and money behind the artwork smuggling venture. His name was Graymond Sharkey.

'Looks like pay day's come early,' Rory grinned broadly.

Graymond smiled back, a little more reservedly. The twenty-three year old had risen to riches and power early in his young life, thanks in part to a series of lucky breaks and fortuitous events, as well as a savvy head for business and a compulsive work ethic. Graymond owned Blackdeane Airfield, along with the private jet charter service which was based there. The airfield was also home to a thriving private pilot training school and accompanying general aviation activity, with a smart clubhouse, restaurant and bar, which was frequented by members of the local community, as well as pilots and crew members. Graymond oversaw all of this with the assistance of his highly efficient airfield manager Caroline Stevens, his senior air traffic control officer Rory Conway and his chief pilot Jimmy Keyes. The last four years had seen Graymond's business go from strength to strength, in particular the jet charter service, which ferried VIPs in luxury across the United Kingdom, Europe and the United States. It was called GS Executive Aviation Ltd., GS being Graymond Sharkey's initials, although Graymond was happy if the GS was mistaken for Gulfstream, the manufacturer of some of the world's most luxurious business jets.

'Do you realise how rich we're all going to be, Gray?' The young air traffic controller's eyes were gleaming in the reflection of the tinted glass of the control tower windows.

'Very,' Graymond replied, a little distracted. 'Why has Jimmy stopped?'

Rory leaned forward in his chair.

'Probably doing after-landing checks.'

'But he's still on the runway.' Graymond narrowed his eyes in an attempt to improve his night vision. He only had a few flying hours in his pilot's logbook; his hectic business schedule did not allow for many more at this time, but he knew that an aircraft should vacate the runway before the after-landing checks were completed, even one that was containing hundreds of millions of dollars' worth of stolen artwork.

CHAPTER THREE

Graymond Sharkey had always conducted his business affairs with scrupulous honesty. He was well spoken and well educated with impeccable manners, and operated at the highest levels of probity and integrity. The summer before, however, a few things changed for Graymond. On the outside, he still appeared to be the same man, but on the inside, he wasn't sure who he was anymore. A series of events had led him to question his values and beliefs and the man he really was. At the beginning of 1998, he had lost his father to a sudden heart attack. A few weeks later, his brother was killed in a skiing accident. Shortly after that, his mother died instantly in a motorway pileup. And then he'd found his longtime and only girlfriend Julia in bed with another man. On the outside, Graymond seemed to take it all in his stride, much to the admiration of his extended family members, friends and co-workers. He threw himself even more into his business, working eighteen-hour days, seven days a week. He kept up appearances whenever and wherever required, and remained the respected, successful businessman that everyone held in high regard.

On the inside, Graymond wasn't sure how to keep it together. He hadn't allowed himself to grieve the loss of his individual family members, and now they were buried and gone, and life had moved on, but Graymond hadn't; he was merely in denial of the feelings that he should have faced up to and dealt with. Graymond was also devastated by his discovery of Julia's affair with Reese Coraini, one of the pilots who flew a light aircraft regularly from Blackdeane. Reese's membership was swiftly terminated and his Piper Cherokee removed from one of the hangars at Blackdeane. A broken man, Graymond felt angry at how life had treated him. He didn't believe in luck, but in six months he had had the very worst of it.

Graymond's work brought with it an occasional trip to London, sometimes to meet with his accountant or solicitor, or occasionally business contacts and potential clients. Before the summer of 1998, Graymond would be on the first train out of town as soon as his business was complete; he rarely stayed overnight, he didn't much like the bright lights of a big city. But this year was different; what was there to rush back home for? Just an empty house to immerse himself in his heartbreak and sorrow and broken dreams. Oliver Jacobs, his accountant, who was rapidly working his way to the top of one of London's most prestigious financial institutions, detected a cry for help from Graymond, and took it upon himself to show his client a good time, on his client's credit card, naturally.

And so Graymond was introduced to fine wining, dining and women, top shelf champagne, VIP suites and more women. He had soon purchased his own penthouse apartment in Mayfair with a price tag as spectacular as the view. When Graymond wasn't working eighteen-hour days in his modest office at Blackdeane, he was working his way around an exclusive party circuit in the City. But the deep hurt and disappointment of the past few months continued to gnaw away at Graymond. He hardly slept and alcohol was his new best friend. It was the only way to ease the torment and the pain of a young life torn to pieces with grief and sadness and tragic loss. In addition, Graymond became bored with the monotonous, everyday routine of his business. Having achieved financial success so early in life, he began searching for the next big risk.

It was in November 1998 that Oliver introduced Graymond to Tobias Anneijes, a Dutch businessman.

'Someone you should meet,' Oliver had said. 'It'll be an exciting little business venture.'

Tobias had a proposal for Graymond. He claimed to be a dealer of high-end artwork for millionaire clients and stately homes across the United Kingdom and Western Europe. He needed a discreet courier service and access to piloted aircraft, to ferry the artwork across the continent from one place to another. He would pay handsomely for the service. A deal was struck between the two men and the work came in, along with swift payment for every job. Graymond never questioned the nature of each job, but after some time, he began to have his suspicions. He had nothing in concrete, no tangible proof, just an uneasy feeling that things were not as they seemed. As far as he had fallen, he knew this was not how he wanted to do business and so he approached Tobias.

'You're in too deep now, Sharkey,' Tobias had replied. 'You know too much. You're too involved. It's too late to get out now. There will be consequences if you do.'

Graymond's worst fears were confirmed. Late one night, alone in a bar in Soho accompanied by a double whisky on the rocks and the barman, Graymond considered the man he once was and confronted the man he had become. Tobias's words played in his mind, like a song played on the radio that he couldn't get out of his head. 'You're in too deep now, Sharkey. There will be consequences...'

'In that case, what's to stop me going in all the way?' Graymond thought out loud.

The barman, cleaning the surface of the bar with a cloth, glanced at him.

'Business,' Graymond slurred. 'What's the point of being honest when the rest of them are corrupt? Why should I play all my cards fairly?'

The barman stopped cleaning momentarily.

'Because it's always easier to maintain your integrity than to try and recover it afterwards.'

'What?' Graymond frowned. He downed the dregs of his whisky, the ice cubes rattling in the bottom of the glass.

'Sure, it might cost you to do the right thing in the first place,' the barman continued, 'but it'll cost you a whole lot more if you abandon your principles and do the wrong thing.'

Graymond swore and the barman went back to the surface cleaning with a shrug. 'Get me another whisky,' Graymond snarled. His mind was made up. Tomorrow, when he was sober, he would approach Tobias with a business proposition. He wasn't going to be a mere courier any longer; he wanted an integral role in the organisation that Tobias was a part of. Whatever it took, Graymond Sharkey was in, one hundred per cent. And so it was, thanks to some introductions courtesy of Tobias, that Graymond's career of moving millions of dollars of stolen artwork around the world began. The cut of the proceeds was lucrative, and it didn't take much persuading to lure Rory and Jimmy into the game. By day, the trio put in an honest few hours' work at Blackdeane Airfield; it was a convenient little cover story. By night, they couriered stolen artwork from one dealer to another. It was just the three of them, and they were sworn to secrecy as if their lives depended on it.

CHAPTER FOUR

The night of August 14, 1999, was their biggest job yet. That afternoon, Jimmy had flown the club-owned Cessna to Alderney, one of the Channel Islands, to collect the stolen pieces of artwork, listed by customs as "soft furnishings". The art had previously been flown in from a private airstrip somewhere in France. In the failing light of the humid August evening, the Cessna had taken off from the cliff-top runway of Alderney, destined for Blackdeane, in Essex. The journey time would be just over an hour, and for a generous pay-off, Graymond's inside man at the UK Border Agency would be turning a blind eye to the late arrival of a private aircraft from non-UK shores.

Rory and Graymond sat in the control tower at Blackdeane. The airfield was deserted and under cover of darkness. It was a still, clear night, perfect for flying. To the north, the stars twinkled brightly against a midnight blue sky; to the south, there was a distinctive copper glow from the light pollution of London. Rory and Graymond were alone at the airfield, the last of the employees having left a couple of hours before. They both wore headsets and were on frequency, eagerly awaiting Jimmy's radio call informing them he was in the vicinity of the airfield, Rory's cue to switch on the runway lights in preparation for the landing. A Ford Ranger truck was parked immediately outside the clubhouse and next to the apron, ready for the artwork to be loaded into the back from the Cessna. Graymond would drive it to his house and in the early hours of the following morning, to an abandoned warehouse somewhere in north London.

'What will you do with your share of the money, Gray?' Rory asked.

'Not sure,' Graymond replied. 'You?'

'Thought I'd get myself a brand new BMW, then I'll treat Sarah and me to a fortnight in Barbados while I decide what to do with the rest of it.' Sarah was Rory's latest soul mate and fiancee number three. Rory had it all worked out.

'Nice,' Graymond remarked casually. It was over a year ago since Julia had cheated on him, and despite the many glamorous women Graymond had had the pleasure of spending time with over the last few months, he still couldn't

bring himself to shelve the feelings he had for Julia. And as for the money, he found little excitement in the thought of spending it, if he had nobody to share it with. Sure, he'd be a rich man, but only in material terms.

As the 16:35 train pulled out of Liverpool Street Station, bound for Essex and then beyond, the ex-prisoner took a sip of freshly ground coffee that he had purchased from the buffet car and studied the scenery of the outside world as he settled into his window seat for the journey home. He took notice of every building, every street, every sign posted along the track advertising storage, health clubs and newly constructed apartments with the enticing wording "If you lived here, you'd be home by now". As the City landscape merged into green fields, Graymond marvelled at the countryside as it sped past in a blur. He admired the trees, the gently undulating terrain; he felt as though he couldn't take in enough of the sights and scenery that for seventeen years inside a concrete compound had been only memories and dreams. Graymond promised himself he would never again take for granted the simple beauties of a sunrise, a sunset, or a rainbow.

He was homeward-bound. Except Graymond wasn't sure what home was any more. Home, as he knew it for the last seventeen years, had been a cell inside a perimeter of concrete prison walls. In a distant memory, in a different world, Graymond remembered home as a happy, joyful place, where he was loved and wanted and needed. Home was where his mother and father had doted on him as their youngest son, of whom they were immensely proud. Back then, he and his elder brother spent lazy summer days biking to a local airfield where they would employ hours watching light aircraft taking off and landing. In those innocent days of his teenage years, Graymond had no inclination that he would one day become the sole owner of this airfield, and that one day it would lead to a life sentence for a murder conviction. Back then, Graymond was just an adventurous young man from a privileged home, with the world at his feet and a lifetime of promise ahead of him.

Graymond wondered what had become of his beloved airfield that had fallen so far from grace since that tragic night in the summer of 1999. Mrs Davidson, the ageing cleaning lady of the Sharkey family home during Graymond's boyhood, had kept in touch with him on and off during his seventeen years inside — she had always had a soft spot for him and had always refused to believe that he was guilty — and in her most recent correspondence, had informed Graymond that Blackdeane Airfield had begun to look tired and run down due to poor maintenance and poor management. The same had apparently applied to Graymond's beautiful home. Paul Greene, a cousin, had been given power of attorney and had been entrusted with the upkeep and running of Graymond's business and estate until his release, with more than adequate funding as required. But Paul had only really been interested in the money he was being paid to do this, and far less so in renting out Graymond's home and overseeing airfield operations.

During the last few months, in the run-up to his release from prison, the tenancy had come to an end for the couple renting Graymond's home and Paul had tied up a few loose ends here and there in preparation for Graymond's home-coming. Few people knew or cared about the exact time and date of this inconsequential event, which suited Graymond. Mrs Davidson had stewardship of the keys to his house, but the former Sharkey family cleaner was out when he arrived to collect them, instead leaving a note to say they had been placed under a flowerpot in the adjoining garage. Graymond was almost relieved that she had not been home; he hadn't been sure how he would face her after all these years and now he had been spared the encounter. Tonight, at least. Perhaps she had planned it that way.

Graymond picked up his suitcase once more, and turned out of Mrs Davidson's gate into the lane. His house was less than two miles away and he had waved away the cab driver who had picked him up from the station, choosing to walk the last part of the journey. There was a chill in the air now as the pale autumn sun slid below the horizon and darkness began to creep slowly across the landscape. It was a clear night, just as it had been seventeen years ago, the only light from a silver-grey moon veiled behind a thin layer of cloud. Graymond's route took him alongside the perimeter of Blackdeane Airfield. The runway, control tower and clubhouse stood in shadow and silence, a far cry from the activity and busyness of the place Graymond had once known and loved so much. Through the blackness, he could just make out a few pale outlines of aircraft parked nearby, ghostly shapes against the darkened framework of the hangars behind. The place seemed to have a neglected, unkempt feel about it; grass that had once been immaculately cut now resembled a nettle-strewn meadow, the gleaming windows of the maintenance workshop were grimy, with paint peeling on the frames. The airfield looked all but abandoned.

Graymond placed his suitcase on the ground beside him and leaned against the rotting wooden perimeter fence. He gazed across to the far end of the runway, where the Cessna had come to a stop, but was not turning onto the taxiway as instructed. Graymond recalled the overwhelming feeling he had had that night in 1999 that something was wrong.

'Rory, get Jimmy on the radio and ask him why he's stopped.' Graymond ordered, snatching up a pair of binoculars and training them on the stationary aircraft at the far end of the runway.

'Calm down, Gray,' Rory replied, placing a hand on his friend's shoulder. 'There's no need to be so uptight, everything's fine.'

'Just do it, Rory,' Graymond insisted. 'Something's wrong.'

'Whatever.' Rory shrugged and picked up the microphone. 'Hey Jimmy, what's taking you so long? Get a move on with those after-landing checks.'

They waited for a reply. None came. Rory glanced over at Graymond who still held the binoculars to his eyes.

'See anything?' Rory asked, uneasily.

'Nothing,' Graymond replied. 'It's too dark.' There was silence for a moment.

'Try the radio again,' Graymond suggested.

'Golf Alpha Kilo, radio check.' Rory used the call sign of the aircraft this time. There was no reply. Graymond placed the binoculars down on the desk and pulled off his headset.

I'm going out there,'

'Gray, wait,' Rory said anxiously.

'We've waited enough,' Graymond replied grimly. 'Something's wrong; I don't know what it is, but I need to get to that aircraft now.' He picked up the keys to the Ford Ranger and headed for the door.

'Be careful, Gray,' Rory called after him. They were the last words Rory would ever say to him.

Graymond walked further along the perimeter fence, breathing in the cool night air. An owl hooted in the distance and something rustled in the grass near his feet, perhaps a rabbit or fox foraging for food. There was an eerie hush over the airfield. It was like a ghost town holding all its forgotten secrets of the past, reluctant to relinquish them after seventeen years of concealment. Almost forgotten, thought Graymond, but not quite. Someone, somewhere knew what those secrets were. He glanced across to the end of the runway again. Someone, somewhere…

The Ford Ranger sped along taxiway Delta towards the stationary Cessna with its strobe light still glowing intermittently in the darkness. Taxiway Delta was the shortest route to the end of the runway from the control tower. As Graymond approached the aircraft, the headlights of the truck shone directly into the cockpit and onto the pilot. Graymond's stomach lurched as he looked in horror at the sight in front of him. He brought the Ford to a rapid stop and leaped out. The propeller was still spinning and the aircraft engine was still running. He ran across the tarmac, his heart thumping inside his chest. Slumped half across the passenger seat of the cockpit was Jimmy. He was covered in blood.

Graymond yanked the passenger door of the aircraft open and climbed into the cockpit. Jimmy's blood was everywhere, spattered across the seats and the controls. Graymond gently lifted Jimmy's head, supporting it in his hands and, in the dim light, saw his neck and chest had been violently slashed with deep stab wounds.

'Jimmy,' Graymond shouted his friend's name hoarsely above the noise of the aircraft engine. He looked around in panic, unsure of what to do. Jimmy's eyelids flickered and for a moment his eyes opened and looked directly at Graymond. His lips parted, as if to speak.

19

Jimmy,' Graymond said again, desperately. 'What happened? Who did this to you?' Jimmy opened his mouth again.

'Gray... help me,' he said, weakly.

'Jimmy, talk to me. What happened?'

Jimmy's eyes closed and his head rolled backwards onto the seat, a trickle of blood dribbled out of his mouth and slowly down the side of his chin. Graymond tilted Jimmy's head forwards again.

'Jimmy, stay with me,' he cried frantically. 'I'll get help, I'll...'

Graymond snatched the headset off Jimmy's head and put it on his own. He pressed the push-to-talk button on the control yoke of the Cessna.

'Rory, it's Gray. Jimmy's been stabbed. Call 999. Rory, do you copy?'

Graymond waited impatiently for Rory's reply. He lifted Jimmy's head off the seat again, but this time there was no response from his friend.

'Jimmy, stay with me,' he screamed. He put a bloodied hand to his forehead in despair and looked across towards the control tower. Where was Rory? He transmitted again.

'Rory, answer me, dammit.'

Silence. Jimmy's lifeless body slumped further down the seat beside him. In desperation, Graymond pulled the pilot's shoulders upright and gently leaned him against the opposite window before positioning himself in the passenger seat. He slammed the aircraft door shut, released the park brake and opened the throttle. With his hands shaking as he gripped the controls, he rapidly turned the Cessna ninety degrees towards taxiway Delta. Suddenly, there was a loud thud and the aircraft lurched violently to the left. He turned to look past Jimmy out of the window; one of the wing tips of the Cessna had struck the top of the cab of the Ford Ranger. The wing was dented and the windscreen of the truck was shattered, the frame twisted and bent inwards. Graymond swore under his breath and slammed the throttle open. With a roar of the engine, the aircraft jerked forwards and Graymond briefly closed his eyes at the sound of metal against metal and glass as the wing of the Cessna slashed through the cab of the truck. Graymond kept the aircraft moving and taxied as fast as he dare to the apron. He had only the dim light of the control tower to guide him. As he approached, he looked up earnestly for Rory, but could see no one through the tinted glass.

Graymond brought the Cessna to a rapid halt on the apron and shut the aircraft down. Forgetting the multimillion dollar cargo of stolen artwork he was *supposed to be unloading, he pulled off his headset, jumped out of the aircraft and ran to the pilot's side where he opened the door, half carrying, half dragging Jimmy's body onto the tarmac, smearing a trail of blood behind them. He felt for a carotid pulse, moving his fingers back and forth on Jimmy's neck in a desperate attempt to locate it. He thought he felt something: a weak, thready beat perhaps. Graymond was shaking. Sweat mixed with blood was trickling down the sides of his face.*

'RORY,' he yelled up at the control tower. He closed his eyes. When he opened them again, Jimmy was still lying there, motionless, in front of him. It would be futile to start chest compressions until he was sure help was on the way. Leaving Jimmy on the tarmac, he ran inside the clubhouse and up the stairs, two at a time. He burst into the control room, gasping for breath. Approaching the high-backed chair that Rory had been sitting in, overlooking the runway, he spun it round to face him.

'Rory, call nine…' he began, but his voice tailed off rapidly as he stood, staring, aghast at what was in front of him. Rory's body was slumped in the chair, covered in blood. He had been viciously hacked to death, with even greater ferocity than Jimmy. As Graymond looked around him, stunned, his eye caught something on the control desk beside Rory. It was one of his own kitchen knives. He went to pick it up, but then stopped himself from touching the bloodied weapon, momentarily suspending his hand in midair. He was breathing heavily, still recovering from hauling Jimmy's body out of the aircraft and running up the stairs to the control tower.

CHAPTER FIVE

Graymond stood motionless, engulfed in the horror of the scene before him. He felt numb and in shock. In the eerie silence he turned his gaze outside the tower into the blackness of the night. He blinked a few times and fumbled for the counter top to steady himself. He looked dazedly across the airfield, scanning the runway and the taxiways, and the apron immediately below. He wasn't certain of what he was looking for. Surely he should make a run for it? His life could be in danger too, couldn't it? And what about the stolen artwork? But Graymond wasn't the hardened criminal he aspired to be. His two friends lay stabbed to death and dying a few feet away from him and he wasn't about to leave them.

Suddenly, he heard the harsh, unmistakable whine of sirens. Leaving a trail of bloodied footsteps behind him, he straightened up and stepped out of the control tower to the rear corridor, where a window overlooked the service road leading to the airfield. Two police cars, with flashing blue and red lights hurtled along it, screeching to a halt in the carpark next to the darkened clubhouse. Doors opened from all sides and police officers leaped out and began running to the control tower.

Graymond felt a surge of panic as he watched, unsure of what to do. There was nowhere to run and hiding was futile; they would find him. How did the police get here so fast? How did they know to get here at all? Graymond stepped back into the control room as hurried footsteps approached; back into the control room where his dead friend slumped grotesquely in a chair and where the knife from Graymond's own kitchen lay on the side, covered in the blood of his murdered companion. As four police officers entered the control room, a flushed, guilt-ridden, blood-spattered Graymond Sharkey slowly lifted his head and looked them in the eyes.

The rustling in the grass stopped momentarily. Perhaps the rabbit or fox had detected the presence of an unwelcome guest and was cautiously eyeing the intruder through fronds of wild bracken and grass. The moon emerged from behind the silvery ribbons of cloud, its stark reflection catching the mirrored windows of the control tower and Graymond stood still, mesmerised as he recalled the final, awful events of that night. The closing scene had tortured Graymond for the last seventeen years; in his prison cell he had lay awake at night reliving every detail; in the consulting room of the prison psychiatrist he had broken down into a sobbing wreck of a man. And now, as he stood so close to where it had all begun, his mind took him back to where it had all ended.

As three of the police officers approached Graymond, the fourth ran to Rory to check for signs of life. He found none, shook his head and at that moment glanced up and out of the control tower window where Graymond had parked the Cessna on the apron below. His eye caught something else.

'We've got another man down out there,' he said looking round at the other officers with a note of urgency in his voice. 'He's stabbed, wounded, just lying there, looks like there's blood everywhere.'

'Kev, Get Tango Four out on the tarmac and call the paramedics,' barked another officer who appeared to have some kind of authority. Graymond felt his arms pulled roughly behind his back and his wrists were handcuffed. Kevin, the fourth officer, had turned away from the window and was speaking into a radio clipped to his jacket.

Suddenly there was a bright flash of light and the loud bang of an explosion, followed by the sound of shattering glass. The control tower floor shook and the whole room was lit up as a ball of flames engulfed the Cessna below. Graymond felt the intense heat from the blast as the control tower windows were blown inwards with the force of the explosion. Covered in shards of glass and debris, Graymond was dragged to the ground by two of the officers amidst a cloud of dust and smoke.

'Jimmy — NO!' Graymond screamed, coughing. He tried to wrestle himself free from the police officers who pushed him back down onto the ground.

'We have to get down there. My friend's out there, lying next to the aircraft, he's badly wounded,' Graymond shouted through the cacophony of noise of rubble settling and more smaller explosions. More sirens wailed in the distance.

'Shut up!' an officer close to him shouted.

'But we have to get down there,' Graymond screamed. 'Jimmy needs help. He was right there, next to the aircraft. He's been stabbed.' His last few words were drowned by another, louder explosion. The acrid smell of burning filled the air and Graymond's eyes watered and stung with the thick smoke pouring into the control room.

He looked up briefly and through a cloud of debris caught the bloodied outline of Rory slumped in the controller's chair, covered with grey dust and shattered glass. The force of the blast had blown the chair and Rory further across the room. Graymond closed his eyes and shielded his face with the ground as a new wave of heat and flames from the furiously burning Cessna could be felt from outside. Graymond suspected the latest explosion was one of the fuel tanks. He knew there was no hope for Jimmy. He would never have survived the blasts. His two friends were dead and there was nothing he could do.

Graymond blinked and turned away from the airfield. He had promised himself he would move on. He had sworn to draw a line under the past and forget it. A free man, he had planned to start this new chapter without the torment of guilt and nightmares. Yet he had been out of prison for less than twenty-four hours and here he was, back at the airfield, reliving every sight, sound, and emotion of that night as if it were only yesterday. Perhaps it was a mistake to return home to Blackdeane. Maybe he should move somewhere a million miles from here. He had the means to relocate to wherever he chose; a simple log cabin overlooking Loch Lomond, an opulent Tuscan villa, a luxury apartment in Monaco. But Graymond knew, deep down, the only thing that would bring an end to the dreams which haunted him day and night, was the truth.

Picking up his suitcase, he looked straight ahead towards the end of the tree-lined lane, which disappeared into a mysterious, shadowy tunnel of overhanging branches. It felt strange to be back for the first time in seventeen years. At least, he thought it felt strange, but Graymond wasn't exactly sure of how he felt. Perhaps his emotions had been hardened by the harshness of prison life. Or maybe it was having to deal with the injustices of a life sentence for two murders that he hadn't committed. Sure, to the average member of the public reading about Graymond's conviction in a newspaper over morning coffee, or to the police officers who had been alerted to the airfield by an anonymous caller that night, or to the jury who had been presented with the undeniable facts, it was an open and shut case. Graymond's fingerprints had been all over the kitchen knife which was forensically proven to have been the murder weapon of both his Chief Pilot and Senior Air Traffic Controller. Both the murdered victims' blood had been found on Graymond and his knife and he was the only other person noted to have been present at the airfield that night.

Graymond had had the opportunity, the means, and without the shadow of a doubt, the motive. Why split the proceeds of millions of dollars' worth of stolen artwork into three, when the entire haul could be kept for himself? He had, after all, been the mastermind behind the whole operation, the one with the contacts and the connections. Jimmy and Rory had been drafted in as hired helpers, yet Graymond had promised them equal shares in the proceeds. It was a shocking amount of money to have to pay out and the jury decided that it would most certainly be a fantastic motive to kill for. Graymond's generosity and loyalty to his friends had only served to make a disastrous situation a whole lot worse. Yet Graymond knew he was innocent of the crimes. Each time he replayed the events of the night of August 14 over in his mind, the many unanswered questions culminated in two main thoughts: first, why didn't he get the hell out of there instead of stick around trying to help his friends; secondly, and more puzzling, *who else was there that night?*

Graymond accepted that he may never know the answer to the first question, but the second gave him sleepless nights and daydreams that ran off at a tangent. As he walked wearily along the lane, another sound startled him: a rustling in the undergrowth on the other side of the fence in the long grass surrounding the airfield. Graymond stopped and listened. The rustling had also stopped. Perhaps it was another midnight animal on a nocturnal hunting escapade, but it had sounded heavier and more deliberate than the earlier sounds.

You're being paranoid Sharkey, Graymond reprimanded himself. You've spent the last seventeen years in a concrete prison; you've forgotten the sounds of the countryside. He pulled his jacket closer round him in the chill of the night, and set off with a purposeful stride. As he emerged from the tunnel of overhanging tree branches, the silvery moon appeared once more from behind a cloud, illuminating a grand, Tudor-style house which stood back from the road behind a forbidding set of wrought iron gates and two six-foot high copper beech hedges running parallel to each other. The place stood in darkness as Graymond set his eyes on his home, Blackdeane House, for the first time in seventeen years.

CHAPTER SIX

Four weeks had passed since Graymond Sharkey's release from prison and return home. He had mostly kept himself to himself, partly through choice in that he wasn't sure how well-received his presence in the community would be and partly through the busyness of integrating into an everyday normal life. Graymond didn't miss prison life, but he did miss the familiarity of a world and an existence that he knew. Grim as it had been, it had had a sense of routine and belonging. Establishing a routine was something Graymond knew he could work out over time, but he wasn't sure if he would ever feel as though he truly belonged here again.

Although Graymond's reputation had been shattered, his personal finances had remained secure. With the exception of the regular outgoings for the number of properties that Graymond owned, the airfield and Paul's attorney's fee, the rest of his money remained untouched, accumulating interest, due to the restricted access to his bank accounts while in prison. It was thus that on his release, although Graymond found himself lacking in many things, money was not one of them. At least he could be rich and lonely, he reminded himself gratefully, although he longed to have a job again, a role in society, a status, goals to reach, deadlines to fulfil.

Graymond had been a workaholic suddenly plunged into a life with no meaning or direction. And now things had come full circle; he had been preparing himself for a new life of freedom for months, but now he was living this life, it was difficult to grasp and take in. He knew he needed to give himself time to readjust, but Graymond was impatient. He knew things would never be as they had been, before the night of August 14; indeed, Graymond had never been one to look backwards, preferring always to move forwards towards the next challenge, but sometimes the past felt inescapable, as if its bitter, remorseless clutches would never quite let go.

Graymond had decided to steer clear of the airfield for now. He had a meeting set with Paul in a few days' time with an agenda to discuss items of business in detail, but as far as Graymond could tell, Mrs Davidson had been right; Paul had made an excellent job of running both Blackdeane Airfield and GS Executive Aviation Ltd. into the ground. With GS Executive Aviation being a limited company, Graymond himself had not been affected financially. However, he felt sad and disappointed that the business hadn't continued with the flourishing success it had once known. Paul had neither the brains, the integrity, nor the work ethic of Graymond. Following in the footsteps of the young entrepreneur had been fruitless for a man who preferred to spend his Saturday afternoons in front of the television with a takeaway and a six pack of beer, rather than putting in overtime at the office.

Graymond had read as widely as he could whilst in prison and had devoured whatever books and up to date news he could get his hands on in order to remain in touch with the outside world. During his time inside, Graymond had watched the prison television in horror as two airliners flew into the twin towers of the World Trade Centre on September 11, 2001, changing the airline industry forever. In January of the following year, he had been fascinated to observe the introduction of the new euro currency, by the European Union.

Although not available to inmates, in 2004 Graymond was intrigued to read of a social networking site on the Internet called Facebook. He took a great interest in technology and, with the many developments taking place, in his mind he regularly updated the web page design of GS Executive Aviation Ltd. On Boxing Day of that year, Graymond was finishing up the last of the Christmas leftovers in the prison recreation room while watching a report of a devastating tsunami, which hit Indonesia and many surrounding countries, resulting from the second largest recorded earthquake in history in the Indian Ocean.

The following July, Graymond read of the coordinated suicide bomb attacks in Central London on the Underground and a double decker bus, in a discarded local newspaper. In June 2016, shortly before his release from prison, he was fascinated with news of the EU referendum which took place in the UK. From the confines of prison walls, he watched the rest of the country exercise its democracy, which resulted in a majority vote to leave the European Union, surprising the nation and the rest of the world. And so he followed every major world event, political, social, economical and technological, always hoping that one day he might be a part of it again.

The prison library proved to be not as poorly stocked as one might imagine. Although his time there was restricted, when admittance was granted, Graymond found he was able to gain access to a variety of reading material from a couple of Harry Potter novels to an iPhone manual for dummies. The library was one of Graymond's favourite places and he relished the limited time he was able to spend there. One chilly December morning, the year before his release, he had been leafing through some older books in the corner furthest from the librarian's desk. He had never paid much attention to these books before. They were mostly ageing, dusty encyclopaedias which had since been replaced with more appealing-looking resources. Graymond had pulled out a smaller book, which was missing its dust jacket. Without looking at the cover, he opened it up and flicked through some of the pages. With disdain, he realised it was a Bible and was about to put it back on the shelf when some words at the top of the page caught his eye: "But let justice roll on like a river, righteousness like a never-failing stream!". It was from a book of the Bible he had never heard of before, called Amos, in the Old Testament. Graymond stared at it for a moment and then snapped the book shut with contempt. Justice, he thought to himself bitterly, what a load of rubbish. There's no justice anywhere in this world, that's for sure. His allotted time in the library was up and suddenly he didn't want to be there anymore anyway. He signed out a manual entitled "Teach Yourself iMac in Easy Steps" and was escorted back to his cell, carrying his new book with him.

It was thanks to the resources of the prison library and the young tech-savvy store assistant, that when Graymond purchased his first iPhone from the nearest Apple store, he was quick to catch on to the latest communications development, another facet of his new life of freedom which needed grappling with. Although technology had moved on at an alarming rate since the year 2000, Graymond was a fast learner and was soon navigating the touch screen like a seasoned pro. He keyed Mrs Davidson's telephone number into the contacts section of the cell phone, and then Paul's.

After thinking for a moment, he wasn't sure there was anyone else he could add. He was certain there would be plenty of acquaintances from his old life in the London party scene who would be pleased to welcome him back. With little regard for morals or integrity, they would care nothing about his past; his prison sentence may even add a little extra kudos to his reputation. And with his bank balance still intact, he knew he could easily be back in the clique, but Graymond had learned his lesson. It was this life that had dragged him into a downward spiral of depravity in the first place. He had lost his two best friends, seventeen years, half of his twenties, all of his thirties and any shred of reputation he may have possessed, because he'd allowed himself to become sucked into the wrong crowd.

But it wasn't their fault. He knew he was responsible for his own actions and he'd been weak and easily swayed, perhaps by greed, but Graymond knew the real reason was his inability to deal with the tragic loss of his family. He'd turned to drink, to women, to work, to anything that would fill the aching void of such a loss, instead of facing his grief and emotions and dealing with them. But seventeen years of prison life and multiple sessions with a counsellor had given Graymond the time and mindset he needed to come to terms with his feelings, and to decide what sort of a man he would choose to be on his release.

Graymond suddenly felt an intense pang of loneliness as he sat by himself in the spartan, oak-panelled study. He missed his family more than he would ever bring himself to admit. He missed his two best friends, Jimmy and Rory, who had lost their lives because of his greed. But he knew the remorse he felt could never bring them back. The only thing he could do for them would be to avenge their deaths. Somewhere out there, their murderer still roamed free and Graymond would find him. But let justice roll on like a river...

With the words still echoing in his mind, he stared out of the French windows into the fading light of the late autumn evening. The study overlooked the freshly cut lawn, which stretched down to the neatly trimmed copper beech hedges, the deep burnt orange of the autumn leaves a stark contrast against the dark grey clouds of the November sky. A light rain had begun to fall, droplets rhythmically tapping on the windowpanes. Graymond momentarily closed his eyes and listened to the soothing patter. A piercing sound suddenly startled him; it was the ring tone of his cell phone. He snatched it off the desk in front of him and noted the caller ID: Mrs D. He swiped the answer button with relish; this new technology still excited him.

'Mrs Davidson, hi,' he heard himself say.

'Oh Gray, I'm so glad I've got through to you,' Mrs Davidson's breathless tones began. 'Roy and I are having a few friends over for dinner tomorrow evening and we wondered if you'd like to join us?'

Graymond detected a hopeful, expectant note in her voice. He paused for a moment. He appreciated the effort she was making in order to help him reconnect with the community. He was also grateful for the extent to which she was going to reinforce her continued belief in him that he was innocent. And heaven knows he craved acceptance and human companions, the opportunity to socialise and be invited to dinner parties, business meetings and lunch with friends. He swallowed nervously. It was too soon.

'Er — thanks Mrs Davidson but I — er — I've got some house stuff to sort tomorrow evening so I don't think I can make it.'

'Oh that's a shame, Gray,' came the reply. He knew the Sharkey family cleaning lady didn't believe a word he had just spoken. She had known him since he was two years old. 'Well, never mind, hopefully you'll be available next time.'

'I — er yes — I'm sure I will.'

'Gray, is there anything you need?'

He was shocked at the tears which suddenly welled up in his eyes.

'Uh, no thanks, Mrs Davidson, I'm okay.' He cleared his throat noisily.

'Let me know if there is, won't you dear?'

'Yes, I will,' he replied abruptly.

'Take care Gray. You know where I am.'

Mrs Davidson hung up. Graymond placed his cell phone back on the desk and hurriedly wiped his eyes with his hand. He felt annoyed at this sudden show of emotion. His only friend in the world was an elderly lady in her seventies.

Mrs Davidson, the loyal cleaning lady of the Sharkey family for many years, had updated Graymond with the odd tidbit of information from his home town now and again while he was in prison, usually along the lines of births, deaths, marriages, or a juicy piece of village gossip she thought Graymond might like to hear. Any report from home was of interest, but Graymond found that Mrs Davidson's idea of captivating news was a little different to his own. He listened intently when she visited him, however, and read all her letters patiently and carefully.

The only person he'd had very little information on, but whom he dearly wanted to know about, was Julia Tripp, the only girl he ever remembered falling in love with, but who had betrayed him for another man. He wondered what had become of her. A couple of years younger than him, she'd be in her late thirties now. What was she doing now? Was she married? To whom? Would he recognise her if he saw her? Graymond had had very little interaction with women over the last seventeen years, with the exception of the female prison wardens and a couple of prison nurses. Now and again he had thought about Julia. His feelings for her were somewhat capricious; some days he despised her for cheating on and abandoning him, and other days he had all but forgotten the betrayal and was willing to forgive the only woman he thought he had ever cared about, other than his mother. Forgiveness had been an important part of the therapy while he was inside. But why should

Julia want to rekindle the relationship? She had never come to visit him in prison. In fact, their relationship had been over before that night in August. She had moved on, but Graymond hadn't.

Graymond was stirred from his thoughts once more, this time by a low-pitched bell-like sound. It was the buzzer outside the wrought iron gates at the end of his driveway. One of Graymond's first jobs on returning home to Blackdeane House was to have his state of the art security system upgraded. He felt it a prudent move in light of his history. He tapped a couple of keys on the keyboard of his new iMac and instantly the live feed from the security camera overlooking the front gates flashed up on the screen. It was raining much harder now, and heavy black clouds hung in the graphite sky.

A hooded figure clad in a dark-coloured raincoat stood looking up at the tall gates, oblivious to the concealed camera. The driving rain made it difficult for Graymond to identify the figure other than that perhaps it was female. As he studied the screen, it was suddenly lit by a flash of white light. For a second everything stood out in an unnatural and distorted glare, like an overexposed photograph. The darkness that immediately followed was accompanied by a sharp crack of thunder and the sound of the rain, which seemed to surge and swell, hurling itself against the window panes.

Graymond watched as the figure reached out a slender hand enshrouded in the raincoat and pressed the buzzer again. The figure looked up and around, and for a brief moment Graymond caught a glimpse of a face. It was that of a young woman, probably in her mid to late thirties, although it was difficult to tell. Graymond didn't recognise her. He pressed a button on his desk and spoke into a little microphone.

'Can I help you?'

The woman turned instantly to the speaker grill embedded in the brick wall that held one of the wrought iron gates.

'Hi, yes — I'm not sure if I've come to the right place, but I'm looking for the home of Mr. Graymond Sharkey.'

It was a crisp, well-spoken tone; each word articulately pronounced.

'Who are you?' Graymond asked rudely. He was intrigued by his unexpected visitor, especially in the dark in the middle of a violent storm, but prison had ingrained in him a suspicious, untrusting nature.

At that moment, the sky was lit up again by a brilliant shock of white, a succession of flashes, like a 1920s black and white silent movie. It was immediately followed by a crackle of thunder, which crescendoed into a deafening crash. The young woman's reply was drowned by the noise and she started again, shouting over the roar of the rain.

'You don't know me, but I know you quite well, at least I have for the last seventeen years.'

Graymond frowned. Was "seventeen years" supposed to be significant? She was right in that he didn't know her, but how could she know him when they had never met? And why was she here now?

'What do you want?' Graymond asked, reluctant to let her in without a convincing explanation. Another flash of lightning and deafening rumble of thunder drowned out the rest of his sentence.

'Look Mr. Sharkey, I'm getting pretty soaked out here.' The young woman continued to raise her voice in order to be heard above the torrential rain. Graymond could hear the wind howling through the microphone. 'Why don't you open these gates and let me in and I'll explain how I know you?'

Still frowning, Graymond tentatively held a finger over the access button to the front gates and pressed it. A green light glowed on the iMac screen and he watched as the heavy wrought iron swung open effortlessly on newly oiled hinges. The woman's small frame hurried through and up the tree-lined gravel driveway as the gates swung shut and the locks clicked into place. Graymond watched her every move as she approached the imposing grandeur of Blackdeane House, the lightning flashing around her, illuminating the garden with a stark, white, ghostly glare followed by deafening cracks of thunder. Graymond pushed his chair back from the desk and stood up. Who was she? Had he just made a big mistake? He made his way down the wide staircase into the hallway to the large, oak front door. It was time to meet his uninvited guest.

CHAPTER SEVEN

The young woman stood on the Persian rug in the vast entrance hall of Blackdeane House. She was soaked through and a fresh spray of raindrops fell onto the rug as she lowered the hood of her raincoat. She looked at the puddle forming on the rug and stepped quickly back onto the tumbled marble floor behind her. 'Oh I'm sorry, I've made your carpet wet.'

'It'll dry,' Graymond said gruffly. He wasn't precious about the rug; it was just another expensive purchase he'd never particularly cared about. There was a pause and then Graymond spoke again.

'Do you need a towel?' he asked, slightly awkwardly. He surprised himself at this unexpected show of politeness.

'Oh yes, thanks.'

As Graymond disappeared back up the grand staircase, two at a time, his unexpected visitor stood in silence and glanced around the magnificent vaulted hallway, slightly awestruck. To her right was a wide archway leading into a spacious living room with more exquisite Persian rugs covering a marble floor, well-worn brown leather sofas and two huge wrought iron chandeliers at either end of the room. The focal point was a magnificent fireplace constructed from floor to ceiling with reclaimed bricks, although the full-sized concert grand piano at the far end of the room was a serious contender as the main feature. She wondered if it had ever been played.

Through another wide archway to her left, a spool of light from the hallway fell into a dark, oak-panelled kitchen. It appeared as vast as the living room with an impressive stainless steel cooking range and a large, cream marble-topped island in the centre of the room with high-backed white-leather chairs pulled neatly up to it. As lavish as they were, the rooms gave more of a show-home impression than one of being loved and lived in.

Ahead of her, Graymond was coming back down the polished oak staircase with a large grey bath towel.

'Will this do?' he asked.

'It's fine. Thanks, Mr. Sharkey,' the young woman replied, smiling. She took the towel and patted her hair and face dry.

Graymond had not entertained a guest in his home for over seventeen years and was unsure of what to do next. Not that this young woman was exactly a guest. She was more of an intruder. What did she want, showing up, uninvited, in the middle of a storm on a dark November night? He'd play along for now, but already he didn't trust her.

'Can I get you anything?' he inquired. 'A glass of water or something?' He hadn't exactly gone out of his way to stock up his food and drink cupboards since he'd been home.

'Could I have a cup of tea?' the woman asked, squeezing her long dark hair with the towel.

'I think I can manage that,' Graymond nodded.

'I'll join you in the kitchen.' She followed him through the archway and watched him pick up a remote control and press a button. The room was instantly bathed in a warm glow from three rows of LED down-lights. As Graymond launched himself into his best efforts at hospitality with the tea-making, his guest slid onto one of the chairs and placed the towel on the marble work-surface of the island next to her.

She observed Graymond for a few moments. With the exception of a few extra wrinkles and some grey hairs visible in his close-cropped hair, seventeen years in prison appeared to have been kind. In spite of his sullen expression, his handsome features remained from when she had last seen him, although perhaps this time he looked a little more tired and sad than he had in the courtroom. Graymond placed two mugs of tea on the counter-top of the island, pulled out another of the chairs and sat down. He watched her carefully as she took a sip of tea. He wasn't sure his entertaining skills were up to scratch these days, even with tea making.

'Thanks Mr. Sharkey,' the young woman said gratefully, setting the mug back down on the work-surface. 'Just what I needed; it's such a terrible night out there.' She nodded to the window where the rain battered the windowpanes in streaks rather than droplets.

'What were you doing outside in the storm?' Graymond asked. 'And why are you here? You said you know me…'

His guest took another sip of the hot tea.

'Oh sorry, how rude of me, I haven't even introduced myself,' she said apologetically. 'My name's Alicia Clayton, but please call me Alicia.' She held out her hand. Graymond shook it cautiously and said, 'Okay, Alicia. I guess you can call me Gray; it's what my friends call me. Called me,' he corrected himself and Alicia detected the sadness in his voice.

'I'm very pleased to meet you, Gray. Finally,' Alicia replied.

'Finally?' Graymond was confused. 'You said you know me. How?'

After another sip of the hot tea, Alicia settled herself into her chair and put her mug down on the marble top. Graymond hadn't touched his tea. He wasn't thirsty and his mind was whirling. It hadn't escaped his notice that Alicia was stunning. Her long, dark hair, still damp from the rain, framed the features of her face: dark brown eyes, high cheekbones, lips with a perfect pout and skin with a flawless complexion. As discreetly as he could, he cast an inconspicuous glance at the rest of her. She was wearing a simple black tight-fitting shirt and dark blue jeans, which looked as though they had been tailored especially for her long legs. If they had met before, surely he would remember someone like her? Graymond's mind was already beginning to wander to other things; seventeen years was a long time.

'Sixteen years ago I was a trainee journalist, a rookie, and a small-time features writer for a little-known newspaper in my spare time,' Alicia began. 'I was studying hard for a journalism degree, working every hour I had for the newspaper and desperate for a big story. It was the summer of two thousand and I was asked to help cover a murder trial with one of the senior reporters for the paper.'

Alicia paused. She had Graymond's attention.

'I was in the courtroom every day of the trial. I researched the case like it was an obsession, I visited the scene of the murders countless times and pulled a dozen all-nighters to get my articles written for publication.'

'What was the outcome of the trial?' Graymond knew the answer to his own question.

'It was pretty much an open and shut case,' Alicia continued in a matter-of-fact tone. 'The evidence was all there: the murderer was found at the scene with his two victims, both stabbed to death with one of his own kitchen knives. Forensics found the blood of both friends on him as well as the knife, which was covered with his fingerprints; nobody else's prints were found, just his. He had means, motive, and opportunity. The jury, naturally, found him guilty as hell and he went down for murder with a life sentence.'

There was a brief silence before Graymond took a deep breath and spoke.

'Sounds like he got what he deserved.'

'He didn't actually.' Alicia's words startled Graymond. He tried to swallow but there was a lump in his throat.

'What did you say?' he asked. Alicia shook her head.

'It wasn't him.' She paused. 'Someone else did it.'

Graymond was speechless. He spread his hands out on the counter in front of him and focused on them. He looked back at Alicia.

'What are you talking about?' he asked, hoarsely. 'What do you know?'

'That's just it,' Alicia went on. 'It's not so much what I know, but more what I *don't* know, if that makes sense?'

'It doesn't,' Graymond replied. 'If an entire jury, an entire *courtroom*, not to mention the rest of society, thought I was guilty, what makes *you* think I didn't do it?'

'Oh I don't just *think*, Gray,' Alicia said quietly. 'I *know* you didn't do it.'

CHAPTER EIGHT

Graymond Sharkey had been stunned and yet mystified at Alicia's confidence in his innocence. As the judge had read the verdict in the crowded courtroom on that hot August day in 2000, Alicia described her sense of unease that all was not what it seemed. True, the evidence was clear — well, most of it, according to Alicia — and a guilty verdict reflected that, but Alicia's enquiring mind wasn't convinced. Some things did not add up, but Alicia was not sure why. She had never met Graymond Sharkey and did not know him as a person. She had never paid him a visit in prison, although was tempted to a number of times. She continued her own little investigation for a while, following up a number of leads, some of which appeared promising, but ultimately, she could never quite connect the dots. It was as though she had a pile of mosaic tiles, which made up a picture, but she had no idea how to arrange the tiles, assuming she had them all, of course.

Over the months and years, life as an ambitious journalist had been a busy one, travelling the country and then the world as a Crime Editor of a major national broadsheet newspaper. She had covered many stories over the fifteen years she had worked as a journalist, but there was one she had never been able to forget.

'I feel as though I have an unfinished story,' Alicia said soberly. 'There's still one more article that hasn't been written. Yet.'

'All right then, Nancy Drew, what evidence do you have to vindicate me, that the police don't?' Graymond said, with a hint of scorn.

Alicia thought for a moment.

'I don't exactly have any tangible evidence,' she replied, ignoring Graymond's taunt. 'Just a lot of questions.'

'Such as?'

'Such as who the anonymous 999 caller was that night and why did he never come forward?' Alicia began.

Graymond thought for a moment.

'Maybe he just didn't want to get involved,' he shrugged.

'Maybe.' Alicia was not convinced. 'A witness nearby reported hearing the Cessna land at around ten-twenty p.m., the anonymous telephone call was made at ten twenty-one p.m., which was *before* Rory's time of death, and the police arrived on scene at ten forty-four p.m. It all happened a bit too quickly.'

'It felt that way too,' Graymond couldn't disagree. 'I often thought about that anonymous caller.'

'What I don't get is why did he make the call?' Alicia said. 'Why call to report a "disturbance" at the airfield — I think that was the word used in the police report — when, at that point in time, there was nothing more than a light aircraft landing, albeit a little later than usual. Why call the police about that? It's hardly a disturbance; everyone knows what an aircraft sounds like around here, and as we know, it's not the first time you'd flown in a shipment of stolen paintings late at night.'

'Well, maybe...'

'But why didn't he come forward despite multiple appeals from the police? The only identification he gave at the time was that he was a concerned local resident,' Alicia interrupted. 'There are just a few houses within earshot of Blackdeane Airfield, including yours Gray, and nobody in the area claimed to be the caller. And when the police searched the area immediately surrounding the airfield, they found no one. So *who* was the caller, why did he really call and why did he never come forward?'

Graymond shrugged again. He had nothing to say.

'*I* think he called because he needed the police to arrive in time to have you framed for the murders. He wanted it to look like you murdered Rory and Jimmy so you could take all the stolen artwork for yourself, but you were interrupted by the police before you could dispose of the bodies and the knife and clean up the mess in the tower,' Alicia said resolutely. 'It's the only explanation.'

Graymond wanted to say he had considered that possibility a long time ago, but there was no proof.

'Although the call was recorded, the voice was muffled and unrecognisable, again, it's as if the caller never wanted to be identified.' Alicia added. 'And there's another thing that's always bothered me; you shut down the engine of the Cessna before you returned to the control room, didn't you?'

'Of course I did. I took the key out, ran to the pilot's door, dragged Jimmy's body out, checked for a pulse and then ran up to the control room to call for help because I couldn't get Rory on the radio,' Graymond replied, adding, 'because by then, he was already dead.'

'So why did the Cessna spontaneously combust?' Alicia asked, raising her eyebrows at Graymond. He shook his head. Don't know.

'Did anyone ever find out what caused the explosion during the investigations?'

'Fuel, oxygen and heat.'

'Very funny,' Alicia said dryly.

'I don't think they ever found a specific cause,' Graymond said seriously. 'The investigative report said that the explosion was so severe and the temperature of the fire that engulfed the aircraft so hot that there was very little evidence to go on. No items of the stolen art were ever discovered in or around the wreckage of the burned out shell of the Cessna and Jimmy's body was so badly burned up he had to be identified by dental records.'

'But that's what I don't understand,' Alicia went on. She was not done yet. 'The Cessna was well-maintained, right?'

'Down to the tiniest rivet.' Graymond managed a smile. 'Hell, we couldn't afford anything to go wrong with that aircraft when it was being used to courier millions of dollars' worth of stolen artwork.'

'And it had just flown back from the Channel Islands, so the fuel status was minimal, correct?' Alicia continued the interrogation.

'Correct,' Graymond said. 'You've done your research, Alicia; I'll give you that. Yeah, the fuel tanks would've been pretty much empty by the time Jimmy landed at Blackdeane; he used to put in as little aviation fuel as he could get away with to keep the weight of the aircraft down.'

'Fine,' Alicia agreed. 'So we've got an aircraft in immaculate working order, empty of fuel, with the engine shut down on the tarmac and it spontaneously explodes into a raging inferno. Does that make sense to you, Gray?'

'No,' Graymond said resolutely. 'It doesn't. But they said in court that while I was supposedly busy stabbing Jimmy to death, I either forgot to shut the engine down properly, or I deliberately rigged the aircraft to explode in an attempt to make it look like an accident.'

'But the police found the key of the Cessna in your pocket when they arrested you, right?' Alicia had apparently memorised every detail of the case, which she had also apparently stored in her brain for sixteen years.

'Yes, the key was in my pocket, but they went with the theory that it was a spare,' Graymond replied. 'They had an explanation for everything.'

'So if it was a deliberate act on your part, why would you destroy your own aircraft loaded with hundreds of millions of dollars' worth of stolen goods?'

'That's what my lawyer argued at the time, but the jury didn't buy it,' Graymond said. 'The police tried to suggest that I'd realised I'd been caught and attempted to destroy the evidence: all the stolen paintings and Jimmy's body.'

'But you didn't know the police were on their way until you were in the control room. And even if you had time to run back down and rig an explosion, why would you run back up to the control room to deliberately frame yourself for Rory's murder?'

'Apparently the jury thought I was stupid enough to do all of that,' Graymond said. He was suddenly bored. He had been over this more times in the last seventeen years than he cared to remember. Tonight was no exception. They were getting nowhere. Still, in a strange sort of way, he felt a sense of comfort that he had had a kindred spirit all this time. Someone, aside from Mrs Davidson, believed in him and was on his side. He decided to be kind.

'Alicia,' Graymond spoke. He even managed to force a brief smile. 'I appreciate your interest in my case, but so far, all you've brought to the table are a bunch of questions that I've been asking myself for seventeen years. Do you actually have anything worthwhile? You know, tangible?'

Alicia appeared to pause for thought for a moment and then her deep brown eyes looked directly at Graymond.

'I nearly forgot,' she replied. 'Did you ever unload any of the stolen artwork from the Cessna that night?'

Graymond looked almost offended. The remnants of the smile rapidly vanished.

'Definitely not,' he retorted. 'Jimmy was bleeding out everywhere; what was I supposed to do? Tell him to hang in there while I transferred all the paintings from the aircraft to the truck and then we'd head back and I'd call the paramedics when I was done? I don't think I even thought about the paintings at that point. But how does that come into it?'

'So, to your knowledge, all of the stolen artwork was still in the aircraft when it burst into flames?' Alicia needed further confirmation.

'Yes,' Graymond replied, almost savagely. 'Why does that matter now?'

'When you work as a journalist, you trade favours with people, you trade information, you gain sources, informants.' Alicia spoke matter-of-factly. 'Over sixteen years, I've built up a nice little empire of information channels in many different arenas. I've got sources in every industry you can think of, Gray, friends of friends on speed dial who can get me inside information on any story you want.' She had a faint sparkle in her eyes. 'One of my most,' she paused, searching for the right word, '*valued* sources, happens to know a little about the art world.'

Graymond frowned, unsure as to where this new string of conversation was headed.

'I've got one final question for you, Gray, and then I'll be going. I've already kept you far too long,' Alicia said. 'If all the stolen paintings were still in the aircraft when it burst into flames, how is it that three of those paintings showed up on the black market last year?'

'What?' Graymond asked with a look of astonishment.

'Did you sell them from prison, Gray?' Alicia asked, almost accusingly.

'No!' Graymond replied, insulted. 'Of course I didn't.'

'I have to ask,' Alicia said. 'It's pretty easy these days, especially for a smart guy like you.'

'Well, I didn't,' Graymond said again. 'I thought all the artwork was destroyed.'

'So did everyone, including my contact and me,' Alicia said, 'until last year when these three paintings popped up out of the blue.'

'Are you sure they were the real deal?' Graymond asked sceptically. 'How do you know they weren't forgeries?'

'Oh my contact is very, *very* good,' Alicia replied with conviction.

'Where did they come from? Who had them?' Graymond asked incredulously. 'Are you sure you've got the right paintings?'

'They're unmistakably three of the pieces of artwork listed in the inventory during your court case. They were transported by Jimmy from the Channel Islands and supposedly destroyed in the Cessna explosion,' Alicia replied. 'They're not copies, they're the real thing. My source may not be entirely honest, but she is entirely unrivalled in her field.'

Alicia drained the last of her tea, which was now cold.

'And there's one other thing,' she added. 'It's perhaps the most puzzling of all.'

'Some *tangible* evidence, perhaps?' Graymond suggested hopefully.

'It's not so much tangible evidence as "a look,"' she replied.

'A look?' Graymond asked doubtfully. He closed his eyes in disappointment before looking straight at Alicia. 'I'm wondering why you even bothered to come tonight. So far, you're hoping to clear my name and reveal the true murderer with the help of a corrupt art dealer and "a look". Gee, thanks Alicia, we're off to a great start.'

'I think it all looks very promising,' Alicia said brightly, sliding off the chair and picking up her raincoat, spraying another shower of raindrops onto the kitchen floor.

'It's not a game, Alicia,' Graymond snarled. 'You're not the one who's been locked up for seventeen years for a crime you didn't commit.'

Alicia looked directly at Graymond with her deep brown eyes and for a brief second, he felt goose bumps on the back of his neck.

'I know it's not a game, Graymond,' Alicia spoke quietly. 'I'm deadly serious.'

'Why are you doing this?' Graymond asked suddenly. 'What's in it for you?'

Alicia tipped her head on one side.

'Easy,' she replied simply. 'I'm a Crime Editor. I'm always on the lookout for the next big story.' She continued with a lower voice. 'And I want closure as much as you do on an unsolved mystery that has haunted me for the last sixteen years. Perhaps it's because it was the first major story I ever worked on. I feel as though there's one more piece that needs to be written, Gray, the final chapter.'

They stared at each other for a long moment, before Alicia turned for the hallway.

'Can I see you to, er, your car?' Graymond asked.

'No thank-you, Gray, I can see myself out,' Alicia replied. She placed a hand in her coat pocket, pulled out a business card and offered it to Graymond.

'Here's my number. If you think of anything else, call me.'

Graymond cautiously took the small, glossy card and stepped ahead of her to open the heavy front door. The storm had passed and the heavy rain had settled into a light drizzle. Dark clouds obscured the stars and the light of the moon, and the humid scent of damp grass hung in the air.

As Alicia made her way briskly down the long driveway to the wrought iron gates and disappeared into the night, Graymond stood on the doorstep, his mind in turmoil. He looked down at the card in his hand which read '*Alicia J. R. Clayton, Investigative Journalist T: 07700 945722*'. Was she really the person she claimed to be? How did he know she was telling the truth? She certainly seemed to know every detail of his case. He didn't remember her from the courtroom sixteen years ago, but then he hadn't exactly made an effort to make eye contact with anyone, especially someone representing the media. At any rate, he had another name and number to add to the contacts list on his iPhone.

CHAPTER NINE

Over four large cups of Columbian coffee, freshly brewed in a brand new, state-of-the-art coffee machine, Graymond Sharkey planned his day ahead. With the prison coffee resembling liquid from a sewage treatment plant in both colour and taste, a fancy coffee machine was one of the small luxuries Graymond had promised himself on his release. He savoured every cup as he devoured two slices of toast and two newspapers, whilst mentally mapping out the next twelve hours. A part of his self-designed plan to get him up to speed as quickly as possible with the world in 2016 was to read two broadsheet newspapers a day, including the sports and business sections. The more he read, the more he realised the world had changed, and was now very different to the one he had left outside those prison gates seventeen years before.

On the marble work-surface next to his coffee was Alicia's business card, which Graymond glanced at from time to time. A part of him wanted to call her, even if it was just to prove that the number was false and that he had been deceived. Maybe he'd never see her again. Even the bright sunshine streaming through the kitchen blinds seemed to be telling him that last night had never happened. Graymond decided to leave any telephone calls for now; there was work to be done.

As he pulled out of his driveway in his new truck, Graymond headed in the opposite direction to the airfield. The gates slid shut behind him and he accelerated down the road, careful to observe the speed limit; the last thing he needed was a speeding ticket. The new truck was new to Graymond, but certainly not new in any other sense. It was a blue 2008 Toyota Hilux SUV, its three litre diesel engine having clocked over two hundred thousand miles.

Although he loved fast cars, Graymond had decided to go for something which blended in and would attract as little attention to himself as possible. He had paid for it with cash and had purchased it from a small garage, out of town, a few days after his release, although it had to be delivered to his home as his new, updated driver's licence had not yet arrived in the mail. The garage owner, who introduced himself as Andy, had insisted on going through every scrap of documentation accompanying the vehicle. Graymond wasn't sure whether this was because Andy had something to hide or because he was an honest businessman. Although it was a far cry from the sporty BMW that had once been his pride and joy, and that cousin Paul had managed to write off two months into Graymond's life sentence, the new truck had, so far, proved to be a reliable choice and Graymond was becoming quite attached to it.

The first stop was the supermarket. Like the garage, it was out of town. Graymond preferred the anonymity of public places some distance away from his home turf and he also loved the freedom of driving wherever he chose. Driving was one of the things he had missed during his time inside, and now he cherished that feeling of being behind the wheel, on the open road, negotiating the sharp bends on the winding country lanes of the English countryside with the skill of a seasoned professional. He reversed expertly into a space in the parking lot of the supermarket, pleased that he hadn't lost his touch, and headed for the entrance, grabbing a trolley. He felt invigorated from the drive on such a beautiful morning and once again relished the feeling of freedom that he had vowed he would never become accustomed to.

Striding purposefully to the fruit and vegetables, he surveyed the attractive display. Thanks to his prison diet and exercise routine, he'd been in pretty good shape on his release and he intended to stay that way. He'd also been watching a number of cookery shows on TV since he'd been home and was keen to try a few new recipes. He made his way along the aisles, checking out the ingredients labels on packets, marvelling at the vast range of new products that had arrived on the shelves since 2000. He turned a corner and made his way along the furthest aisle from the entrance, the aisle displaying alcoholic drinks. Graymond stopped and looked around him. He'd been drinking heavily in the last few months before the night of the murders, but he hadn't touched a single drop in the seventeen years he'd been in prison. Graymond pushed his trolley slowly down the aisle. He stopped at the bottles of Jack Daniel's Tennessee Whiskey and took a longing look. *What's the problem?* An innocent voice in his mind spoke quietly. He was a free man, wasn't he? There was nothing wrong with an occasional drink. *But it won't be, will it, Gray? In your mind there's still no such thing as "just one drink," is there Gray?*

Graymond lingered a moment more before resolutely pushing his trolley to the end of the aisle. Not today, he told himself, firmly. Not any day. He would be strong. He suddenly remembered he'd forgotten to pick up some granola. It was a "superfood" he'd read about in a magazine supplement in one of his Sunday newspapers. He thought he'd try it. Back in the cereal aisle, Graymond studied the rather overwhelming range of varieties of granola. To his left, he noticed a young woman, a little on the heavy side for her height, attempting to reach a box of cereal high up on a shelf. Graymond glanced around anxiously, hoping there was a store assistant nearby to come to her rescue. There wasn't. He studied the granola boxes intently and was about to make his selection when a voice to his left said:

'Excuse me, you couldn't reach that box of Sugar-Pops for me, could you?'

Graymond froze. There was something familiar about that voice. He recognised it from a long time ago, in his distant past, another life. He pretended not to have heard.

'Sorry but you wouldn't mind would you?' the voice said again.

Graymond scowled and turned slowly to face the young woman who was stretching to the top shelf. As she looked round at him, she gasped.

'Graymond Sharkey?' she asked in disbelief.

'Julia Tripp.' Graymond said slowly.

'Oh my gosh, Graymond; it's you, it's really you,' Julia said, wide-eyed.

Graymond felt a tinge of embarrassment. The cereal aisle of a supermarket was not the Hollywood-style reunion he'd spent seventeen years dreaming about.

'I heard you got out of prison; that's great news!' Julia said enthusiastically.

'Isn't it?' Graymond agreed, with somewhat less enthusiasm.

An awkward silence ensued.

'So what've you been doing with yourself?' Julia asked.

None of your business, Graymond thought.

'Oh, you know, stuff,' he replied as courteously as he could manage. 'Taking each day as it comes, getting back into the pace of life.'

'That's great!' Julia was hanging on his every word. It was annoying. He looked her up and down. She was just as he had remembered her, except a little older and perhaps a little heavier. Graymond felt that she had let personal upkeep slide over the years, although the outfit she was wearing that could have doubled as pyjamas may just have been her casual look for supermarket trips. In any case, this was not the Julia he'd dreamed of winning back all those nights in prison. He wondered if she and Reese were still together. The wondering lasted all of four-seconds.

'Julia,' came a loud voice from further down the aisle. An equally rotund body accompanied the voice and came into view, thundering past the breakfast cereals with an overloaded trolley.

'Julia,' the voice said again. 'Oh, there you are. Where've you been? I've been looking for you every...' The voice trailed off as he caught sight of Graymond.

'Hello Reese,' Graymond said quietly. For the first time since he had discovered the two of them in bed together, he looked Reese in the eyes.

Reese momentarily stopped chewing on the nicotine gum his jaw was frantically working on.

'Graymond Sharkey. What are you doing here?'

Graymond couldn't work out whether it was a voice of surprise or disdain.

'Food shopping, strangely enough,' he replied sarcastically. How did Reese ever manage to get his private pilot's licence, he thought to himself. 'How about you?'

'Well, yeah, we're stocking up with a few bits too,' Reese replied, still recovering from the shock.

'I can see that,' Graymond said, surveying the groaning trolley.

'Just a quick mid-week shop to tide us over,' Reese waved his hand casually over an impressive collection of microwaveable pizzas, popcorn and frozen cheesecakes.

'Absolutely,' Graymond agreed. 'You wouldn't want to run out of essentials.'

'Definitely not,' Reese nodded.

'What are you both up to these days?' Graymond asked in a vague attempt to be polite, although in his mind he was already debating the quickest way to get the hell out of there.

'Reese works nights as a delivery driver.' Julia rejoined the conversation.

'Yeah, that's right, and Julia's just got a job as a chef at that new residential home that opened a few months ago. You know the one?' Reese was suddenly making a gallant effort to be friendly.

'No actually, I don't,' Graymond replied, 'but that might be because I was only released from prison four weeks ago. I'm sure I'll get round to catching up with all the newly opened residential homes one of these days.'

'Oh yeah, sure, sorry mate,' Reese looked away, embarrassed. He turned back. 'Listen mate, about what happened all those years ago…'

'Yes?' Graymond gripped the handle of his trolley.

'How about we draw a line under everything that happened? No hard feelings and all that?' Reese looked hopefully at Graymond.

No hard feelings? You slept with my girlfriend, you sonofabitch, Graymond thought angrily.

'Sure,' he forced a gracious smile. 'It's all in the past, all forgotten.'

'Oh great,' Reese breathed a sigh of relief. 'Thanks Gray. I know Julia's keen for us all to be friends now you're back in the real world!'

Graymond almost choked on his own saliva. You're mistaking me for someone who actually wants to be friends, he thought indignantly.

'Sometimes I think these things are meant to be,' Reese went on. 'I mean, after you banned me from keeping my light aircraft at Blackdeane, I moved it to a local grass strip where I met my current boss who gave me my delivery job!'

'Isn't that amazing?' Julia added excitedly.

'Isn't it?' Graymond wasn't sure how much further his acting skills could be stretched. 'Still flying, Reese?' he asked.

'Oh no,' Reese shook his head. 'Had to sell the Cherokee to pay for a wedding.' He cast a sickly look at Julia who beamed back. 'And then we bought a house and, well, you know how life goes.'

Graymond wanted to say that no, he didn't know at all how life goes because he happened to have spent the last seventeen years of it locked up behind concrete walls. It was time to leave.

'Well, it was great to catch up,' he said, casually, 'but listen, I've got to dash, so — er — I'll let you finish your shopping.' He turned back to his trolley.

'Yeah, it was good to catch up,' Reese said quickly.

Liar.

'Gray, you must come to dinner some time,' Julia called after him.

Like hell, Graymond thought to himself. I'd rather serve another life sentence.

'Sure, we'll be in touch,' Graymond replied over his shoulder. He rounded the corner of the aisle and made his way to join one of the lines to pay for his groceries. For a brief moment, he was tempted to head back to the Jack Daniels aisle. Not today, Gray, he reminded himself. Not any day.

CHAPTER TEN

With the exception of the unfortunate reunion between himself and Julia and Reese, the day was going well. Graymond was back on the open road, enjoying the late autumn sunshine and the freedom of driving wherever he chose, whenever he chose. He switched on the radio of his truck. A dance-pop song that he had never heard before was playing. He wasn't sure he liked it. He switched to a classical channel, to a slow, depressing ballad that was being slaughtered by a violin. The third channel he tried was a talk show on gardening that lasted a record-breaking thirty-seconds before Graymond switched channels a fourth time. He agreed he was a little behind with current music trends and media in general, having missed out on nearly two decades' worth, but he was beginning to wonder whether it wasn't such a bad miss after all. Suddenly, a song he knew and loved, but had not heard for over seventeen years pounded through the speakers of the truck. The driving rhythm and familiar guitar riffs of She's A River filled Graymond with a sudden sense of yearning for times gone by.

Back in those endlessly carefree days, Graymond and his brother would take turns to drive his convertible Volkswagen to the beach every weekend, with the roof fully down and stereo volume fully up. The old Volkswagen had only a compact cassette deck and the Simple Minds track was played and rewound until the flimsy magnetic tape wore out and finally snapped. Graymond's mind flooded with memories of those days and he found himself singing along to the lyrics as if he had only sang them yesterday. As the last chorus of the song faded, his thoughts returned to the present. He reflected on Alicia's hope in proving his innocence and wondered if he could bring himself to share the same dream. He thought of another river; the one in the prison Bible: "But let justice roll on like a river". He wondered how there could ever be any justice reclaimed for an innocent man who had served a life sentence for two murders that he didn't commit. How could such a wrong ever be made right?

In spite of this temporary distraction, Graymond felt invigorated and upbeat as he pulled into the parking lot of his next stop: a clothing outlet mall. He needed some new clothes. He'd been alternating a couple of shirts and two pairs of jeans since his release, but he was getting tired of the washing and ironing and decided it was time to expand his wardrobe. He thought it was probably wise to stick with classic staples for the time being, the last seventeen years of prison clothing having leeched out any sense of style he may once have had. His old clothes remained in a box in a spare room in Blackdeane House. He wasn't sure he'd ever wear them again. It was time for a fresh new look.

As Graymond wandered along the pavements of the outlet mall, he marvelled at the vast range of stores. Shopping had never been one of his hobbies, but these days, everything seemed to be interesting and exciting. He found a John Lewis, a large department store, a household name that he was familiar with, and headed to the men's department on the second floor. As he stepped off the escalator, he was met with an overwhelming collection of menswear from swimming shorts to dinner suits. He stood still, unsure where or how to start shopping, and was approached by an attractive young shop assistant with a name badge declaring her name was Kate.

'Can I help you sir?' Kate asked kindly. She spoke with a soft Irish accent.

Graymond was about to follow his usual pattern of declining any offer of help, but reminded himself that he probably did, in fact, need some assistance, if this particular shopping expedition was to be a success. Kate proved him right, and soon he was the proud owner of a selection of four tailored shirts, four casual polo shirts, two smart pairs of chinos, two pairs of jeans and a navy sports jacket, which Graymond thought he'd wear for his forthcoming meeting with Paul. Graymond thanked Kate and flashed a smile at the equally attractive assistant who took his payment. She smiled back and almost seemed to be flirting with him. She wasn't wearing a wedding band. He wasn't sure of the current dating etiquette these days, but wondered if it would be awkward to ask her if she'd like to get a coffee some time. He decided against it. What was the rush? He still hadn't worked out how he would account for the last seventeen years of his life to a potential new girlfriend. He wasn't sure what kind of nice, well-to-do young lady would be interested in a relationship with an ex-con who'd just served a life sentence for a double murder. He felt good about the compliment though.

Back in the truck, Graymond checked his watch. It was four o'clock; still time for the final stop of the day, the library. There was a large one on the outskirts of town that would have what he needed. The internet confirmed the closing time as six p.m., plenty of time to conduct the necessary research. Graymond parked the truck in the library car park and headed inside, with a degree of apprehension. He couldn't recall the last time he had visited a public library and wasn't sure if the layout of the books and other resources was the same as in the prison library that he had become so familiar with. Graymond was also concerned that this further delving into the past may bring back memories he would rather keep buried, but he knew if he wanted justice, he would have to open the book of the past, one final time, in order to close it forever.

Graymond decided he would have to resort to seeking some assistance, once again, in order to find what he was looking for. He approached the librarian's desk where a long-faced, middle-aged woman looked up at him and raised her eyebrows. Graymond cleared his throat.

'Hi, I wonder if you could help me?'

'With what?' the librarian asked curtly.

Almost as friendly as the service in the prison library, Graymond thought.

'I'm looking for some newspaper archives dating back to nineteen ninety-nine,' he continued.

'They're all online now; I'll show you where the computers are.' She got up wearily from her chair and beckoned to Graymond to follow her. They headed to the rear of the library which was partitioned by a glass wall. Beyond the glass was a room filled with lines of desks, each with its own computer. The computer room was almost empty, with the exception of a young college student and an elderly gentleman. The librarian led Graymond to a computer just inside the sliding glass doors and rattled off a list of instructions on how to access the newspaper archives, none of which Graymond understood. She left before he had chance to ask her for clarification.

Graymond keyed a few words into the search box, and scrolled and clicked from page to page for a few minutes until he thought he had worked out how to navigate the library's online archive resource. He briefly glanced around him. On the other side of the glass, a mother was helping her young child choose some reading books. The librarian was back at her desk. There was nobody else nearby. The library was deserted.

Graymond took a deep breath and began his search. He started by typing his own name into the search box. Sure enough, a surprisingly large number of articles were listed on the screen, from a wide range of different newspapers, including some international ones. Graymond scanned a few paragraphs of some of the articles, but he wasn't particularly interested in reading the sensationalised stories; he had been shocked at the time at how far the facts had been distorted. As he scrolled through the newspaper pages on the screen in front of him, he looked for one thing: the name of the journalist who had written each article. The first twenty pages revealed nothing. Graymond wished he had asked Alicia which newspaper she had been employed by as a rookie journalist. It was probably one of the local ones. He continued to scroll. Perhaps she had a different surname back then? Graymond found an article by an A. Hartley. Could the "A" have stood for Alicia? He read an extract from it. Poorly written, he thought, and extremely accusatory in nature with all sorts of exaggerations and lies. He decided that this wasn't Alicia's work.

The article beneath it was short, but concise and well-written and had been published in a newspaper called The Blackdeane News which Graymond knew was now defunct. The headline of the article was simply "Jury convicts Graymond Sharkey" and contained the facts of the case, the outcome of the trial and no editorial. The author of the article was Alicia Clayton, Crime Reporter.

Graymond narrowed his search for other stories that had been published in "The Blackdeane News" with the same key words. Sure enough, Alicia had contributed a number of articles relating to his case. He slowed his search and began to read them with interest. Instead of jumping on the guilty-as-charged bandwagon that a lot of journalists appeared to have done, Alicia had kept an open mind with her reporting and had concentrated on presenting the facts without editorialising. There was one exception in which she had been granted a single page Features article where she had clearly set out the evidence from Graymond's trial along with a well-argued case as to why the jury who gave him a life sentence may have made a mistake. Graymond noticed the date on this article was April 2001, a short time after he had begun his life sentence. He was also intrigued to see a small photograph of Alicia's face next to her name; she looked a little younger, with rounder cheeks, but it was unmistakably the same woman who had paid him a visit the previous night. Graymond leaned back in his chair and let out a deep breath.

Alicia Clayton was who she said she was. He glanced casually over both shoulders before pulling his cell phone out of his pocket and taking a snap shot of the Features article on the screen, including the picture of Alicia. He wondered whether to continue his search a little further, but decided against it. He had what he came for.

As Graymond turned into the entrance of his driveway and slowed the Toyota Hilux to walking pace, he pressed a little button on his key fob and the heavy wrought iron gates began to swing open, perfectly timed. Graymond smiled to himself with satisfaction; he loved technology. As he inched the truck through the gates, in his rear view mirror he noticed a car pull out of a lay-by on the other side of the road, a little further down. It was a black Volkswagen Sirocco with tinted windows. He didn't recognise it and neither could he make out the driver, but it followed him into the driveway and closed in behind the truck as he drove through the gates, which were programmed to shut once all vehicles had cleared the sensors at the entrance. Which meant that they would remain open until the black Sirocco was also inside. Graymond accelerated, sending a shower of gravel over the windscreen of the Sirocco. At the end of the driveway, Blackdeane House, his home, stood imposingly in the dim twilight.

Graymond slid the truck to a halt, the wide tires carving out sharp lines in the gravel. He wondered briefly who the intruder was and what to do with him. The warmth from the vehicles activated the passive infrared sensors on the array of spotlights positioned strategically around the outside of Blackdeane House, lighting up the front of the building and the driveway like searchlights from a maximum security prison. Graymond opened the door of the truck and jumped out, turning towards the Sirocco which had parked immediately behind. The driver's door opened.

CHAPTER ELEVEN

'I hope you're prepared to pay for the new paintwork on my car after spraying gravel all over it.' Alicia's voice could be heard before she was seen. She climbed out of the Sirocco laden with a black shoulder bag and two large brown paper bags.

'Alicia!' Graymond was startled. The second unexpected visit in twenty-four hours. He was surprised, but not disappointed. 'What are you doing here?'

'I'm touched; another warm welcome. I suppose prison isn't really the place for honing your people skills though, is it Gray?'

Graymond scowled, but felt a touch of embarrassment.

'What do you want?' he asked with a sour tone. 'If you've come here to lecture me on my social skills then you can leave now.'

'You really do have a wonderful gift of making people feel welcome,' Alicia replied. She held up the brown paper bags. 'I guess I'll be eating this Indian takeaway by myself then. See you later Gray.' She stepped back towards the Sirocco.

'Stop. Wait.' Graymond stepped towards her and held up his hand. 'I'm sorry, okay?' he said defensively. 'I'm just not used to… people, socialising, all that stuff. It's not that I don't want to; it's just going to take a while, that's all.'

Alicia smiled and pushed the door of her car shut with her elbow.

'Consider this the first step in reacquainting yourself with basic social skills.'

'I suppose you'd better come in,' Graymond sighed. He nodded at the brown paper bags, 'I haven't had an Indian takeaway for a while; it must be at least seventeen years.' He hastily grabbed the shopping bags from the passenger seat of his truck and caught up with Alicia who was on the steps leading to the large oak front door. He was suddenly starving.

They sat at the kitchen island in the same chairs they had occupied the previous night. Graymond had tentatively offered to remove the dust sheets from the table and chairs in the large dining room, but Alicia had decided that the kitchen island was cosier and more homely. As she set about removing foil boxes from the paper bags, a rich aroma of spices filled the kitchen.

'Smells delicious,' Graymond said as he peered at the contents of each box.

They loaded up their plates and ate in silence for a few minutes. Graymond attacked the unexpected feast in front of him with vigour, savouring each mouthful with satisfaction. Finally, he spoke.

'You really believe it, don't you?'

Alicia took a sip of water before replying.

'Believe what?'

'That I'm innocent.'

Alicia nodded and looked him in the eyes.

'Yes, I do.'

Graymond pulled his cell phone out of his pocket and put it on the table in front of them. He tapped and swiped until the photograph of Alicia's Features article was on the screen.

'I read this at the library today.' He cast a sideways glance at Alicia as she turned the phone towards her. He wasn't sure how she would respond to the knowledge that he had completed some background research on her. A faint smile played on her lips at the realisation of what she was looking at.

'So you've been doing some homework on me?' she laughed. 'I think that's perfectly fair, considering how much I know about you. I remember writing this; I knew it was too late for anything to be done, but I just felt — I'm not sure — perhaps it was *anger* at the thought of someone taking the blame for a crime they hadn't committed. It was interesting though, after this article was published a number of people wrote to the paper to say that they felt the same way. In fact, a member of the jury even contacted me anonymously to say that he was never completely convinced of your guilt, but in the presence of overwhelming evidence against you, and the absence of any other suspects, he was left with little choice but to go along with the rest of the jury.'

She stopped and piled another spoonful of chicken korma onto her plate.

'I read a number of other articles that you wrote at the time,' Graymond said. 'I admire the way you didn't allow yourself to be influenced by speculation and popular opinion; you always stuck to the facts. Thanks for doing that.'

'You're welcome,' Alicia replied. 'I love a sensational story as much as the next journalist, but I'll never compromise the truth, in spite of the saying that you should never let the truth stand in the way of a good story. Speaking of which...' She pulled a thick legal pad and a pen from the shoulder bag at her feet and placed it next to her. 'We have work to do.' She picked up the pen and held it poised over the legal pad.

'We need to start with a list of suspects, and then for each, we'll consider means, motive and opportunity.'

Graymond looked at Alicia incredulously. 'You're not serious about this?'

'Deadly,' Alicia shot back. She tapped the pad with her pen. 'Names, Gray.'

'But... there weren't any,' Graymond stammered helplessly. 'I mean, I know there must be someone else, but at the time I was the only suspect.'

'Correction,' Alicia said, 'you were the only suspect the *police* had, but what about *your* list Gray? Who was on *your* list of suspects?'

'*My* list?' Graymond looked perplexed. 'I didn't have a list.'

'Of course you did,' Alicia insisted. 'You're thinking of someone right now, someone you suspect could have been involved. Give me a name and we'll work it up from there.'

Graymond paused in thought. Alicia was right. There was a name in his head, a name that had always been there, as a possible accomplice at least, but Graymond wasn't sure how he fitted into the picture.

'Give me the name anyway,' Alicia said.

'I saw him today,' Graymond said thoughtfully.

'Name,' Alicia said again.

'Reese Coraini.'

'Tell me how he's involved,' Alicia scribbled the name "Reese Coraini" under the heading "Suspects" at the top of the legal pad.

'I... It's complicated,' Graymond flushed slightly.

'Murder generally is.' Alicia was unperturbed. 'We're not diving for the truth in the crystal clear waters of the Caribbean, Gray; we're digging about in the muddy waters of a rubbish-strewn ditch, so get used to it. I want every detail.'

Graymond sighed. He was quite sure he wouldn't be giving Alicia every sordid detail of Reese's affair with his ex-girlfriend, although he guessed that she would find out eventually anyway. Keeping his voice cool and detached, Graymond began an abridged version of his estranged relationship with Reese: they had once been friends, pilot buddies, Reese had kept his Piper Cherokee aircraft at Blackdeane Airfield. One afternoon, Graymond had walked in on Reese and Julia who were, *well never mind,* he said to Alicia, *use your imagination.* After a heated argument, Graymond had told Reese to leave the airfield and take his aircraft with him. Reese had taken off in the Piper Cherokee later that day and had not made any contact with Graymond since. Julia subsequently ended their relationship and moved in with Reese soon afterwards, leaving Graymond a heartbroken, devastated wreck for the months that followed.

'Did he know about your little sideline as an art courier?' Alicia asked.

Graymond frowned.

'I never told him anything,' he said after a few moments, 'but I remember once after I put up the hangarage fees for the airfield, Reese wasn't too impressed. He stormed into my office, said he'd refuse to pay, and said something like why did I need to put up the prices anyway, wasn't I earning enough from my "other business". When I asked him what he meant, he said something like he knew I was involved in some shady enterprise, almost trying to hold it over me as leverage, you know? Like he wanted a "special rate" in order to keep his mouth shut. I wasn't about to be blackmailed and he never went through with it, so I just assumed he didn't know anything after all. And soon after, he left Blackdeane and didn't have to pay the new hangarage fees anyway. He was pretty angry at being asked to leave though.'

'Which gives us motive,' Alicia said, half to herself.

'But not opportunity,' Graymond added. 'He had an alibi: he was at home with Julia all night.'

Alicia looked up from her notes.

'That's no alibi,' she said scornfully. 'As far as I'm concerned, Julia's word is about as watertight as the Titanic. If he was involved, then she was too.'

'But even if that's the case, how do we go about disproving it now, nearly twenty years later?' Graymond asked helplessly.

'Trust me, we'll figure it out,' Alicia said firmly, scribbling "yes" next to the word "opportunity" on her legal pad.

'Who else?' she asked, looking back at Graymond.

'I always wondered about Caleb Fonteyne,' Graymond said, scooping some mango chutney onto a piece of naan bread.

'Caleb Fonteyne,' Alicia said slowly, as she wrote. 'And who is Mr. Fonteyne?'

'He was one of the aircraft mechanics I employed at the airfield,' Graymond replied. 'I caught him stealing on a number of occasions; specialist tools, aircraft parts, cartons of oil, all sorts of stuff. Had to let him go in the end.'

Alicia smiled to herself as she wrote.

'What's funny?' Graymond asked.

'It's a little ironic that by day you were an upstanding, model citizen of humanity, utterly shocked when you found your girlfriend cheating on you and firing one of your employees for stealing, yet by night you were the most devious, deceitful sonofabitch around.'

Graymond swallowed a mouthful of naan bread and paused.

'I've never thought of it like that,' he said. 'I guess you're right though; I was living two separate lives, sort of a Jekyll and Hyde thing.'

'At least you were only half bad,' Alicia grinned.

Graymond didn't reply. He was lost in thought.

'Why don't I make us coffee?' Alicia asked suddenly. She pushed her plate to the edge of the counter-top and stood up.

Graymond recovered himself, looked up in agreement and nodded, good idea.

'Let's finish this in the living room,' he said, taking a final bite of the naan bread. 'I'll get the fire lit.'

When Alicia brought the mugs of coffee through from the kitchen, Graymond had made up a roaring fire. The flames danced and flickered and crackled, casting a warm orange glow into the living room. The soulless grandeur of the room the previous night was transformed into a cosy, intimate setting, almost romantic, Graymond thought, although he immediately dismissed this from his mind. Alicia settled herself into one corner of the large leather couch and spread her numbered pages around her. Graymond sat at the other end and took a sip of his coffee.

'Where were we?' Alicia said, shuffling through the papers on her lap. 'Ah yes, Caleb Fonteyne. We've got means, we've got motive — you'd just fired him — what about opportunity?'

'I think he was at the cinema watching a movie with a friend at the time,' Graymond said.

'Which movie?'

'How should *I* know?' Graymond couldn't remember.

'Which friend?'

Again, Graymond wasn't sure. He reminded Alicia that none of these "suspects" were ever actually suspects because Graymond was the only possible guilty party in the police investigation. Therefore, none of these people had ever been formally interviewed by the police as a suspect, and Graymond's knowledge of each person's whereabouts on the night in question was gleaned entirely from unofficial sources and conversational snippets here and there throughout the years, mainly from Mrs Davidson. Alicia wasn't fazed and wrote the word "yes" next to "opportunity".

'What've you done that for?' Graymond asked with a puzzled look. "He was in the cinema, with a friend, a watertight alibi.'

'Like I said, Gray, nothing's watertight anymore. We're starting over. What if the friend was in on it too? They could've purchased their movie tickets, sat down on the back row and then snuck out without anyone noticing. A ticket doesn't prove they were watching the entire movie all night.'

Graymond shrugged. Alicia was right, but he just wasn't sure how they would ever begin to challenge an alibi from seventeen years ago. He didn't even know where Caleb lived or worked these days.

'Who would know?' Alicia asked. Graymond shrugged again.

'Mrs Davidson, I guess,' he suggested.

'When we've got this list together, we'll pay her a visit. You can take her some flowers or something, and we'll see if we can get any information out of her,' Alicia said.

'Won't she think it's weird?' Graymond asked. 'Surely it's the last thing she'd expect me to want to talk about?'

'Don't worry Gray, you can talk about the weather and gardening and stuff; leave the investigative work to me,' Alicia said.

Graymond looked doubtful.

'Trust me,' Alicia reassured him, 'it's my job.'

By the time the chimes of a clock somewhere in the hall struck midnight, Alicia and Graymond had, between them, drawn up a list of possible suspects; those who may have known of or had access to information about Graymond's shipment of stolen art on the night of August 14 and who would be motivated in some way to frame him for murder. Each suspect had next to his name the means, the motive and the opportunity, regardless of whether they had an alibi or not. Alicia placed the last of the pages on the colourful Persian rug in front of the fire and surveyed their work. At the bottom of the final page, she drew a large question mark.

'What's that for?' Graymond asked frowning.

'It's for the unknown,' Alicia replied. 'There's possibly someone else in the equation, someone we don't know about yet, someone in the background, lurking at the bottom of the muddy ditch. You must never assume that your list of suspects is complete. In fact, there may be more than one unknown; remember that no traces of stolen art were found in the burned-out remains of the Cessna and then three of the stolen paintings came up for sale on the black market last year. Someone unloaded those paintings from the aircraft that night, in the time between when it landed and when you drove up to it in the Ford Ranger.'

'I guess we had maybe three or four large bags to unload,' Graymond said thoughtfully, 'but I remember from previous shipments that a lot of the artwork was surprisingly bulky and heavy. There were no frames or anything, just rolled-up canvases, but it sure weighed a ton.'

'As well as transferring the paintings from the aircraft to a waiting truck, there was the additional task of immobilising and stabbing Jimmy,' Alicia continued.

'That wouldn't have been easy; he wouldn't have gone down without a fight,' Graymond said with a little smile.

'And the whole time you saw absolutely nothing?' Alicia quizzed Graymond again. 'No sign of anything going on from your vantage point in the control tower or out on the runway?'

Graymond shook his head firmly.

'No, really Alicia, I didn't see anything unusual,' he replied resolutely. 'I wish I had. Maybe I would've driven out to the aircraft sooner and been able to save Jimmy. I don't care about the artwork, they could've had it all if it meant Jimmy being alive today.'

'How much time between the aircraft coming to a stop on the runway and you driving up to it?' Alicia asked.

Graymond gazed at the glowing embers in the fireplace as he tried to recall.

'It's difficult,' he said. 'It all happened so fast.'

'Give me a ball park,' Alicia said gently.

'Maybe ten, fifteen minutes tops,' Graymond replied, 'no more than that.'

'So in fifteen minutes, someone in a hidden truck, waiting somewhere along the edge of the runway, drives up to the landing Cessna, stops Jimmy in his tracks and stabs him to within an inch of his life, and then unloads three, maybe four large duffel bags of artwork into the truck and disappears without a trace.'

They looked at each other without smiling.

'That's a pretty risky operation,' Graymond said grimly.

'But whoever it was, pulled it off,' Alicia said. 'How? Because he knew he could. He knew how the whole thing would play out. He knew the airfield would be deserted except for you and Rory in the control tower. He knew in which direction Jimmy would be landing and which taxiway he'd take to get to the apron. He'd probably even calculated how much time he'd have before you got curious and showed up on the runway.'

'That's a lot to do in fifteen minutes,' Graymond remarked soberly.

'Which brings us back to the possibility that there was more than one person involved in it all,' Alicia continued.

For a long minute, neither of them spoke. Alicia was going over the intricacies of the killer's cleverly constructed plan in her mind, while Graymond was wondering how he could possibly have missed so much action right in front of his nose.

'There were definitely two people,' he said suddenly.

Alicia raised a questioning eyebrow.

'While I was driving the Ford Ranger over to the Cessna, someone else was busy stabbing Rory in the control room,' Graymond said. He looked appalled at the thought of being so easily manipulated from one place to another in order for the killer to successfully complete his mission and escape, framing Graymond at the same time.

'Unless he, or she, was already driving towards the control tower by another route while you were driving out to the Cessna,' Alicia speculated. 'Would there have been enough time to get into the control tower and stab Rory while you were out on the runway?'

'I guess there would,' Graymond said. 'There's also a little road around the perimeter of the airfield that takes you from the runway to the control tower which he could've used. If he drove without lights, I would never have seen him. I was too busy focussing on the aircraft anyway.'

'And then he adds one final touch to his cunning plan,' Alicia concluded. 'He waits for the police to show up and sets off his little firework display, making sure Jimmy's caught in the explosion. He probably poured a few gallons of aviation fuel over everything to speed it all up and create a handy little distraction, while he tip-toed away into the night with two hundred million dollars' worth of stolen artwork.'

Graymond sighed and looked forlorn.

'I was an idiot, wasn't I?' He was burning with shame and couldn't bring himself to look at Alicia. She leaned across and squeezed his arm.

'We can all say that about the mistakes we've made,' she said gently.

'Yes, but two people lost their lives that night,' Graymond protested. 'Sure, I was stupid and greedy, but no one was supposed to die.'

'Don't get mad at yourself,' Alicia said. 'You've more than paid the price for your part in it all. It's someone else's turn for justice now.'

'But I don't see how we'll ever find him,' Graymond said despondently, 'not with what we've got here.' He picked up a page from the floor and tossed it bitterly to the side.

'Someone, somewhere, knows what happened that night,' Alicia said seriously. 'One day, he'll make a mistake, because people always do eventually; the truth doesn't stay buried forever.'

In the dim light of the glow from the fire, Graymond looked at the pages spread around in front of them. He pulled Alicia's page entitled "Suspects" towards him and studied it carefully.

'Every person on that list is under suspicion until we find the killer,' Alicia declared firmly.

She yawned suddenly and looked at her watch.

'I'd better go, it's nearly one o'clock and I've got an article to finish editing before I can even think of sleeping tonight.'

She gathered the pages neatly together and placed the little bundle into her shoulder bag. As she stood up, she turned to Graymond.

'We'll find him,' she said with conviction.

'Alicia, thank-you,' Graymond said. It was difficult to say. His eyes briefly met hers.

'I hope you realise I'm expecting exclusive rights to the story,' Alicia smiled, 'and my own personal interview with one Mr. Graymond Sharkey!'

'Sure, whatever you want,' Graymond replied. He managed to return the smile.

As he watched Alicia's Sirocco disappear towards the gates at the end of the driveway, he wished she wasn't leaving. He closed the front door and stood alone in the silent hallway. He rather liked the idea of an exclusive interview with Alicia Clayton.

Suspects:

Name: Reese Coraini
Means: Yes
Motive: Revenge for being asked to leave Blackdeane Airfield (was also having affair with Julia Tripp)
Opportunity: Yes (only Julia's word to provide an alibi)

Name: Caleb Fonteyne
Means: Yes
Motive: Former employee of Gray (aircraft mechanic); revenge for being fired after caught stealing
Opportunity: Yes (watching movie at local cinema with friend; only friend's word as alibi)

Name: Alisdair Brooks
Means: Yes
Motive: Former restaurant/bar/clubhouse manager of Blackdeane Airfield; revenge as unhappy with Gray after his refusal to give a promotion and a pay rise, threatened to leave
Opportunity: Yes (at home alone)

Name: Oliver Jacobs
Means: Yes

Motive: Gray's accountant; desperate for financial success, whether achieved legitimately or not, saw how much Gray was making from each shipment of stolen art and wanted a cut or to run the operation for himself (especially as he had initially introduced Gray to the art courier work)
Opportunity: Yes (at a party in London, but could have slipped away unnoticed)

Name: An Unknown Person
Means: Naturally
Motive: Plenty to dislike about Gray
Opportunity: Goes without saying

CHAPTER TWELVE

Graymond awoke the following morning to the vanilla rays of a pale winter sun streaming through his bedroom windows. It was mid November and particularly mild for the time of year. There was not a cloud in the sky and the wind was light; a perfect flying day. A visit to Blackdeane Airfield on such a beautiful day should have filled Graymond with excitement, but as he pulled on his navy sports jacket over one of his new white shirts, he felt only apprehension and nerves.

It was time to discuss business with Paul Greene, the cousin who had been responsible for the running and upkeep of Graymond's estate and business while Graymond was in prison. Graymond had reviewed some recent figures relating to his assets, properties and enterprises and was quite certain that Paul had not been the greatest choice to manage the estate. He had, however, been the only person available at the time; the decision to arrange for someone to be given the power of attorney had been made in haste and Graymond was grateful to Paul for stepping in and taking the reins. Paul had, naturally, been paid handsomely for liaising with letting agents and taking precious little interest in Blackdeane Airfield and GS Executive Aviation Ltd. and therefore, Graymond was rather relieved, if a little daunted, at the thought of regaining control of his businesses. He was aware that many things had changed over the last seventeen years: technology, the economy and the law, to name a few. He had decided that he would initially tread carefully with his strategy for reclaiming the success he had once known, one step at a time. If it took him a few years to bounce back, that was fine.

A life sentence in prison can change the priorities of a man; Graymond had decided he would conduct every aspect of his work with the honesty and integrity of a choir boy; he would be scrupulous with every business decision he made, he would gain the reputation for being the most bona fide, law-abiding business-man and a model citizen. There would be no hidden agendas in anything he did, no ulterior motives, just clean, fair and square, lay-it-on-the-line business dealings.

Graymond's truck pulled into the car park of Blackdeane Airfield. The Toyota was nondescript and could have belonged to anyone, and nobody even glanced at Graymond as he climbed out, some-what hesitantly, and headed for the entrance to the clubhouse. He had promised himself he would remain dispassionate and de-tached throughout the visit — a life sentence in prison made this significantly easy — and that regardless of the mess Paul had made in his role as attorney, he would be gracious and polite, thankful for his help, and they would leave on good terms. Graymond's lawyer would also be present to ensure that any necessary documentation was signed and everything was aboveboard for his fresh start.

Graymond tried to avoid a glance at the control tower and across at the runway, and taxiway delta. Where once he would have stopped to observe a small aircraft taking off into the cloudless sky, he kept his head down and hurried through a set of glass doors into the reception area. The receptionist, a middle-aged lady with thick make-up and platinum blonde hair, who wouldn't have looked out of place in a drag queen show, was busy applying a further layer of bronzer to her cheeks. She looked up and gave him a smile revealing red lipstick-stained teeth. A piece of card in a plastic holder in front of her had the name Angharad Hearn printed on it. She would have to go, as well as Paul, Graymond thought to himself.

'Good morning sir, can I help you?' Ms. Hearn asked, not rec-ognising the founder and former owner of GS Executive Aviation Ltd. Graymond didn't recognise her either.

'Looking for Paul Greene,' he replied, struggling to make eye contact. He remembered Alicia's comment regarding his lack of social skills.

'He's not in his office yet; it's a bit early for him.' The voice had a pronounced accent from the East End of London. 'You're very welcome to wait in the waiting area over there.' A hand with claw-like, red finger nails beckoned to some faded black leather sofas next to the entrance. 'Can I get you some coffee?'

Graymond looked at his watch in annoyance; it was ten o'clock on a Thursday morning and Paul hadn't yet arrived for work. He thought back to the days when he was in the office by seven every morning and tried to remind himself that everyone had a different work ethic. Declining the coffee, he sat down on a corner of the sofa facing the clubhouse door. Angharad put the bronzer in a desk drawer and went back to answering phones and shuffling papers around the cluttered desk. Two young men in pilot's uniforms entered the reception area, chatting about the weather, before disappearing through a door to the left of her. She ignored them and carried on talking into the phone.

From his corner in the reception, through the tinted floor-to-ceiling windows, Graymond watched people coming and going outside the clubhouse. He had a good view of the runway and watched a few aircraft taking off and landing. There were a couple of Cessnas and a larger business jet, perhaps an Embraer Phenom 300, Graymond wasn't sure. Seventeen years ago, he would have recognised it instantly, but his knowledge of aircraft had become a little rusty in prison. He gazed around the reception area; except for looking a little tattier and worn around the edges, it hadn't changed much. Even the sofa he sat on was the same one he had purchased nearly twenty years ago. Clearly, Paul had not bothered to invest in the airfield facilities or update them in any way, despite having full access to any funding that he required for this purpose.

The two pilots were back. They exchanged a few pleasantries with Angharad who suddenly pretended to be busy in a flurry of activity. The pilots disappeared through the glass entrance door. They didn't even notice the man in the navy sports jacket sat alone in the corner. It was a strange feeling to think that seventeen years ago, he could not have walked anywhere around the airfield without being recognised and greeted as the MD, the CEO, the man in charge. He had been respected, if not liked, by every employee (whom he knew by name) of Blackdeane Airfield and

GS Executive Aviation Ltd. Today, he was an unknown guest, an anonymous visitor. He picked up a magazine on the coffee table in front of him called Flyer. It was dated May 2014, two years out of date. It seemed to reflect the general feel of the place.

Noticing someone he recognised, Graymond dropped the magazine back on the table and stood up. He watched as a man in his fifties, red in the face and a little overweight, approached the entrance to the reception. He was wearing a black pin-striped suit and was carrying a black briefcase. Pushing open the glass door, he stepped inside and looked around, slightly out of breath. Angharad was talking earnestly into the telephone and ignored him. Graymond stepped towards him and held out a hand.

'Avery, thanks for coming, glad you found the place okay,' he said with a smile. People skills, he remembered.

'Morning Gray, yes, I hadn't forgotten how to get here,' Avery panted, giving Graymond's outstretched hand a firm shake. 'It's been a while though. Place looks a bit rundown to me.'

Graymond nodded grimly.

'When you're back at the helm I'd say you've got your work cut out for you round here,' Avery remarked, looking around the jaded reception area, 'but I suppose you could do with a challenge, you know, something to get your teeth into. Personally, I don't envy you.'

Avery Sherwood-Johnson and Graymond were old friends. They had known each other for nearly twenty years, ever since the time that Blackdeane Airfield and GS Executive Aviation Ltd. had begun to flourish and enjoy serious financial success. Avery was a lawyer from the City who had managed all of Graymond's business affairs, financial matters, taxation and, following Graymond's murder conviction, his overall estate, including setting up the power of attorney status for Paul Greene on Graymond's behalf. Avery had never been involved with Graymond's sideline of couriering artwork from the Channel Islands and had dealt solely with the law regarding the legitimate business dealings of GS Executive. Avery himself, not the most scrupulous of lawyers, lamented Graymond's demise only for the fact that he had been caught in the act, rather than for the act itself. Secretly, he wished Graymond had involved him in the illegitimate artwork courier business; it would have been a nice little bit of extra-curricular work for him, off the books, and a nice little top-up for the bank account. At any rate, Avery admired Graymond's business ethics — particularly the immoral ones — and was happy to provide legal assistance, once again, even if Graymond had emphasised that everything was to remain above board.

'Where's Paul? Shall we get started?' Avery asked. He had to be back in the City for a meeting at one o'clock.

'Paul's not here yet,' Graymond replied, trying to hide a note of frustration. Angharad looked up from her desk and interrupted.

'He's normally in by about eleven,' she reassured them.

Graymond rolled his eyes.

'Are you sure you don't want some coffee?' Angharad asked again.

'Coffee would be wonderful.' Avery had never been one to refuse an offer of food or drink. 'Cream and two sugars,' he added, lowering himself heavily onto the tired sofa.

'I'll take mine black,' Graymond said.

'I'll get those right away for you.' The height of efficiency herself, Angharad was already out of her chair, high heels clip-clopping across the laminate floor to the coffee machine.

Paul and the coffee arrived at the same time and without any apology for his tardiness, he ushered Graymond and Avery through to his office. He exchanged some flirtatious banter with Angharad, whom he referred to as "Harry" — clearly she was more than just his receptionist — and asked her to bring him "his usual" when she had a moment.

The three men seated themselves in Paul's office, with Paul behind a large desk made of teak — the place where Graymond once sat — and Graymond and Avery facing him on the other side. Hanging on the wall behind Paul, Graymond noticed a calendar with the picture of the month showing a barely clad woman pole-dancing in what appeared to be a strip club. As Avery pulled a bundle of papers out of his briefcase, Harry appeared at the door with Paul's "usual" which looked like a simple latte to Graymond.

After the obligatory repartee, consisting mainly of what seemed to be private jokes, she disappeared with a little wave at Paul. Graymond felt nauseous.

'Well, gentlemen, let's get started, shall we?' Avery brought the meeting to order. 'The purpose of today, as I'm sure we're all aware, is to thank you Mr. Greene for the, er, outstanding job you've done acting as Mr. Sharkey's power of attorney for the last seventeen years, and to officially bring this role to an end in order for Mr. Sharkey to resume full responsibility of his properties and business interests.'

'It's been a pleasure to help out while you were inside, Gray,' Paul said, feigning a pleasant smile. He took a slurp of his latte and a layer of milk foam stuck to his upper lip. *Yeah, I'll bet it's been a pleasure*, Graymond thought to himself, *you've simultaneously run my businesses into the ground and turned the clubhouse into a downmarket playboy den for you and that trashy receptionist. All for a ridiculously inflated fee.*

'As you can see, I've kept the place flourishing with the usual business acumen you'd expect,' Paul continued.

Graymond, who at that moment was taking a sip of his coffee, nearly choked.

'Are you okay?' Avery looked at him in alarm.

'I'm fine,' Graymond replied, still coughing. 'It's a little hot, I think I'll let it cool for a minute.' He placed his coffee mug back on the desk.

'I think you'll agree that GS Executive Aviation has gone from strength to strength over the last seventeen years.' Paul was still talking. 'I take pride in the fact that through my shrewd leadership, intuitive business sense and visionary approach, the company has enjoyed unrivalled success.' Another fake grin. What was his agenda?

Graymond gave Avery a sideways glance.

'Yes well, thank you Mr. Greene, as I've said, Mr. Sharkey is very grateful for...'

'It is on the basis on this success that I was hoping Gray would consider employing me, full time, as the Vice President of GS Executive,' Paul interrupted Avery and looked earnestly at both gentlemen. He took another sip of the latte and replenished the milk foam on his upper lip before finishing the sentence, 'with perhaps a small pay rise?'

Graymond's eyes widened and a few sentences of colourful language came into his mind before he reminded himself of his original game plan to be polite and gracious in the process of abdicating Paul from his duties. One of the things he had learned within the confines of prison walls was patience, and now was the time to exercise some verbal restraint and self-control. Avery could do the talking; it was safer that way.

'Mr. Greene,' Avery said firmly, 'I am quite sure that Mr. Sharkey has taken note of your interest in a position at his company and will bear that in mind once he has assumed his role as managing director. Now if we could...'

'I was sort of hoping we could discuss it now,' Paul said insistently.

Graymond looked across at Avery and gave a shake of his head. He didn't care if Paul noticed or not.

'That's not the purpose of today's meeting, I'm afraid, Mr. Greene,' Avery said loudly. He leaned forward and pushed the bundle of papers over the desk towards Paul.

'If I could ask you both to sign these documents, starting with you Paul, to end your power of attorney over Mr. Sharkey's estate, including his properties, his businesses and assets, and then we'll go over a few other small matters before we finish up.'

Paul fell silent. He looked like a wounded prey who knew he was beaten as the papers were signed and collected by Avery. The lawyer then rattled through a few other points of the law, somewhat briefly for him, while producing more documents to read, check and sign. Graymond rapidly scanned each one, taking in every word; Paul struggled with the first sentence on each before giving up and signing anyway. As Avery collected the final few pages, there was a knock on the door followed by Angharad's head peering around the doorframe.

'Sorry to interrupt you boys,' she said, sounding anything but apologetic, 'but Paul — er, Mr. Greene — there's a Philip Yewdale here to see you. He says it's about the jacuzzi that you ordered;

would that be for the training room you're converting to your personal treatment room? Should I show him in there for you?'

'Your *what*?' Graymond snarled at Paul, who almost jumped out of his seat in fright. 'Your *own personal treatment room in one of the training rooms*? What the hell d'you think this place is Paul? A country club?'

Paul held up his hands in protest.

'It's not what you think, Gray,' he said defensively.

'No? What is it then?' Gray snapped back.

'Well, I...' Paul began.

'Don't bother answering,' Gray interrupted. He turned to Angharad. 'You can tell Mr. Yewdale that Paul won't be meeting with him this morning and that he'll be cancelling the order for the jacuzzi.'

Angharad cast a confused look in Paul's direction. Paul nodded weakly and she disappeared.

'Well, I think that concludes our business for today gentlemen,' Avery said briskly, stuffing the bundle of papers into his briefcase. 'I'll be getting back to the office now.' He stood up and shook the hands of Paul and Graymond adding, 'if there's anything else, feel free to give me a call any time.'

'Thanks Avery, I'll be in touch,' Graymond said and gave Paul a hostile look. 'I suggest we meet later this week for you to get me up to speed with everything. I doubt it will take too long. I'll expect you to have everything in order in preparation for the hand over.'

Paul was nodding. His face wore a shell-shocked expression. The party was over.

'And don't be late,' Graymond said over his shoulder as he disappeared through the office door, leaving it open.

Without looking back, Graymond strode out of the clubhouse and across the car park to his truck. He had intended to spend a little time at the airfield after the meeting, looking around the place, perhaps checking in with a few of the current employees, getting a feel for it all again. Not today, he decided. He knew from the figures and from Paul's infrequent visits to him in prison that the business had been poorly managed, but what really angered him was Paul's ignorant belief that he had made a good job of it, as well as his audacity at the expectation of being offered a senior position in the company.

Graymond slammed the door of the Toyota, started the engine and shifted it into gear. He looked straight ahead as he drove away in a cloud of dust, past the long unkempt grass and the fading Blackdeane Airfield sign at the entrance. There was a lot of work to be done. Graymond remembered a younger version of himself to whom such a challenge would have been met with excitement and determination. Today, he could only feel disheartened at the daunting prospect of resurrecting GS Executive Aviation Ltd. to its former glory. He accelerated away from the airfield, unsure of where he was headed. Perhaps he'd just drive around for a bit. The sun was still shining and he had no other place to be. He needed to think things through. He'd built his business from nothing twenty years ago; he knew he could do it again and it would be even better this time around.

CHAPTER THIRTEEN

Alisdair Brooks would be lying if he said he hadn't taken more than a casual glance at the attractive red head who had sat alone at the bar for over an hour now. She sipped Moët & Chandon Impérial delicately from a flute glass with a wistful look. He slid a couple of bourbons across the counter to two businessmen, acknowledged the generous tip and coolly stepped over to the red head. The champagne was almost finished.

'Is there anything else I can get you, madam?' he asked, picking up a wine glass and starting to polish it carefully.

The red head looked up at Alisdair with beautiful, dark eyes. He melted.

'Actually I'm waiting for someone,' she replied, 'but I guess I could have another of these.' She touched the now empty flute glass. 'Unless, of course, you can recommend one of your cocktails?' Through puppy dog eyes, she looked seductively at Alisdair, who's newly divorced heart almost began to fibrillate.

'Well,' he flashed a charming smile, 'I think I may be able to do just that. A particular favourite with my more fashionable clients is the Red Passion; I think you'll enjoy the blend of Maraschino liqueur, rose and passion fruit.'

'Oh that sounds divine,' the red head replied, managing a small, but captivating smile in return.

'Certainly madam,' Alisdair beamed. With the flamboyance of a Las Vegas stage show, Alisdair began preparing the drink. He always enjoyed the attention and the looks of admiration as he tossed and spun bottles and cocktail shakers; he was certainly getting plenty of those from the mysterious red head. He may be balding and greying slightly and his waistline may be narrowing the gap with his age in inches, but apparently he'd still got it. She slid a silk scarf off her shoulders, revealing flawless skin and a low-cut neckline of a charcoal satin camisole. Around her neck was the most stunning diamond necklace, glittering with brilliance in the subdued lighting of Hoolaghan cocktail bar and club, a favourite haunt of the rich and famous, City bankers and celebrities.

With a flourish, Alisdair placed a lace doily in front of his beautiful admirer onto which he carefully put a glass containing an exquisitely garnished liquid, bright red in colour.

'One Red Passion for the lady,' Alisdair beamed. He waited breathlessly as she took a sip.

'Oh my,' the red head exclaimed, 'I've never tasted anything quite like this before. It's heavenly. You have a rare talent Mr.?'

'Alisdair, please!' he blushed.

'Melissa Pendergast-Jones,' another seductive smile, revealing dazzling white teeth, perfectly aligned, 'but please call me Melissa.'

'Honoured to meet you, Melissa,' Alisdair was almost bowing. To his annoyance, a customer a few bar stools away signalled for his attention.

'I'll be right back,' he faithfully promised Melissa. She nodded understandingly; she wasn't going anywhere.

'Where did you become such a talented bartender?' Melissa purred with a bell-like voice when Alisdair returned, following another demonstration of flawless mixology skills.

'Oh here and there,' Alisdair replied, blushing all over again. 'I've picked a few things up over the years.'

'Along with what is clearly a natural flair.' Melissa stretched a slender arm with a single diamond-encrusted bracelet across the bar, while resting her chin on the other hand. Her hands and nails were perfectly manicured, and without a wedding or engagement ring on the left, Alisdair noticed.

'Oh well, maybe, perhaps a little,' he replied coolly.

'I bet you could work anywhere in the world, in any bar you wanted,' Melissa smiled.

'Well, I'm not sure I...'

'Oh Alisdair, you're so modest.' Melissa toyed provocatively with the lace doily. 'You know, I'm actually looking for a talented, handsome bartender — such as yourself — to take care of the bar onboard my private yacht. I usually entertain an exclusive group of guests for a New Year's Eve party and then we sail around the Caribbean during January and February.'

'Exclusive guests?' Alisdair was intrigued. He had served his share of celebrity clients at Hoolaghan, but this could be a step-up to bigger and better things.

'Oh I can't possibly divulge the guest list,' Melissa said with a wink, 'although I have no doubt I could rely on your absolute discretion Alisdair.'

'Oh you could, you can,' Alisdair stumbled out his words. He liked the way she said his name; she half-whispered the "-dair" part. 'Did you say the Caribbean?'

'Yes, that's right,' Melissa smiled. All the time she spoke, her dark eyes were fixated on Alisdair, who was mesmerised. 'We may have a little stopover on my private island too; it's only small but simply delightful. It even has its own runway for my private jet.'

'I love the Caribbean,' Alisdair said dreamily. 'I worked on cruise ships for a few years, frequently sailed around the Caribbean, visited all the islands, I think it was one of my favourite destinations.'

'Oh you would just *adore* my private island,' Melissa flashed the bar tender an alluring smile. They were briefly interrupted by another patron and Alisdair's skills were again on display. This time he played for his captivated audience of one.

'Did you say you were here to meet someone?' Alisdair asked on his return to Melissa's end of the bar.

'Oh yes, I was,' Melissa looked suddenly upset and glanced at a diamond studded Rolex watch with mother-of-pearl face. 'Either he's very late or I've been stood up.' The sorrowful, puppy dog eyes quickly replaced the seductive ones.

Alisdair gave his best look of sympathy and understanding. Who would stand this beautiful, attractive woman up? What a jerk that person must be. Still, if Alisdair could do anything to help, he was right here.

'I'm so sorry,' he said with empathy. 'Can I make you another drink? It's on the house.'

Melissa closed her eyes and touched her head with one of the perfectly manicured hands for a moment, as if the pain of the betrayal was too much to bear.

'I'd love another Red Passion,' she said, emphasising the word "passion".

'Coming right up.' Alisdair grabbed a glass and set to work. After placing a second Red Passion on a fresh lace doily in front of Melissa, he poured himself a whisky on the rocks. Drinking on the job was strictly forbidden, but to hell with the rules, this was a special occasion, Alisdair told himself.

'Have you ever been on board a private jet, Alisdair?' Melissa was asking.

'Er — a couple of times,' Alisdair replied. 'Not in flight or anything, just on the ground. I used to manage the restaurant, bar and clubhouse of a small airport on the outskirts of London.'

'Oh?' Melissa took a sip of the cocktail. 'Which one?'

'It was years ago,' Alisdair looked suddenly uncomfortable.

'I occasionally fly from Blackdeane Airfield in my private jet,' Melissa said. 'It's a little run-down these days but they do so well with taking care of privacy and discretion. If I'm flying with celebrity companions you can guarantee there'll be no waiting paparazzi. Do you know Blackdeane, Alisdair? It's very conveniently located just outside of London.'

'That's the airfield I used to work at,' Alisdair replied, his face suddenly darkening. He downed the whisky and poured himself another.

'Oh what a coincidence,' Melissa remarked with a surprised expression. 'When did you work there? Our paths may have crossed before, although I'm sure I'd remember someone as... charming as you, Alisdair.'

'I was there in the nineties,' Alisdair replied. 'Worked for a chap called Graymond Sharkey; you might have heard of him, he was a millionaire businessman — owned the airfield and a private jet charter company called GS Executive Aviation — but he blew it when he murdered two of his employees in cold blood. They were involved in some illegal artwork smuggling racket; he got greedy and decided he wanted it all for himself.'

'Oh Alisdair, that's quite the story,' Melissa was wide-eyed. 'What happened to Mr. Sharkey?'

'Got banged up for murder with a life sentence, didn't he?' Alisdair said, rather smugly. 'Serves him right though, be sure your sins will find you out and all that.'

'So he was guilty?' Melissa inquired.

'One hundred and fifty percent,' Alisdair replied. 'He always protested his innocence but it was a no-brainer as far as the jury was concerned; they came to an unanimous verdict of guilty as charged.'

'Did *you* believe he was guilty Alisdair?' Melissa asked suddenly. 'I mean, you knew him, he was your employer. What was he like?'

Alisdair had been on a role, but now he hesitated. Melissa watched him finish his second whisky which was certainly freeing up the flow of information. He looked into the glass, debating whether to pour himself a third.

'I don't think anyone would mind if you had a little fun to-night,' Melissa teased.

Needing no further invitation, a third whisky was poured and Alisdair continued the story.

'I didn't like him much to be honest. He was a good boss when he started out and we got on all right, but then he had a few personal things happen — family tragedies, girlfriend cheating on him, stuff like that — and he lost it a bit. He sort of became hard and cold, and full of himself too, he was pretty arrogant. Success too early is never a good thing; he was twenty-one when he made his first million. I guess I'd say he was always very hardworking, very fair, never cared about popularity or anything and always wanted to do the right thing whether people hated him or not, but there wasn't much love lost between me and him.'

'Why?' Melissa asked.

'There were a few things we didn't see eye to eye on,' Alisdair said. 'I asked him for a promotion and a pay rise a couple of times, said I wanted to get more involved in the running of the place — I knew I was up to it and all that — but he wasn't interested, told me I could leave if I didn't like the job or the pay. Things got quite heated a couple of times.'

'What an idiot,' Melissa rolled her beautiful eyes. 'Clearly he had no idea how lucky he was to have a man of your talent working for him.'

'Exactly right,' Alisdair nodded, fuelled with the finest Jameson Gold and Melissa's charms.

'What did you do?' Melissa asked.

'I stuck around for a bit and then after the night he murdered his two employees — he did it at the airfield, you know, stabbed them to death and then blew up one of his own aircraft to hide the evidence — well, after that night the whole place was a mess. It was a crime scene for ages, none of the employees knew what was going on, or whether they still had jobs, the reputation of the airfield was in shreds and I thought Alisdair, it's time to get out of here; start over, big adventures ahead. I travelled for a bit; Mexico, Hawaii and the South Pacific, stayed in some pretty exotic places and then got a gig on a cruise ship which was hard work but a great experience, and now I'm back here in the City.'

'Did you know your boss was moonlighting as a courier for millions of dollars of stolen artwork?' Melissa asked.

'I did, actually,' Alisdair replied. 'One of my buddies, a private pilot who kept his aircraft at Blackdeane found out and told me about it.'

'Wow! What did you think when he told you? Were you surprised?' Melissa hung on every word. As much as Alisdair could think of a thousand more enjoyable topics of conversation, he clearly had Melissa's undivided attention with his story-telling. He would ensure he portrayed himself as the unsung hero that he was.

'In my line of work, Melissa, nothing surprises me,' Alisdair replied casually, with the air of a man who has seen the world. He went on. 'I don't know how my buddy found out about Sharkey's little sideline, but he'd also managed to get a copy of a list of dates which detailed when the shipments of stolen artwork were to be flown into the airfield by night. The two employees Sharkey murdered were in on it: Rory, an air traffic controller at Blackdeane, and Jimmy, the chief pilot at GS Aviation.'

'Go on,' Melissa's eyes were sparkling, Alisdair's eyes were becoming a little glazed.

'We went to the airfield one night when we knew an art shipment was being flown in by Jimmy,' Alisdair continued. 'Sure enough, the aircraft arrived on schedule — from the Channel Islands I think — the three of them unloaded four duffel bags, which I guess were holding the artwork, into Sharkey's truck, then they shut down the control room and Sharkey took off. We tried to follow him, but we lost him. I've no idea where they were taking the artwork to.'

'Did you ever speak to Mr. Sharkey about it?'

'No.' Alisdair shook his head. 'We were going to, but then that night happened and it was all over.'

'What was the name of your friend?' Melissa asked.

'Reese,' Alisdair replied. 'Reese Coraini. He didn't have much time for Sharkey either; he started dating Sharkey's girlfriend and was asked, in no uncertain terms, to leave Blackdeane and take his aircraft with him. Reese told me things got quite nasty between them. That doesn't surprise me either; Sharkey definitely knew how to make enemies.'

'Sounds like these amazing talents of yours were wasted at that place anyway,' Melissa smiled. 'I do love a man with a bit of daring and adventure.'

Alisdair basked in the glory of Melissa's compliments. Another customer had a cocktail order and he was briefly distracted. The whisky seemed to enhance his bar skills immensely. When he returned to his station opposite Melissa, she was speaking earnestly into her cell phone, a concerned look on her face.

'I'm on my way,' she finished the conversation and looked up at Alisdair.

'Something's come up; I have to go,' she said apologetically. Alisdair looked crestfallen.

'I'd really like to see you again, Melissa,' he said, slurring his words slightly, 'and I'd definitely be interested in the job on your private yacht.'

'Oh absolutely, Alisdair,' Melissa threw the silk scarf over her shoulders, 'we'll certainly see each other again. Do you have a pen and paper?'

Alisdair was all over it; the pen and a scrap of till receipt paper were instantly in front of Melissa. She scribbled her name in flamboyant handwriting and a cell phone number.

'Call me,' she winked at Alisdair as she pushed the piece of paper towards him. He picked it up in a daze.

'Thank you,' he replied breathlessly, 'I'll be sure to.'

'And thank you for the drinks,' Melissa said, picking up a large designer handbag from the bar stool next to her. Alisdair watched in awe as Melissa strode gracefully towards the door and disappeared. He glanced down at the till receipt paper and smiled to himself. He'd always known he was destined for greater things.

CHAPTER FOURTEEN

On the street outside, Melissa hailed a cab to Liverpool St. Station. It was quicker than taking the underground at this time of the evening when most of the rush hour traffic had dispersed. A cab would also give Melissa a convenient ten minutes to dispose of the red wig and change out of the Louboutins into a pair of flat shoes that she could actually walk in. Stuffing the wig into her large handbag, Melissa pulled out the clips securing her long dark hair and shook it free. As the cab hurried along the London streets, brightly lit against the winter darkness, she unclasped the diamond necklace and bracelet and slid them carefully into velvet lined boxes. She'd return them to her trusted jeweller companion tomorrow.

The cab swung to a stop just outside Liverpool St. Station and Alicia Clayton stepped out onto the pavement. Before entering the station, she pulled a plastic container out of her handbag containing a reddish coloured liquid and tossed it into a trash can, wondering just how drunk she might have been had she consumed it all. She smiled to herself at the thought of Alisdair dialling the cell phone number she had given him; it was the WhatsApp number of a television daytime chat show. The smile quickly faded as she remembered the call she had taken in Hoolaghan, which had necessitated her hasty exit. She had, by that time, obtained all the information she was hoping for and was ready to leave, so the call was timely, if a little concerning. She read the text message that had been sent to her cell phone following the call, which contained the name of a bar in a nearby town not far from Blackdeane. It would require Alicia to get off the train from London a couple of stops early from where she'd take a cab to the bar. Filled with a sense of unease and dread, she turned and jogged up the steps to the entrance of Liverpool St. Station. This wasn't how she had envisioned the ending to a successful evening of detective work.

As the cab pulled up outside a dive bar called The Gold Room, Alicia paid the driver and stepped onto the pavement somewhat apprehensively. Two bouncers in black suits, probably with a combined weight approaching five hundred pounds, guarded a dark entrance with steps leading downwards. Above the entrance was an old Hollywood-style yellow neon sign lit up with the words: The Gold Ro-m. One of the "o"s of the word Room had lost its neon glow. The dirty sign was attached to a red brick wall covered with a variety of interesting exhibits of spray-painted art and floral language.

Alicia approached the bouncers with a casual aloofness and they waved her through, down the stairs into a long, dingy room — almost resembling a corridor — with a bar stretching along its length. The only light seemed to come from two widescreen TVs which were showing a football match and a late night chat show, although Alicia noticed small, dim lamps on haphazardly arranged tables opposite the bar. For nearly eleven o'clock at night, the place was relatively quiet, with most of the customers sat at the bar glued to one of the TV screens. Alicia approached the bar and signalled to the barman, who was probably approaching sixty, with long grey hair tied back in a ponytail.

'Get you somethin' darlin'?' he asked.

'I'm here to collect someone,' Alicia began. 'I had a call earlier from a Torben Yorke.'

'That's me,' the barman replied. 'You'll be Alicia Clayton, right?'

'Right,' Alicia nodded.

'He's over there.' Torben motioned with an arm covered with an intricate tapestry of tattoos to the far end of the bar where a man sat slouched against the wall with his eyes closed and mouth slightly open.

'What happened?' Alicia asked without moving.

'Came in here, late afternoon, had a couple of beers, moved onto shots, all the while telling me this crazy story that he's just served a life sentence in prison for two murders, which he didn't commit — they all say that, don't they? — an' now he's looking for the truth, looking for justice. We're fairly relaxed here, but it got to the point where I told him he'd had enough to drink, you know what I'm saying? He got pretty aggressive and, well we don't tolerate threatening behaviour here, I try to keep a civilised 'stablishment, don't want no trouble. Told him if he didn't leave, I'd have to call the police, get him escorted off the premises…'

You'd let this place burn to the ground before you had the police in, Alicia thought, looking around her, but let it pass.

'Anyway,' Torben was still talking, 'he suddenly backed off, begged me not to call the police, said he'd leave right away, but by that time he could barely stand, let alone walk. I couldn't throw him out on the street, so I propped him up over there and asked him if there was anyone I could call to come and get him. He asked for you.'

Wonderful, Alicia thought.

'He's all yours,' Torben said with a sympathetic shrug. 'Let me know if you need a hand getting him out to your car, speaking of which…' Torben reached under the bar and pulled out a bunch of keys. 'Couldn't let him drive, could I?'

'Thanks.' Alicia took the keys and made her way towards the man passed out at the back of the room, ignoring the stares of the rest of The Gold Room's dubious clientele.

'Gray,' Alicia said as she approached him. No response.

'*Gray*,' Alicia said, a little louder. '*Graymond.*' She placed a hand on his shoulder and shook him. He rolled his head towards her, slowly opened his eyes and tried to focus on her face.

'Gray, you idiot, what did you think you were doing?' Alicia raised her voice as loud as she dare. Graymond allowed his head to loll back again the wall.

'No, wake up, you're coming home,' Alicia said firmly, shaking him again.

'Really? With you? Happy to.' Graymond's words slurred together. 'Whatever you want beautiful,' he added with a leer. One of the bouncers appeared behind Alicia and she stepped to one side to let him through.

'Shut up, Gray,' Alicia snapped. She nodded to the bouncer who manhandled Graymond off the bar stool and guided him through the room and up the stairs. As they emerged through the narrow entrance onto the street, Alicia pressed the key fob of Graymond's truck keys and looked around. A few cars along, there was a bleep and flash of orange, indicating where he had parked the Toyota.

'Over there,' she signalled to the bouncer who half-walked, half-dragged Graymond along the pavement.

'Wait a sec,' Graymond suddenly said, putting up a hand in distress. He began to retch and pulled away from the bouncer, who rapidly let him go. He stumbled into the gutter, fell onto his hands and knees and vomited into a drain. The bouncer smirked at Alicia who gave him a weary look. Graymond vomited again before wiping his mouth with his hand. Alicia produced a bunch of tissues from her handbag and gave them to him.

'Clean yourself up, Gray, and get up,' she said abruptly, 'and if you puke all over the inside of your truck on the way home, that's your problem. I'm just glad it's not my car.'

With the expertise of one who had completed the manoeuvre many times before, the bouncer assisted Graymond to his feet and guided him to the truck where Alicia held the passenger door open. Between them, they helped him climb in. The combined smell of alcohol and vomit was overpowering as Alicia stretched the seat belt across him. She nodded thanks to the bouncer and joined Graymond in the cab of the truck in the driver's seat. Graymond's head, resting on the seat-back, rolled to the side to look at her.

'I can drive us home,' he said, the words barely comprehensible.

'Gray, it's late, you're drunk and you're wasting my time,' Alicia said sharply. She started the truck with a roar.

'I'm fine,' Graymond's glazed eyes were still desperately trying to focus. 'Never felt better. Where are we going?'

'I'm taking you home,' Alicia said again. She gave a frustrated sigh. 'How could you do this, Gray? How could you let this happen?' There was anguish in her voice.

'What?' Graymond slurred.

'Never mind,' Alicia replied wearily. She put the truck into gear and reversed out of the parking space.

By the time they pulled up outside the front door of Blackdeane House, Graymond was snoring loudly in the passenger seat.

'Wake up,' Alicia said loudly, jabbing him in the ribs, 'you're home.'

Graymond jumped and looked around him in bewilderment.

'Where am I?' he asked.

'Home,' Alicia said harshly. She jumped out of the truck and ran to the passenger side.

'Get out Gray,' she said, yanking the passenger door open. She waited impatiently while Graymond fumbled with the seat belt release button. When he had finally managed to disentangle himself from it, he stepped down out of the truck unsteadily. He put an arm around Alicia's shoulders for support and breathed the stench of vomit and stale alcohol into her face again. Before they made it through the front door, Graymond had had to take a few minutes to puke some more before he wiped his mouth and continued inside.

Alicia had never been upstairs in Blackdeane House. She considered putting him in the lounge to sleep it off, but decided he'd probably be better in his own bed, if they could make it up the staircase. Thankfully, Graymond managed to remember where his bedroom was in the vast expanse of the first floor and Alicia flipped on the light. She looked at him in disgust. The new sports jacket and shirt were covered in vomit and, to her dismay, Alicia realised that it had also been transferred to her designer jacket. She threw it onto the floor, followed by Graymond's own jacket and shirt. Graymond half fell, half sat onto the bed and Alicia pulled off his trousers, soaked from more vomit and from kneeling in the gutter. In different circumstances, she would have been impressed by his toned upper body. She left his boxers on and threw the duvet over him as he collapsed back into his bed and immediately began snoring again.

As annoyed as she was with him, Alicia decided to stay put with Graymond overnight; the thought of him inhaling his own vomit wasn't a pleasant one and would, of course, put an end to the investigation into the truth of the airfield murders and the subsequent chance of a high-profile crime story. In addition, she was tired. It was past midnight and she had no means of getting home as her Sirocco was still in the car park of Blackdeane Station. She switched on a bed side lamp and flipped off the main light, before padding through to an en suite bathroom next door where she took a hot shower. After drying herself with a towel, she found one of Graymond's shirts in a chest of drawers in the bedroom before settling herself into a chair by the window. The blinds were still open and she gazed through the wooden slats into the darkness outside. It was a clear night and she contemplated the infinite number of twinkling stars, like tiny diamonds glittering in the blackness of a winter's night sky. She glanced across the room at Graymond who was breathing heavily in his drunken slumber. Pulling her knees up to her chest, she turned back to the window and mulled over the evening's events.

CHAPTER FIFTEEN

His head was throbbing and the thirst was unbearable. Graymond opened his eyes which seemed to be stuck together and immediately closed them again; the light was too bright. He attempted to open them again, more slowly. His vision was blurred, he was almost seeing double, his head was pounding and he desperately needed a drink of water. He eased himself up on his elbows and looked around. Where was he? Across the bright room, he noticed someone sat in the chair, quietly watching him. He blinked.

'Alicia?' he croaked. His voice was hoarse. He licked his lips; they were cracked and dry.

'Good morning Graymond,' Alicia said icily from across the room. She didn't move.

'What happened? Where am I? What are you doing here?' Graymond sat up a little more and rubbed his forehead, confused.

'You don't remember?' came the frosty reply.

Graymond thought for a moment.

'I remember the meeting at the airfield yesterday, with Paul and Avery,' he said slowly. 'Paul just made me so angry, I just… I went for a drive and — and then I went to a bar. Just for a couple of beers.'

'A couple of beers?' Alicia asked reproachfully.

Graymond looked at her. His ability to focus was a little better and the light not as blinding. He noticed she was wearing one of his shirts. She looked good in it.

'It wasn't just a couple though, was it?' he said sombrely. He looked down at the crumpled duvet and suddenly felt a sense of shame.

'It wasn't,' Alicia said.

'I remember asking the barman to call you,' Graymond said. 'I don't remember much else. I'm sorry Alicia.' He looked up at her, embarrassed. 'Thanks for coming to get me. There was no one else to call on.'

'You can't do this, Gray,' Alicia said. 'You can't let this happen again.'

'I know,' Graymond replied soberly. 'Alicia, can we discuss this over coffee? And I need some aspirin too.'

'I'll get the coffee on. Come down when you're ready,' Alicia replied. She stood up and Graymond cast a lingering gaze at her long legs as she stepped out of the room. He cursed himself for driving to a bar and giving in to the temptation of a couple of beers, but most of all, he bitterly regretted Alicia seeing him like this. What had possessed him to ask the barman to call her?

He pulled on a t-shirt and a pair of jeans and carefully made his way down the stairs to join Alicia in the kitchen where she had a glass of water, two aspirin and a freshly made pot of coffee waiting. She perched on a chair furthest from him, with her own mug of coffee.

'Thanks,' Graymond said, swallowing the aspirin and gulping down the water in one go. He poured himself some coffee and took a seat, wincing at the pain in his head.

'What happened Gray?' Alicia asked.

Graymond took a sip of coffee. He felt better already, but he wished he wasn't having this conversation.

'A combination of things, I suppose,' he replied. 'I'm grateful to be out of prison and I love this new life of freedom, but trying to fit in with society again, the change of pace, it's so different to prison life, everything's different; the world's moved on and evolved and I'm still trying to catch up with it all.'

Alicia listened but didn't reply.

'I met with my cousin Paul and my lawyer Avery yesterday,' Graymond continued, in between sips of coffee. 'Paul has had the power of attorney over my businesses and my estate. Alicia, I can't tell you what a disaster he's made of everything. I knew things were bad but I didn't realise how bad. He's pretty much run everything into the ground and I'm almost going to have to start over. It's going to take so much work to get things back to how they were before and I don't know if I can do it. I just felt... overwhelmed with it all, with life, with the businesses, with everything.'

Alicia stared at him, unfeelingly. The air was tense and awkward between them.

'I promise it won't happen again,' Graymond said earnestly.

'I need you to stay focused, Gray,' Alicia said finally. 'You can't just head to a bar and drown your sorrows every time you think you feel overwhelmed with life.'

The screen of her cell phone suddenly lit up and it started to vibrate across the marble work surface. She studied the screen for a moment before answering it.

'Kam, hi,' she said. She listened for a few seconds and then replied. 'Perfect, I'll be there. Thanks for this, Kam. I'll see you later.'

Placing the phone back onto the work surface, she looked at Graymond.

'That was my contact. She's an independent artwork consultant, the go-to person for art dealers. She can spot a high-end forgery a mile away with a blindfold on, and often facilitates negotiations and smooths paths between buyers and sellers with millions of dollars' worth of art. She owes me one and thinks she might be able to help with tracing those three paintings that showed up on the black market last year.'

'How?' Graymond asked.

'She wasn't involved in the original negotiations, but she thinks she knows which art dealer may have been. He was the man to take care of things if you had a high-end painting that you wanted to get rid of quickly and quietly. The problem with these pieces of artwork back then was firstly that they were stolen. The paintings, although valuable, weren't going to be easy to get rid of, especially when they had been all over the news after having been stolen, illegally flown into an airfield and burned up in an aircraft explosion. They would've been a real headache for anyone trying to get rid of them. Apparently this art dealer was quite the magician when it came to such pieces of artwork.'

'What about my own art dealer contacts from the nineties? We could track them down too and see if they know anything,' Graymond suggested.

'Tobias Anneijes, your Dutch contact and Sonny Duclair, your man this end, were both caught in an undercover sting operation a few months after you were sent to prison. I've studied the reports made at the time and I don't believe they had anything to do with any of the stolen artwork listed in the inventory at your trial. There's another reason I don't think they were involved: with the media frenzy surrounding the events of the airfield that night, whoever murdered your two companions and took the stolen artwork would've had to lay low for a while; they couldn't risk trying to get rid of the paintings with so much interest in the case. With the police and the media all over the inventory of stolen artwork, it was too dangerous to try to offload the paintings until things had quietened down, by which time Anneijes and Duclair's dubious activities were under investigation, ergo another dealer had to be sourced.'

'Sonny and Tobias were caught?' Graymond looked shocked. 'I had no idea. Where are they now?'

'Don't know,' Alicia replied. 'They're both out of prison, probably involved in some illicit trading somewhere. Kam might know. But they're not our guys.'

'So what happens next?' Graymond asked. He massaged his temples and poured himself some more coffee. The hangover was dulling his senses and he wanted to take in every detail from Alicia.

'I'm meeting with Kam later this morning,' Alicia said. 'I'll call you when I've heard what she's got for me.'

Graymond nodded.

'There's one other thing I should tell you,' Alicia continued. 'I checked out your creepy friend Alisdair Brooks yesterday evening.'

'You saw Alisdair?' Graymond said with surprise. 'What's he doing now? How did you find him? And he's not my friend. Never has been.'

'He works at a swanky club in London called Hoolaghan,' Alicia replied.

'Never heard of it,' Graymond said flatly.

'No, well you wouldn't, you've been off the radar for seventeen years,' Alicia remarked, with a hint of a smile. 'And it's not important how I found him.'

'Did you tell him who you were?' Graymond asked.

'Yeah I said I was a crime reporter and I was trying to find out if he was the one who framed you for the murders of Jimmy Keyes and Rory Conway.'

'Very funny. So how did you get him to talk?'

'Without a whole lot of difficulty,' Alicia said with amusement. 'He's a sucker for a bit of flattery and hollow charm.'

'You got the right man then,' Graymond laughed.

'Gray, he and Reese Coraini knew about your shady courier work, right down to a comprehensive list of dates and times of shipments of the artwork,' Alicia said seriously. 'They even followed you to the airfield one night and watched you unload the paintings from the Cessna into the truck.'

Graymond closed his eyes for a moment.

'I should have known,' he said, 'I should've taken Reese's threat more seriously.'

'Perhaps,' Alicia said. 'But there was no love lost between you and Alisdair — he admitted to that — which gives him ample means and motive. We already know he had opportunity. Not only that, he also had a possible accomplice in Reese.'

'Supposing Alisdair, Reese and Julia were in on it together?' Graymond asked suddenly.

'Exactly,' Alicia agreed. 'It's interesting that soon after you were sent to prison, they all apparently came into a significant amount of cash. Considering Reese had to sell the Cherokee to pay for the wedding, how did they suddenly manage to afford a rather nice detached pile in five acres of woodland? And Alisdair admitted to having some time off to go travelling around the South Pacific. He didn't work or anything; just bummed around. How did he pay for it? The money could easily have come from the sale of a couple of stolen paintings, although we don't know exactly how many were taken from the aircraft that night. Just the three? Or perhaps the whole lot. Kam's been on the lookout for me for some time now. There were seven paintings in total listed on the inventory. Stolen artwork can be a nightmare to turn into cash, but even if they just sold three at a percentage of their true value and divided the proceeds, that's hundreds of thousands of dollars' worth right there.'

'A lot of money,' Graymond said thoughtfully.

There was silence between them for a full minute before Alicia looked at her watch.

'I should get going,' she said, jumping up from her chair. 'I'll get my clothes and then you'll need to give me a ride to the station, Gray; my car's still parked there from yesterday. That's if you're not still too drunk to drive?' She gave him a reconciliatory smile which he acknowledged.

'This morning's hangover is punishment enough,' he remarked. 'Keep the shirt, by the way. You look good in it.'

CHAPTER SIXTEEN

Over a week passed before Graymond and Alicia were able to discuss their investigation further. Alicia also had yet to report back on her meeting with Kam, but a heist in one of London's most exclusive jewellery stores had kept her busy for most of her waking hours, reporting on developments in the case and editing the work of the junior reporters.

Graymond busied himself with some long overdue home and garden renovations; the trees and shrubs around Blackdeane House had grown considerably over seventeen years and parts of the garden had become severely overgrown. Graymond tackled what he could, but decided that a tree surgeon and a gardener were required for the more substantial tasks.

Between attacking out-of-control shrubbery and wrestling with wild thorn bushes, Graymond made a number of visits to his office at the airfield where he set about the monumental task of recovering GS Executive Aviation Ltd. from a downward spiral into disaster. After their final meeting, cousin Paul had gathered his belongs and vacated Graymond's office. Graymond had not heard from him since and intended on keeping it that way. Harry, Paul's drag queen of a receptionist had also left without so much as a goodbye; another small blessing for which Graymond was truly grateful. He would find another receptionist in due time, but for now he had decided to resort to obtaining any front desk staff on a short term basis from a recruitment agency.

He missed Caroline Stevens, his former Business Manager, who had effortlessly overseen the running of both the airfield and the charter company with the greatest efficiency. The last he had heard, she was working for a highly successfully property company in London, and doing well at it. They had not remained in touch, at Graymond's insistence. He had known she was destined for bigger and better things and any association with a convicted murderer may have hampered her career.

Graymond had managed to set up meetings at the airfield with a few current employees which, to his mind, had gone reasonably well. Time is a great healer and seventeen years was a long time. Most people either had no idea of or had appeared to have completely forgotten about his background history, for which he was thankful. He had taken a few walks around the airfield surveying the runway and the decaying hangars. Not a scrap of renovation work or maintenance had been carried out since Paul had been at the helm. Graymond had made a careful inspection of the Gulfstream business jets of GS Executive Aviation Ltd., as well as the light aircraft at Blackdeane Airfield and was shocked to find out-of-date technical logs, and expired maintenance contracts and servicing documentation. He had always been meticulous with the upkeep and maintenance of his aircraft from the largest Gulfstream to the smallest Cessna and immediately grounded the entire fleet for urgent servicing and necessary upgrades.

Graymond obtained quotes from various carpenters, electricians and building contractors for renovation work on a larger scale for both his home and the buildings at the airfield. He realised he'd have to use a considerable amount of his own money for the airfield renovations as GS Executive Aviation was all but bankrupt. The more he became involved in the work, the more Graymond became excited and motivated with setting the company back on its feet and the more he began to believe that there was hope for a prosperous future once more. Avery was on hand to assist and advise with the increasing amount of bureaucracy and red tape which seemed to have escalated in the last seventeen years. Graymond knew he could never catch up with seventeen years' worth of twenty-first century developments in seven days, but embraced the task with impressive energy and enthusiasm, nonetheless.

Compared to the mundane prison routine, the energy required for his new life of freedom was so much more, and the busyness and activity of each day ensured Graymond went to bed exhausted most nights. Sleep often evaded him, however, as his mind was distracted with yesterday's problem-solving and tomorrow's planning. And then his thoughts would drift to Alicia. To his surprise he missed her more than he dared to admit. He counted the days that she didn't call, and debated whether to call her himself. They had parted on good terms, hadn't they? He wasn't entirely sure. For the time being at least, he opted for a teetotal existence. Any amount of alcohol would be dangerous and there was too much at stake right now.

And so it was when Graymond met Oliver Jacobs, his former accountant, for dinner in London one damp, foggy evening in late November, he ordered a lime and soda to accompany his enchiladas.

'Not like you, Gray,' Oliver frowned, as he perused the wine menu of the Mexican joint he had chosen for the reunion. 'Lime and soda's a bit lame for a man who's spent the last seventeen years in the clink, isn't it? Shouldn't you be celebrating your freedom? Living life a bit? Recapturing all those lost years?'

'I don't see how an evening drinking myself into oblivion can possibly be considered as recapturing lost years,' Graymond remarked curtly.

'Suit yourself,' Oliver replied. 'The Graymond Sharkey I once knew used to be first off the bat with the drinks orders. I guess prison's beaten all the fun out of you. We'll work on that one, I'll soon have you back off the wagon.' He grinned at Graymond, then at the waitress. 'Get me a beer,' he said, pointing to the menu.

When the waitress had disappeared with their order, Oliver leaned back lazily in his chair. He was the same age as Graymond, but seventeen years of a hardcore party scene fuelled by all-nighters, alcohol and cocaine seemed to have worn down his appearance far more than Graymond's seventeen years behind prison bars. At the age of forty, he was already on tablets for high blood pressure and high cholesterol, and the various diets he had tackled somewhat half-heartedly, had done nothing for his waistline which bulged over the top of his trousers and through the spaces between the buttons on his shirt.

Shortly after Graymond's life sentence in prison had commenced, Oliver had paid him a visit — the one and only — to offer some sort of consolation for his unfortunate demise.

'Of course you didn't do it,' he had said,' I'm one hundred per cent behind you Gray, can't believe they found you guilty, it's obvious you're innocent, I'll do everything I can to get you out of this hell hole.'

It was the last Graymond had seen of Oliver, although he had received a letter about a year later enquiring after life in prison and informing him that he had got some money together and had set up his own accountancy firm. A few more letters followed over the years, detailing the success of OJ Accountancy Ltd., the grand openings of new offices somewhere in the United States and the Caribbean (a convenient little tax haven, Graymond thought) and the acquisition of various assets essential for the running of the business including a beach condo, a private jet and a supersize yacht. Apparently OJ Accountancy Ltd. had gone from strength to strength with a considerable number of high net worth individuals on the books. It had been Oliver's idea to meet for dinner to celebrate Graymond's new freedom, although Graymond suspected it was to be more of a platform for Oliver to impress him with stories of the success of OJ Accountancy Ltd.

'So then, Gray, ' Oliver said, the wicker chair creaking and straining under its load, 'how does it feel to be a free man?'

'It's...' Graymond began.

'Well, technically you're under licence or something, isn't that what it's called?' Oliver interrupted, 'but hey, essentially you've been let loose back into society, the heinous murderer that you are!'

He winked and let out a loud, boisterous laugh. Graymond forced a smile. Oliver's sense of humour had always proved to be a little on the edge, but it appeared to have worsened with time.

'Seriously though, Gray,' Oliver attempted a look of sincerity which wasn't entirely convincing, 'I've always maintained that you were innocent.' He looked Graymond straight in the eye, which

Graymond found a little unnerving from a man who was not known for his honesty and integrity.

'I've always said you were framed for those murders.' Oliver went on with the speech. 'I'm telling you Gray, the sonofabitch who had you sent away for seventeen years deserves to be hung for what he did.'

Graymond couldn't agree more, but he preferred not to dwell on the past.

The waitress was back and a brief silence ensued as Oliver watched her reach over the table with a leer, as she placed their drinks in front of them.

'I could do with some of that,' he said to Graymond in a low voice, his eyes following her as she walked away from their table. 'I guess your need is greater than mine right now though?'

Another wink followed by another loud laugh. Graymond was beginning to feel mildly annoyed. He took a sip of his lime and soda.

'Anyway Gray,' Oliver attempted to regain some composure, 'how's business these days? I've seen what a disaster Paul Greene's made of running the show at Blackdeane and as for the state of those aircraft hangars, hell, I've seen wartime relics in better condition. I think I'd feel safer walking through a condemned building.'

'I'll bring it round,' Graymond said coolly. He began to resent every question Oliver asked. 'Give it a couple of years and I'll build the business up again, bigger and better and even more successful than before.'

Oliver let out another laugh.

'Good luck with that!' he said, almost choking on his beer. Graymond wanted to punch him in the face. He took a deep breath.

'So what about you, Oliver?' The sooner he could divert the conversation away from himself and onto his egocentric companion, the better.

'Oh life's never been better,' Oliver replied. 'Business is booming; my company's got offices in New York, Los Angeles, Las Vegas, Chicago and a couple in the Caribbean. Matter of fact, I'm headed out to one of the islands next week if you fancy joining me; there's rum on tap, gorgeous girls, and sailing and snorkelling that's out of this world. You should come Gray, you're looking a bit pale; a bit of sea and sun, and plenty of sex would do you the world of good. What d'you say?'

'Thanks for the offer, but I haven't got my passport sorted yet,' Graymond replied, 'and anyway, as you've so kindly taken the trouble to remind me, I'm out on licence; I'll need permission from the Probation Service to travel abroad which could take weeks.'

Oliver shrugged.

'Up to you Gray. Let me know if you change your mind.'

The waitress arrived with the enchiladas and Oliver was distracted for a few moments. He winked at Graymond who ignored him. If anyone wasn't getting enough, it was Oliver, Graymond thought to himself. There was a brief respite from Oliver's garish conversation as they took synchronised bites of their enchiladas. Table manners hadn't been high on the list of priorities in prison, but Graymond's dining etiquette had escaped relatively unscathed from seventeen years inside. Oliver's social graces, however, were somewhat lacking; as he shovelled the enchilada into his mouth, pieces of meat and vegetables oozed out of one side of the corn tortilla onto the table. Graymond looked across at him in disgust; he managed to make meal times in the prison dining room look civilised.

'So any lucky ladies on the scene right now Gray?' Oliver asked, still with a mouthful. He wiped his mouth carelessly with his cloth napkin. Graymond wasn't sure he was prepared for that question and neither could he be bothered to answer it, but Oliver appeared incapable of discussing precious little else.

'I thought as much,' Oliver replied, all-knowing. 'Tell you what Gray, when I'm back from my business trip overseas, you and I will have a night out on the town, just a bit of light-hearted fun, a few clubs, a few drinks, pick up a few girls, all that typical playboy shit you and I used to do, let me show you a good time.'

'Thanks Oliver, but I think I'm...'

Oliver held up his hand, in an I'm-not-listening gesture.

'That's settled, I'll be in touch,' he said firmly, adding, 'I owe it to you, Gray.'

'How's that, Oliver?' Graymond asked inquisitively.

'Well, I — you know — I think you've had a rough deal being locked up for some shit you didn't do, missing out on the best years of your life,' Oliver replied smiling broadly. 'I think life needs to cut you a bit of slack these days; it must be hard enough to get back into the routine of things without wondering how it could've been. If I was you, I'd constantly be thinking what life would've been like if…' Suddenly unsure of how to continue, Oliver took a quick gulp of beer.

'If what?' Graymond asked. 'If you hadn't have set me up with Sonny and Tobias?'

Oliver looked suddenly embarrassed.

'Hey, no, wait,' he spat out in defence, 'you can't put that one on me Sharkey, I just provided the introductions, the rest of it was your doing.'

'I'm not putting anything on you Oliver,' Graymond replied calmly. 'I take full responsibility for every business decision I ever made, good or bad. You benefitted from both if I remember correctly.'

'The rough and the smooth all come with the job,' Oliver shrugged.

'Even after I went to prison,' Graymond ventured. He watched Oliver closely; his companion suddenly appeared uncomfortable, unsure of how to respond. He took another gulp of beer and fidgeted in his chair, deliberately avoiding eye contact.

'Soon after I was sentenced, you left the accountancy firm in London and started your own show,' Graymond continued deliberately.

'So? What's wrong with a bit of entrepreneurialism?'

'By your own admission, your financial success went from strength to strength pretty rapidly,' Graymond said. 'How was that, Oliver, considering that towards the end GS Executive was pretty much your only client at the accountancy firm? It's not like you had a portfolio of existing clients to take with you when you left. And where did you get your start-up cashflow from?'

'Hard work,' Oliver replied, 'and a couple of lucky breaks here and there. But mostly hard work. Can't argue with that.'

'Let's be honest, Oliver, you've never been known for working hard.'

Oliver sat up in his chair, which creaked alarmingly.

'What are you saying exactly?' he asked in a low voice.

'I'm wondering if you saw how much I would've walked away with if that night in August hadn't gone south. Even a small percentage would've got you a nice little startup fund to go it alone.'

'Look, Gray,' Oliver said as loudly as he dared, 'I don't know what you're insinuating, but I don't like it. If you're accusing me of having something to do with those murders, you're completely out of order. I've always been your biggest supporter, always believed in your innocence, and you dare to imply that I set you up somehow.'

Oliver's face burned a shade of scarlet. Graymond had seen less dramatic hues of red on the brighter section of a Dulux colour chart and thought briefly of the high blood pressure problem with a smile.

'Seriously, Gray,' Oliver snarled through gritted teeth, 'how you can have the audacity to even *suggest* I might be involved is just…' His voice trailed off. He glared angrily at his dining companion, temporarily lost for words but desperate to say something.

'Well?' he barked.

'Oh, I'm sorry Oliver,' Graymond replied coolly. 'Was there a question in there for me somewhere?'

Graymond had lived through seventeen years of interacting with angry fellow inmates and argumentative guards; he wasn't about to be intimidated by an enraged accountant with an out of control blood pressure. A routine prison day could start with everything running smoothly, but could suddenly turn into a violent brawl due to all manner of reasons from a fight over drugs to an inmate who felt they'd been unfairly treated.

'You sonofabitch,' Oliver snatched his napkin off his lap and thumped it onto the table with a crash. The soft chatter of nearby diners was briefly stunned into an awkward silence.

'Oliver, you're overreacting.' Graymond assumed the role of an innocent party.

'*Overreacting?*' Oliver growled in disgust. 'You're accusing me of murder — a crime a jury found *you* guilty of, I might add — and theft, and you think I'm *overreacting?*'

'I'm not accusing you of anything,' Graymond said in an indifferent tone.

'Go to hell,' Oliver replied angrily, this time making no effort to lower his voice. Ignoring the stares from the other diners, he seized his coat from the back of his chair and stalked out of the restaurant, pushing roughly past the waitress who had served them earlier.

Graymond sat silently for a few minutes as the excitement subsided and the surrounding conversations resumed once more. He hadn't meant his words to sound like an interrogation, yet he had touched a raw nerve with Oliver on some level. He wondered what had caused the angry outburst. Oliver had always had a fiery temper, but flareups could usually be justified. Was it possible that he had indeed been involved in some way in framing Graymond back in August 1999? Had Graymond come just a little too close to the truth? Oliver's reaction had been unexpected and one that he wasn't sure how to read. He wished Alicia were here; she would undoubtedly have handled things better. She would also have had Oliver right where she wanted him all evening; he would probably have confessed to anything for her. Instead, Graymond appeared to have ruined all hope of further conversations and thus, if Oliver had been involved in the murders of Rory Conway and Jimmy Keyes, he had also ruined all hope of proving it.

The waitress approached the table, slightly nervously.

'Can I get you anything else sir?' she asked timidly.

'Just the bill,' Graymond said shortly.

'Certainly sir.'

Graymond left a modest tip and kept his head down as he navigated his way through the tables and chairs to the door of the restaurant. Outside it was dark and cold, the hazy orange glow of the street lights above veiled by a thick, damp fog. Graymond buttoned up his jacket. There was an icy chill in the air, which seemed to seep into every part of his body. A dog barked relentlessly in the distance as Graymond made his way along the deserted street towards the car park where he had left his truck. Although it was Oliver who had made a scene and stormed out of the restaurant, Graymond was annoyed at himself for the way things had gone.

Badly done, Gray, he said to himself. *It's hardly surprising you've got no friends if you go around accusing them of murdering people.* But one of them was lying. One of them knew more than he — or she — had ever let on. Graymond knew he had to find the truth that had been hidden for seventeen years, even if it cost him his friends.

CHAPTER SEVENTEEN

It was the first Saturday in December and Graymond had spent the day in his office at the airfield. Progress was slow in every aspect of business, partly due to the excessive amount of bureaucracy and red tape there appeared to be these days, and perhaps partly due to the fact that it was only three weeks until Christmas. Graymond wasn't sure how he would be spending his first Christmas not locked in a prison cell since his twenties. He had, naturally, received an offer from Mrs Davidson to spend Christmas Day with her and her husband Roy, and grown-up son Landon, which he had, naturally, declined. He had decided he'd rather spend a day working, alone, in his office, than attempting to socialise around an artificial Christmas tree with people whom he had nothing in common any more. He couldn't think of anything worse.

Graymond vaguely remembered Landon Davidson from when they were teenagers, but had not particularly liked him back then. Landon was a few years younger than Graymond, although Graymond couldn't remember exactly how many. In fact, Graymond couldn't remember much about Landon Davidson at all. While Graymond had always had a daring, adventurous approach to life, Landon had preferred to play it safe. Graymond had despised his cautious, cowardly nature and Landon had been somewhat intimidated by Graymond's continual dance with danger. While Graymond had excelled at whatever he did, coming top of his class in almost every subject, Landon lagged behind and didn't appear to have a natural ability for anything, or the drive to achieve.

Subsequently, they had never been close. The only common ground they shared was a passion for flying, although even in this, they had their differences. While Graymond took to the skies with enthusiasm and excitement, Landon was having lessons for six months before his instructor deemed him competent for a solo flight. During one of her prison visits in the early days, Mrs

Davidson had proudly informed Graymond that Landon had been accepted at an airline pilot training academy. Graymond learned much later that he had dropped out after just a few months. His mother informed Graymond that he hadn't got on well with the instructors, although reading between the lines, Graymond guessed that it was because he had been unable to keep up with the requirements of the course.

He had returned home to live with his parents, getting a job working night shifts at a local supermarket. His home and work life had remained unchanged since then. Graymond had not seen him following his release from prison and he intended to keep it that way, Christmas Day included.

As Graymond drove home from the airfield that evening, a light snow began to fall. Although it was only five o'clock in the evening, it was already dark, with the light from the moon and stars obscured by thick snow clouds. Leaving his office so early in the evening was unusual for Graymond, even for a Saturday. He would often remain at his desk until ten or eleven at night, however, this evening was an exception. Alicia's artwork consultant Kam had been in touch. The art dealer whom Kam suspected had arranged the quiet sales of the stolen paintings retrieved from the Cessna seventeen years ago was hosting an exclusive exhibition and auction of his current collection of high-end art. It was to be held at his private residence in Mayfair, a five storey townhouse with basement parking, and all proceeds of the auction would be donated to a charity for homeless people. Entry was strictly by invitation only and the guest list was more elite than that of Paul's Baby Grand, a cocktail lounge at the Tribeca Grand Hotel in New York that Graymond had once visited with Oliver, known for its tough door.

Securing two names on the guest list of Borja Moreno-Fernandez, whose notoriety as a high-end art dealer had earned him celebrity status in both the legitimate art world and the black market, appeared to have been of no consequence to Alicia, however. Kam, who owed Alicia a favour from way back, was a close companion and personal consultant to Mr. Moreno-Fernandez, and had arranged not only tickets to the event, but a promised introduction to the prominent art dealer. He had been in the art business for over forty years and it was rumoured that he could recall every painting that had ever passed through his hands and every buyer and seller that he had ever conducted business with. He was rarely seen in public and reportedly lived the life of a recluse, therefore a private event and personal introduction were rare opportunities that could not be missed.

Alicia had given Graymond firm instructions as to what to wear. *It's a very exclusive event,* she had informed him, *with a very strict, black-tie dress code. You need to make an instant impression at the door, otherwise the security detail won't let you in, even if you have a ticket. Don't let me down, Gray,* she had said firmly. Graymond had insisted he was capable of organising his own attire. He still wasn't sure if Alicia was being a little aloof with him following his drunken escapade two weeks' before and was determined to show her that he could both look and behave as though he were the next James Bond. He had spent an afternoon at a tailor's in London recommended by Avery where he was painstakingly measured for a custom-made white dress shirt, a black bow tie and a black double-breasted suit.

'What's the special occasion, Mr. Sharkey?' the tailor had asked as he positioned his tape measure at various points on Graymond's body, scribbling numbers on a reporter's notebook after each measurement.

'It's — er — it's a charity ball,' Graymond had mumbled. He had hoped this was the first and last lie he would have to tell, but he certainly wasn't going to discuss the art exhibition.

'A charity ball, oh how delightful,' the tailor had exclaimed, still carefully measuring.

Graymond had glanced down nervously as the tape measure was carefully positioned at the top of his thigh. The tailor, an elderly, grey-haired gentleman worked with extreme precision. Graymond had tried to remind himself that this was a good thing, although he wasn't entirely comfortable with every aspect of the experience. He was even less comfortable with the price, which, in his mind was extortionate for an outfit he had planned to wear just once. To make matters worse, an additional premium had been added as the deadline by which the suit was required was in days rather than weeks. The tailor had lived up to Avery's glowing recommendation, however, and Graymond was now in possession of full black tie dress with a brand new pair of black Oxford dress shoes, again with a little help from Avery.

En-route home from the airfield, Graymond stopped at a small florist called Faireclough Flowers. He remembered passing the flower shop many times as a young man. As he entered the store, the scent of pine cones and fir tree branches filled the air from the attractive Christmas wreaths and arrangements on display. He approached the counter somewhat apprehensively. From somewhere at the back of the store, he heard a female voice:

'Be with you in a minute.'

As he waited he looked around at the attractive floral displays and was briefly tempted to invest in a Christmas wreath for his front door. The thought was dismissed almost as quickly as it had arisen. Graymond's attitude to Christmas made even an unreformed Ebenezer Scrooge look as though he was the life and soul of the festive season.

'Can I help you?' A middle-aged lady wearing a pink tabard appeared with a bundle of sprigs of holly covered with glitter spray. She placed them on the counter top and wiped her hands on the tabard.

'Yeah, I need a dozen red roses,' Graymond said shyly.

'I think I've still got a dozen left,' the flower shop lady replied, turning to a corner of the store behind the counter. 'Red's a popular colour this time of year.'

Graymond nodded in agreement and watched as the lady selected twelve large red roses from a large metal canister.

'Beautiful, these ones,' she said, placing the large bunch carefully on the surface of the counter. 'Need them wrapped?'

'I just need them to look nice, in some kind of arrangement or something.' When it came to flowers, Graymond was out of his depth. There had been no such thing inside the prison walls, but thanks to the expertise of the Faireclough Flowers lady, Graymond was soon walking back to his truck holding a dozen red roses, beautifully arranged and tied with an attractive silver ribbon. He placed them on the passenger seat next to him as he got in and pulled out of the car park, turning in the direction of Blackdeane House. The snow was falling thick and fast now and was beginning to settle on the ground, covering the landscape with an unspoiled carpet of the purest white.

As Graymond pulled into his driveway and the wrought iron gates slid shut behind him, he looked through the falling snow towards the large, dark building ahead of him. Parked in front of his house was a silver Bentley Continental GT, right where the rental delivery guy had left it that morning. He stopped his truck behind the Bentley and, cradling the bunch of roses, Graymond jumped out and walked towards the car, gazing at it with the excitement of a child with a new toy on Christmas morning. He slid his hand along the gleaming surface of the highly polished bonnet, he peered through the driver's window at the stunning purple leather interior, and smiled at the thought of the throaty roar of the six litre twin turbo-charged W12 engine. He allowed himself a few more moments of admiration before he turned to the steps leading to his front door. He let himself in, placed the roses on the counter top of the kitchen island, threw his jacket across the bannister in the hallway and ran up the staircase, two at a time. Alicia had informed him she would arrive on the dot of seven. He had less than an hour to shower, shave and change into his new suit.

CHAPTER EIGHTEEN

At exactly seven o'clock, as Graymond was struggling with a cuff-link, he watched on the security monitor as Alicia's black Sirocco pulled up to the gates at the bottom of his driveway. He pressed a key on his lap top and almost immediately the gates began to open, silently and slowly. He noticed that the heavy snowfall had all but stopped and the snow clouds had parted to reveal a full moon, its iridescent light reflecting eerily on the blanket of white that covered the garden and the fields beyond. The security lights, activated by the warmth and movement of Alicia's car, switched on in perfect synchronisation. Graymond observed Alicia step gracefully out of her car. She glanced up at one of the hidden cameras; she knew she was being watched. Casting a puzzled look at the Bentley Continental parked in front of Graymond's truck, she made her way to the front door.

With the cufflink finally in place, Graymond pulled on his jacket, buttoned it up and ran down the stairs in a whirlwind, just as the door bell sounded. His heart was pounding in his chest from nervousness and excitement in equal measures. He grabbed the roses from the kitchen and took a few seconds to compose himself before he pulled the solid oak front door open.

Alicia stood on the doorstep in front of him. She looked stunning and Graymond couldn't think of any words to say just then. She wore a long red dress with a plunging neckline revealing pale, flawless skin, enhanced by the most magnificent diamond necklace that Graymond had even seen. It was the same one that Melissa Pendergast- Jones had modelled a few days earlier. Alicia's long, dark hair was elegantly pinned into a French chignon twist with wisps of hair framing her face. Her makeup was so immaculate that she looked as though she had just stepped off the cover of a fashion magazine, yet so natural that she could have applied it in thirty-seconds flat.

'Wow!' Graymond could only think of saying.

'Thank you,' Alicia replied.

The last time they had seen each other was the morning after Graymond's drunken evening. The last time they had spoken on the telephone, things had still been considerably awkward between them.

'You look… beautiful,' Graymond said, a little shyly.

'You look very handsome.'

Alicia shivered.

'Are you going to ask me in? It's freezing out here!'

'Oh sure, sorry, come on in,' Graymond stepped back hastily, almost tripping over his feet as he held the door for Alicia. She stepped inside and Graymond closed the door behind her. He turned to look at her again; she looked even more alluring in the dim lights of the hallway.

'Alicia,' Graymond said awkwardly, 'these are for you.'

He handed her the roses, feeling a little ashamed. Alicia took them.

'Graymond thank-you; they're beautiful,' she gave him a puzzled smile, 'I love them, but you didn't have to get me these.'

'I did,' Graymond replied. He drew in a breath and continued. 'Alicia, I want to say I'm sorry for the other night. I really am. I won't let it happen again.'

'Gray, you don't need to apologise,' Alicia said softly. 'I'm not mad at you.'

'I know,' Graymond looked away in embarrassment, 'but I'm sorry.'

'Well, you're forgiven,' Alicia smiled. She stood up on tip toe and kissed him on the cheek. She stepped back and they both looked away.

'I guess we'd better get going,' Alicia said, suddenly all business.

'I'll get the car keys,' Graymond replied. As he went through to the kitchen, Alicia called after him.

'Speaking of cars, whose is the Bentley parked outside your house?'

'It's ours,' Graymond said, returning with the keys and a boyish grin.

'*Ours?*' Alicia looked shocked.

'Just for the night,' Graymond replied, still grinning. 'We can't exactly turn up at an exclusive art exhibition in the truck, can we?'

Alicia wasn't about to disagree and allowed Graymond to escort her to the Bentley.

'You didn't stretch to a chauffeur as well then?' Alicia asked as Graymond got in beside her.

'I could, but then I wouldn't have you all to myself,' Graymond replied, casting a sideways glance at his passenger.

Alicia didn't respond and looked away, but to his delight Graymond saw a little smile playing on her lips.

'We agreed you're my boss as our cover story, remember?' Alicia said, gazing out of her window.

'That was your idea,' Graymond replied, starting the Bentley with a satisfying, throaty roar of the engine. 'I thought we could go as a couple; friends with benefits or something.'

'We want to keep up a professional guise here, Gray,' Alicia said quickly, 'we need to blend in as discreetly as possible. It looks better if we're business partners, rather than romantic partners.'

'So you're not the secretary that I'm having a secret affair with then?'

'*No!*'

'Just making sure,' Graymond said with a gleam in his eyes. 'Wouldn't want to give the wrong impression.'

'Very funny,' Alicia's gaze remained outside the window.

Graymond slid the Bentley into drive and the car accelerated enthusiastically down the driveway towards the gates which opened on cue.

'I love this car already,' Graymond smiled as he turned onto the road, covered by a thin layer of snow glistening in the moonlight.

Traffic was light on the journey to London and, much to his delight, Graymond was able to exercise the Bentley's muscles a little, taking care of the slightly slippery roads damp with melted snow. Most of the traffic was headed in the opposite direction, retreating from a day's Christmas shopping in the City, and therefore it took them less than the anticipated hour to reach the West End towards Mayfair. Graymond took a detour along Oxford Street and Regent Street informing Alicia that it was for her to take in the pretty Christmas light displays, although Alicia suspected it was more to do with the fact that he was driving a Bentley Continental worth nearly two hundred thousand pounds.

During the first half of the journey, they discussed where they were at with Graymond's case. Alicia, having spent most of her time working on developments in the jewellery heist story since they last met, had little to contribute, so Graymond talked the most, recounting the details of his evening with Oliver Jacobs which ended rather abruptly. Alicia listened with interest and little comment.

'Not sure I handled it in the right way,' Graymond finished up.

'I think you handled it just fine,' Alicia replied. 'You got him to show his true colours and that's what we need.'

'He always was a bit hot-headed,' Graymond surmised. 'but after that discussion, I just don't think he was involved. He had so many fingers in so many pies, he could've got his start-up money from a dozen dubious different places. I think he would've reacted that way regardless.'

'Don't jump to any conclusions yet, Gray,' Alicia said firmly. 'We need hard evidence before we can prove anything.'

'Even so, I think it's the cool, calm, collected ones that are the most dangerous,' Graymond continued. 'You'd have to be pretty damn cool to plan and execute that night as it went down, and then to follow up with getting rid of the artwork. Oliver is neither cool, calm, nor collected, even on a good day.'

'But his accomplice may have been,' Alicia reminded him.

'Speaking of hard evidence,' Graymond suddenly changed the subject as a thought came into his mind, 'there's something I've been meaning to talk to you about, Alicia.'

'Go on.'

'My kitchen knife, the one that was used to stab Jimmy and Rory…'

'The one with their blood and your fingerprints all over it?'

'Yes.'

'What about it?'

'It went missing from my house about two weeks before that night in August. I could never work out how or why it disappeared.'

Alicia was silent for a few minutes before she spoke. 'Was anything else taken?'

'No, not that I could see,' Graymond shook his head, 'just the knife.'

'You know what that means?'

'It was definitely premeditated.' Graymond glanced across at Alicia. 'I know. I'm sorry, I should've mentioned it before; there was so much going on, I forgot, and then I remembered it the other day.'

'Don't worry,' Alicia said. 'It doesn't change things for us now. Did you tell anyone at the time?'

'Sure, but it was my word against a mountain of damning evidence; I think Pinocchio would've had an easier time of getting someone to believe him.'

'Gray, can you remember who visited your home around the time your knife went missing?' Alicia asked seriously.

'Everyone on that list we made a few weeks ago, plus a whole bunch of other people.'

'I had no idea you entertained so much,' Alicia said with a wicked smile. 'Clearly you were quite the socialite back then, Gray.'

'It's not how it looks,' Graymond shot back, catching Alicia's smile. 'They were almost all business calls. And I didn't use that knife much anyway, so I couldn't work out exactly when it went missing. I just know I went to use it about two weeks before that night and couldn't find it. I thought I'd misplaced it; had no idea it had actually been stolen until it showed up in the control tower next to Rory, covered in blood.'

'Well, I guess I'm impressed with the all the planning and preparation that went into framing you for all that,' Alicia said matter-of-factly.

'I'm even more impressed that whoever it was got away with it and I ended up serving a life sentence for a crime I didn't commit,' Graymond said bitterly.

'So you may have done, but it's not over yet, Gray,' Alicia placed a hand on Graymond's arm.

'That's nice, but I thought I'm supposed to be your boss?' Graymond glanced across at Alicia.

'You are my boss,' she replied firmly, withdrawing her hand, 'and it was nothing more than a reassuring pat.'

'That's a shame,' Graymond said with a mock look of disappointment and fixed his eyes back on the road.

After a short silence, Alicia spoke again.

'Any further thoughts on Caleb Fonteyne's whereabouts? He's the only suspect on your list that we haven't been able to track down yet.'

'I've tried to do a bit of digging here and there,' Graymond replied, 'asked around a bit — some of the guys at the airfield used to work with him — but I've come up with nothing so far. I'll keep digging.'

'Fine, we'll keep him on the list of people to ask Mrs Davidson about when we pay her a visit.' Alicia said.

'Are we going as secretary and the boss for that too?' Graymond smiled.

'*No Gray!*' Alicia laughed. 'We're going as friends.'

'As you wish.'

Silence descended once more. Graymond's mind wandered to an extension of the secretary and the boss conversation. Alicia gazed distractedly out of her window through the snowfall at the streets where late night shoppers trudged along the pavements laden with shopping bags of all shapes and sizes. They drove past a coffee stand where a small group was gathered, bundled up in hats, scarves and winter clothes, warming their hands on steaming paper cups of seasonal coffee and marshmallow-topped hot chocolate. Further along the street was a brass band playing traditional Christmas carols to a small crowd of weary shoppers, the melodic sounds drifting over the cacophony of street sounds, horns and sirens. A giant Christmas tree stood next to the band, shimmering with a myriad of twinkling lights, which reflected in the glass-fronted building opposite.

'I love Christmas, don't you?' Alicia said, turning to Graymond. Her eyes sparkled.

He paused.

'I'm not sure,' he said. 'I've spent the last seventeen locked in a cell and I was thinking of working this one. I'm not really into celebrating Christmas.'

'Really Gray?' Alicia raised one eyebrow.

'Yes, really.'

'I'll make you a deal,' Alicia said suddenly. 'If we find the killer before Christmas Day, promise me you won't work it?'

'Like that's going to happen,' Graymond replied sarcastically. He glanced at the date on his watch. 'In exactly three weeks it will be Christmas Eve. We'll never find the real killer in that time; it could take months.'

'Gray, I think you should have a bit more faith in the magic of Christmas.'

'No such thing.'

'Humbug,' Alicia replied.

'Fine, if we've found the real killer, with hard evidence — which we won't have, obviously — I'll celebrate Christmas, or something,' Graymond put on a deliberately bored tone. 'But if we haven't, I'm working it.'

'That's a deal,' Alicia said decisively.

CHAPTER NINETEEN

At exactly 8:02 p.m. the silver Bentley cruised majestically to a stop outside a grand townhouse in a treelined residential street in Mayfair. Two unsmiling doormen dressed in tuxedoes immediately stepped towards the car, one taking the keys from Graymond, the other guiding Alicia out of her seat and onto the pavement towards the steps leading up to a bright red front door. The first doorman disappeared in the Bentley while the second spoke in low tones into a concealed microphone. Graymond glanced above the door and noticed a hidden camera, inset into the doorframe, barely visible. After seventeen years inside, Graymond had become accustomed to obtaining familiarity with hidden cameras for various reasons, and it was a trait he had decided to preserve. In this case, the purpose of the camera was for facial recognition of guests in order for the security team to identify each person. At that moment, a computer somewhere inside would be matching their facial features to a database containing recent photographs of themselves which Alicia had taken and passed onto Kam a few days before.

Graymond had been reluctant to have his picture on anyone's database so soon after his release, particularly one belonging to an art dealer of dubious integrity, but Alicia had managed to persuade him, reminding him that his face had been on surveillance cameras all over town from the moment he stepped out of prison.

The red front door, on which hung an attractive Christmas wreath, opened suddenly; Graymond and Alicia had been successfully identified and were now invited guests to the party, without so much as an introduction or the display of a valid ticket. Graymond wasn't sure he liked everything about twenty-first century technology; it almost reminded him of being back in prison. The doorman extended a hand to beckon them inside and then was gone, as the door closed silently behind them. Graymond and Alicia found themselves in a hallway with an arched ceiling which opened out into a large circular entrance hall with a glass dome and a white marble staircase, descending on either side of the foyer from a balcony above. The walls were white and covered with various pieces of artwork, none of which Graymond recognised, but then he was hardly a veteran art critic in spite of his illegal art transportation sideline in the nineties. The floor was a black and white checkerboard of glazed tiles.

A young woman in a short black dress approached with a tray of champagne flutes which she offered to the two latest guests. She was followed by a young man, immaculately dressed in the standard tuxedo party wear, who beamed a warm, welcoming smile at the pair.

'Good evening Miss Clayton,' he spoke with a European accent as he gently lifted Alicia's hand and kissed it, 'and Mr. Sharkey.' He reached over and shook Graymond's hand firmly, bowing slightly.

'My name is Diego De Santis, I'll be coordinating our wonderful Christmas charity auction this evening, in aid of various homeless charities throughout London; I'm sure you'll agree it's a worthy cause, especially at this festive time of year.'

Alicia and Graymond nodded sagely as Diego produced two iPad Air tablets and gave them one each.

'Our fine collection of artwork is available for your information on these tablets; as you peruse the eclectic display of carefully selected pieces, just capture the image of anything you like on your iPad and the full details, including provenance and authenticity, will be immediately available to you.'

With a gracious smile, Diego gave a little bow and ushered them towards a door set into the wall of the foyer which slid noiselessly to one side, revealing a large room set out in the form of an art gallery, with paintings lining the walls. In the middle of the wooden floor was a large leopard print rug of thick pile upon which were four pink velvet chaise longues with silver and leopard print cushions. A number of guests, dressed in black tie and holding champagne flutes and iPads, were chatting in small groups or perusing the artwork on display.

'D'you think I should get one of those rugs for Blackdeane House?' Graymond whispered to Alicia.

'It might liven things up a bit with all that beige you've got,' Alicia whispered back.

'Hey!' Graymond feigned an indignant look.

'Enjoy the evening, and if there is anything at all that you need, please do not hesitate to ask me,' Diego was saying in gushing tones.

'Thank you,' Alicia smiled and to Graymond she whispered, 'don't you just love that dreamy Italian accent? Isn't he so polite and charming? Gray, you should be taking lessons from him.'

'I *am* polite and charming,' Graymond replied, 'and I bought you roses and drove you here in a Bentley; what more d'you want?'

Alicia was about to respond when she spotted a familiar face approaching them from a small group.

'Alicia! How wonderful to see you!' The voice accompanied an attractive young woman of Asian background, in her early thirties. She had short, dark brown hair cut into a bob and wore a dark green velvet dress which fish-tailed gracefully behind her. She embraced Alicia with two air kisses and stepped back smiling.

'It's fantastic you could be here!' she said excitedly, 'I can't wait to introduce you to Borja; he's so excited to meet you both.'

Graymond guessed Alicia and Kam tuned their acting skills to whatever was required for the occasion; they had clearly worked together for a variety of undercover, information-gathering roles a number of times.

'Kam, it's great to see you too!' Alicia replied. She gestured to Graymond.

'This is my boss, Gray.'

Kam turned to Graymond.

'It's a pleasure to meet you Gray, I've heard so much about you,' she said with a sparkle in her eye. 'My name's Kamalgeet, but everyone calls me Kam.'

'It's an honour to meet you Kam,' Graymond replied. 'Alicia tells me that your knowledge of today's art world is unrivalled; what you don't know isn't worth knowing.'

'Oh well, I'm not sure about that,' Kam gave a modest smile adding, 'I could say the same about Alicia and the world of crime reporting; she's practically Scotland Yard's go-to person when they need an expert opinion!'

'A slight exaggeration I think, Kam,' Alicia laughed. She looked around the room. 'This is quite the collection.'

'Oh isn't it?' Kam agreed. She took Alicia's arm. 'Let me tell you both about some of these pieces of artwork.'

She led them to a large painting in a gilded frame, a colourful abstract piece that Graymond didn't quite understand, by an artist he had never heard of. He stood staring at the artwork for a few minutes as Kam explained to Alicia the intriguing tale of how the piece came about and the story behind the painting. Kam knew the artist personally and interspersed the narrative with a few amusing anecdotes. She and Alicia moved onto the next painting by the same artist as Kam began a story about the time when they were on his yacht in St. Tropez. Alicia was a captive audience and seemed immersed in Kam's every word. Graymond wondered if she was genuinely interested or if it was all part of the act. If it was, she was a talented actor; no wonder she had succeeded in seducing Alisdair.

Graymond stayed where he was, still gazing at the abstract painting. Pretending to be particularly taken by the artwork, he stepped forward to examine it more closely while at the same time discreetly pouring his champagne into a plant pot containing a small fig tree which stood next to the painting. He had promised himself he would stay away from even the smallest amount of alcohol and he intended to keep that promise. He moved casually towards the next painting, a rather uninspiring portrayal of a vase of flowers on a table. He wasn't sure what made this nondescript painting so special, but studied it with the keen eye of an expert who knew what he was looking at. Alicia and Kam were deep in conversation further down the room; Graymond decided he'd leave them to it.

As Kam finished telling Alicia about the time she was at a celebrity art auction in Ibiza where a box containing thousands of dollars' worth of paintings fell off a transportation trolley into the swimming pool, she glanced back at Graymond who was looking intently at a Van Gogh.

'Your friend — I mean boss — seems nice Alicia.'

'Yeah, he's okay,' Alicia smiled.

'What does he do again?' Kam asked.

'He's got his own aviation business. It's based at an airfield — which he also owns — in a little town on the outskirts of London.'

'That sounds glamorous,' Kam said. She took a sip of champagne and watched a female guest approach Graymond and engage in some kind of discussion about the painting.

'Are you sleeping with him?' Kam asked. 'Please tell me you are Alicia; he's gorgeous.'

Alicia's cheeks turned a shade of crimson.

'No, of course I'm not,' she said quickly.

'And why not?' Kam quizzed her friend. 'I know you too well Alicia; it's obvious you're crazy about him — the way you are around him, even the way you look at him — and I'll bet one of these paintings that he feels the same way about you too.'

'I doubt that very much,' Alicia said, frowning. 'So even if I do like him a bit…'

'A *lot*,' Kam interrupted.

'Okay — a lot, maybe — but now's not the time to get involved.'

'If you don't want him, there'll be plenty of other attractive women who do,' Kam said. She nodded in Graymond's direction. 'Look over there; I think we need to rescue your handsome boss.'

Alicia looked over to see the female guest who had been speaking to Graymond a little while earlier standing considerably closer to him than Alicia was comfortable with.

'Let's go,' she said to Kam who was only too happy to oblige.

'Oh there you are Gray,' she said loudly as she walked towards Graymond and his new admirer. She nodded sweetly at the woman, who took a step back.

'He's my boss,' she said firmly, glaring at the woman. Looking at Graymond, she said: 'There's a stunning Picasso over there; you simply must see it.'

Graymond gave her a relieved look and she shot a rather sickly apologetic smile at the woman.

'Oh I'm sorry, were you in the middle of something? Forgive me for interrupting so rudely.'

'No, it's fine Alicia,' Graymond said quickly. 'Where's that Picasso you want to show me?'

'Right this way,' Alicia said, taking his arm. Kam took the other arm leaving Graymond's disappointed admirer to stare helplessly after them.

'Thanks,' Graymond said to Alicia under his breath. 'I wasn't sure how I was going to get out of that one.'

'Any time,' Alicia replied.

'Case in point,' Kam looked across at Alicia with a wink.

'Noted. Let's move on,' Alicia said quickly.

'What are you talking about?' Graymond looked from one to the other.

'I was just demonstrating to Alicia that if you don't make it clear when you're interested in something, an exquisite painting at auction for example, then you lose the painting to a more enthusiastic bidder.'

'Not that we're here to bid for any paintings.' Alicia shot Kam a warning look.

'Quite, but it does demonstrate rather well the principle of losing out,' Kam went on. 'Now, how about I introduce you to my friend Borja? He is, after all, the reason you're here.'

Kam led Graymond and Alicia to an elite-looking group standing in one corner of the room, chatting quietly. As Kam approached, the group parted. She was clearly well-known and respected in this business. In the centre of the group stood a small man, probably approaching sixty, Graymond guessed, although he could pass for much younger, dressed in a Prussian blue, satin, three-piece suit. The group drifted away on cue as Kam made the introductions.

'Borja,' she said, pronouncing it the Spanish way with the "j" sounding like an "h," 'I'd like you to meet my friends Alicia Clayton and Graymond Sharkey.' There was no point keeping up the boss and employee act with Borja whose security team would have no doubt completed extensive background searches on them both.

'Miss Clayton, Mr. Sharkey,' Borja kissed Alicia's hand and shook Graymond's. 'The pleasure is all mine.'

He turned to a stunning strawberry blonde standing elegantly next to him. She looked at least half his age and had a slightly bored expression.

'Let me introduce you to my beautiful girlfriend Pippa,' he said beaming. Polite hellos were said all round.

'And what do you think of my exquisite artwork collection on display this evening?' Borja asked waving his hand towards the paintings around the room.

'It's wonderfully impressive, Mr. Moreno-Fernandez,' Alicia gushed, 'and in support of such an important cause. The homeless people of London deserve to be remembered at this time of year.'

Graymond was impressed, even if he did not share quite the same measure of sympathy towards London's homeless population as the host of the auction and apparently Alicia.

'What a charming young lady,' Borja smiled broadly at Alicia, 'I'm glad you agree.'

He looked at Kam and raised his eyebrows. She gave him a quick nod which he briefly acknowledged.

'Why don't you come and see my,' he paused, '*other* collection?' He motioned for Graymond and Alicia to follow him. As he led the way through a small side door into a white-washed, arched corridor, Kam spoke quietly to Alicia.

'All the artwork to be auctioned legitimately is displayed in the room we've just been in, for the majority of guests here tonight, but there's another room with another collection.'

'Go on.' Alicia looked intrigued.

'The artwork in this room is genuine, but they're the kind of paintings that Gray would've flown into Blackdeane from the Channel Islands in the middle of the night, if you understand what I'm saying,' Kam said.

Alicia nodded. 'This is a little off-the-record collection?'

'Precisely. You need the right credentials to get an invitation back here.'

'Thanks Kam,' Alicia muttered.

'Don't mention it,' Kam replied, 'I owe you one.'

The corridor opened out into a room, smaller than the first and with the paintings displayed on easels in a much more intimate-style setting. There were fewer people in the room, many of whom appeared to be alone, and the ambiance and lighting were much more subdued. They were immediately offered more champagne and canapés by the discrete but attentive staff. Pippa kissed Borja on the cheek and disappeared somewhere to the back of the room with a flute of champagne.

Borja turned to Kam, Alicia and Graymond.

'Kam tells me you're looking for information on someone?'

'Yes,' Alicia replied, 'from a long time ago. Seventeen and a half years, to be exact.'

'I've got a long memory. Try me,' Borja responded quietly. His eyes gleamed in the dim lighting of the room. 'Kam is one of my closest friends and confidants; I'm always pleased to provide assistance to any friends of hers where I am able.'

'Thank you,' Alicia said graciously. She slid a hand into her bag and pulled out a laminated A5 size card on which she had printed small replicas of the seven stolen paintings from Graymond's ill-fated artwork haul on the night of August 14, 1999. The top three pictures were of the paintings which had recently emerged once more on the black market. She passed the card to Borja who studied it carefully, his eyes revealing nothing.

'I remember each of these paintings,' Borja said finally, 'except these two.' He pointed to two of the small replicas. 'What is it you want to know?'

'The name of the man who came to you with five of the paintings, back in nineteen ninety-nine,' Alicia said, a searching expression on her face.

Borja was silent for a minute and then he spoke.

'I met him twice; the rest of the time he had someone act on his behalf, as many of my clients do. I never knew his name, but then that's not unusual; most of the time my clients are anonymous or they provide me with an alias, so I doubt it would be helpful to you. He first came to me in the summer of two thousand, almost a year after those paintings disappeared. I was extremely surprised to see them, as it was widely thought in the business that they had been tragically destroyed in an aircraft explosion.'

He took a small sip of champagne and placed the glass on a table next to him.

'I realised the delicacy of the situation, following the media circus that had surrounded the drama of the murders at Blackdeane where the artwork was allegedly lost,' he glanced at Graymond but revealed nothing. Graymond had no doubt that Borja knew exactly who he was. 'There was also the forthcoming Blackdeane murder trial later that year. To all intents and purposes, the police had their man, the paintings had been burned up, and yet here were five of them in front of me — the genuine articles — without so much as a speck of charcoal or the scent of burning on them.'

His little audience of three stood listening, spell-bound. Graymond felt stunned and in shock. At least five of the paintings had escaped the fire, had not even been anywhere *near* the fire. It confirmed the theory that they had been rapidly unloaded from the Cessna *while it was still on the runway*, as there would have been no time after Graymond drove out to the aircraft and taxied it back to the apron.

'What about the other two paintings?' Alicia asked.

'I never saw those; perhaps they didn't survive the explosion. I have no idea what happened to them, but they have certainly never come up for sale. The arena for selling the artwork that I am involved in is quite small, even internationally; I would have known if one of these paintings had been sold. I'm afraid I can't be of much help to you,' Borja said apologetically. Detecting the disappointment in Alicia's face, he appeared to debate something in his mind for a moment.

'There was one thing about the man who came to see me that may interest you,' he said slowly. Alicia looked up at him.

'The first time we met he had had some recent cosmetic surgery work done,' Borja continued. 'Quite extensive work, I think; a facial reconstruction and then some work on his body. He still had some dressings on his face, but the rest of him was covered under clothing so I didn't see any of it and quite frankly I didn't want to. I believe he'd had some skin grafts due to injuries from extensive burns, but I can't be certain of that.'

'Burns?' Alicia was wide-eyed.

'I'm not absolutely sure,' Borja emphasised again. 'He was extremely shy, understandably so, as his face was still quite swollen and didn't look terribly pretty, the little I saw of it. When we met the second time, the dressings were off and the scars had healed. If I had not remembered how he had looked a few months before, I doubt I would even have noticed that he'd had any work done at all. The results of the surgery were very, very good.'

'Would you be able to identify him now, if we showed you some photographs taken around the time of the Blackdeane murders?' Graymond asked suddenly.

'I sincerely doubt that,' Borja shook his head. 'It was sixteen years ago. I only met him twice, and one of those times his face was in bandages so I could hardly see any of it.'

Graymond was inclined to agree.

'What about the clinic that he went to for the surgery?' Kam asked. 'Did he ever say anything about that?'

Again Borja shook his head.

'We were discussing the paintings, not the latest facelift treatments. I have no idea, but I think the man who acted on his behalf once mentioned that he had an appointment somewhere on or near Harley Street. Again, I really can't remember; as I said, I was more interested in the paintings. And I never ask questions, personal or otherwise.'

Borja glanced at a gold Rolex watch.

'My apologies, but the auction next door is about to begin and I must be there for the opening bids; I've a few words to say about Christmas and homeless charities before the bidding commences, so if you'll excuse me.' Borja looked at the little group around him.

'Of course,' Alicia replied. 'Thank you for your time.'

'My pleasure,' Borja smiled. 'Please feel free to look around; if there are any pieces that interest you, then Kam will set you up with one of my people. Enjoy the rest of the evening.'

The glamorous Pippa was back at Borja's side with a fresh glass of champagne, and they disappeared into the white-washed corridor, back to the main display room where the paintings with the legitimate procurement credentials were about to be auctioned.

'Was he of any help?' Kam asked, looking from Graymond to Alicia.

'Yes, and no,' Alicia replied slowly. 'Yes, because we now know that the person who took the stolen paintings that were flown into Blackdeane was there that night. In fact, Gray, he was so close to you that he was badly burned in the explosion. He must've been watching you the whole time.'

'I didn't see anything, or anyone,' Graymond said helplessly, 'I was so worried about Jimmy I didn't think to look around; I just wanted to get him back to the clubhouse and get help.'

'Do you know of anyone who's had surgery for facial reconstruction or treatment for severe burns in the past?' Kam asked.

'Therein lies the problem,' Alicia said. 'Three of the four potential suspects have been met by either Gray or me in the last few weeks. None of them appear to have had any facial surgery.'

'That you can see,' Kam interrupted. 'Borja said that even after a few months he probably wouldn't have noticed that the man had had any work done. After sixteen years it would be even less obvious.'

'So our mystery man was accidentally burned in the aircraft explosion and required extensive burns treatment and facial reconstruction, which was apparently successful. Perhaps the cosmetic surgeon was even able to reconstruct his face to as it had been before, without the burns scars,' Graymond suggested.

'Unlikely,' Alicia murmured. 'Once you're burned, you're burned, especially on your face.'

'Some cosmetic treatments are pretty good,' Kam said, 'and he may have had further corrective surgery over the years to make any residual scars even less visible.'

'And perhaps the burns on his face weren't too severe,' Graymond ventured.

'Okay, I'll roll with you guys on this, it is possible,' Alicia conceded, 'but only just. In which case we're looking for someone who disappeared off the grid for a few months immediately after the Blackdeane murders, while he was having the cosmetic work done.'

'There's Alisdair for a start,' Graymond said, looking at Alicia. 'He told you he went travelling immediately after everything happened at the airfield. Was he really in the South Pacific the whole time, or was some of it spent convalescing after surgery?'

'We can also consider Oliver Jacobs,' Alicia continued. 'He left his job in the City soon after and set up his own business, with offices in the States and the Caribbean. Who's to say he didn't have a short surgical sabbatical in between?'

'Do you know of anyone who could verify the movements of these guys around the time in question?' Kam asked.

'We can do some digging,' Graymond said with a note of doubt.

'Is there anyone else on your suspect list?' Kam asked.

'There's the elusive Caleb Fonteyne, one of Gray's former employees,' Alicia replied, 'but we haven't been able to track him down yet; we're still working on it.'

'That's quite a lineup,' Kam said.

'I'm thinking more and more that it's got to be someone who had some kind of a connection with Blackdeane,' Alicia continued. 'He needed to have known about the artwork coming in that night, therefore it had to be someone who knew enough about the people involved and the layout and routine of the place to be able to successfully plan the theft, the murders, the aircraft explosion and, most importantly, the framing of Gray for it all.'

'What about the burns on the rest of his body?' Kam asked.

'Another problem,' Alicia said, with frustration. 'It's winter and we're in England. Everyone's in jackets, scarves, long-sleeves. How do we go about checking arms and legs and body parts for any signs of skin grafts or scars?'

'I agree it's a difficult one,' Kam said thoughtfully.

'At the end of the day, he's a marked man,' Graymond said, somewhat optimistically for him, Alicia thought. 'Contrary to what we originally thought, he didn't escape entirely unharmed from that night and, like me, has some scars; scars that, again like me, he'll have for the rest of his life. If we keep looking, we'll find him, it's just knowing how and where to look. Maybe one, or more, of the suspects on our list knows something or is an accomplice. Or maybe none of them are.'

The three of them fell silent. Graymond and Alicia's search for the killer had a new twist and neither were sure how to pursue this new direction.

'Let's take a look at these paintings,' Alicia said. 'We've learned all we can for tonight. Kam, I'm forever in awe of your ability to be able to tell a genuine from a fake.'

Alicia took a step towards a rather unusual abstract painting with outlines of animals emerging from blocks of colour.

'It's quite simple,' Kam said, taking another glass of champagne from a passing waiter. 'You have to have an eye for detail and know exactly what you're looking for, a bit like solving a murder.' She smiled at Alicia.

'When I look at a painting,' Kam went on, 'I examine things like the brushwork: are there any inconsistencies with the genuine article? Sometimes the perspective can be a bit wrong, or the painting has been cut from its original size, or the colours used weren't actually available when the artist was alive. All these things help point towards the authenticity of the painting. But there's much more to it than that.'

Kam took a sip of champagne.

'It's not just about the painting,' she continued. 'The frame can tell you a lot too. Sometimes frames are altered to make forgeries appear genuine; even the way a painting is hung on the wall can tell you a lot about its authenticity. And then there's the paper trail, the provenance of the piece of artwork, which is essentially the timeline of ownership of the painting. If the artwork has gaps in its paper trail, or no paper trail at all, it's most likely a forgery. And then, of course, if you want to sell a painting, you must have legal title to it.'

They moved on to look at the other paintings in the room as Kam explained in greater detail how to distinguish a forgery from an authentic piece, with anecdotes of various impressive and not-so-impressive attempts at convincing her that a forged painting was a genuine one. Alicia listened attentively, but Graymond found himself thinking about Kam's words: *It's not just about the painting... frames are altered to make forgeries appear genuine... even the way a painting is hung on the wall... and then there's the paper trail...*

CHAPTER TWENTY

It was a few minutes before midnight when Graymond and Alicia bid goodnight and thanks to Kam and made their way down the steps of Borja's Mayfair townhouse to the waiting Bentley Continental which had miraculously appeared on the street from the underground carpark. There was a light dusting of snow on the salted pavement and a gust of icy wind blew a scattering of frozen leaves across the quiet road. As he pulled away from the kerb, Graymond glanced at Alicia who appeared to be deep in thought. He concentrated on the road for a few miles before breaking the silence.

'How about some music?'

Alicia, her attention brought back to the present, looked at Graymond with amusement.

'What did you have in mind?'

'We could listen to some late night love songs on the radio,' Graymond said with a sideways grin at Alicia. She tried not to smile.

'Which jail did they put you in again? Was it the Soft Shell Institution for the tenderhearted? I thought you were supposed to be an insensitive, emotionless ex-con.'

'I am,' Graymond replied, 'I just forget to keep up the act sometimes.'

They were headed east along the Victoria Embankment. The glittering lights of the London skyline were reflected in the Thames River to their right, a mirror image of colours blended and blurred into one another like a child's painting. The traffic was moving fast and Graymond briefly went silent as he manoeuvred the Bentley out of the way of an ambulance approaching rapidly from behind with blue lights and shrieking sirens. Once he had resumed the normal direction of travel, he spoke again.

'So detective Clayton, what're your thoughts from this evening?'

'I'm not sure yet,' Alicia said slowly, 'except that the key to this whole thing is our mystery cosmetic surgery man.'

'Agreed,' Graymond replied. 'Something Kam said got me thinking; she was talking about forged paintings: paintings made to look like something they're not. She was saying how much work people go to in order to prove that a piece of art on the outside is the real deal, but underneath, it's something quite different. It's portraying a totally different image to what it really is.'

'You mean a bit like cosmetic surgery?'

'Exactly. We definitely need to bear in mind that there is someone, somewhere involved in this who is not as they seem, physically, at least.'

'But finding him is easier said than done,' Alicia replied.

'Which brings me to something else Kam mentioned,' Graymond continued. 'She said there always needs to be a paper trail. Sometimes in the art world, there isn't, and that's one of the things that alerts dealers to the fact that a painting may be a forgery. But in the case of private cosmetic surgery clinics...'

'They'll have all kept meticulous records, in one form or another.' Alicia interrupted him.

'Right,' Graymond said. 'If we could only find out which private clinic our man attended for his treatments and work out a way of accessing the records...' His voice trailed off in thought.

'It's a great idea, Gray, but we're talking nearly twenty years ago. There's a good chance that the clinic we want has closed, been taken over by another company, or moved, or gone out of business entirely.'

'There's also a chance it could still be there,' Graymond said, 'complete with records dating back to two thousand. I realise some of these places come and go, like pop-up shops, but some manage to stay the course. Just supposing our mystery man's clinic happens to be one of those?'

'Alisdair Brooks has more chance of a date with Melissa Pendergast-Jones than that happening,' Alicia laughed.

Graymond raised his eyebrows at Alicia.

'Something you want to tell me?' he asked with a smile.

'Not where Alisdair's concerned,' Alicia shot back, 'it's just that I think it's highly unlikely that the private clinic we're looking for is in existence any more.'

'But not impossible,' Graymond said firmly.

'No, not impossible,' Alicia agreed. She glanced at Graymond, adding, 'Where has this new-found optimism suddenly come from, Gray?'

Graymond shrugged.

'I don't know. Perhaps it's your influence. Or maybe it's to do with the fact that there don't seem to be any other leads to follow. Unless you've got a better idea?'

Alicia thought for a moment, and shook her head.

'All right, Gray, you win,' she said, 'so let's make the best of the only idea we do have. We'll start by seeing if there any clinics on or around Harley Street that were there in two thousand. Admittedly, it's a very long shot, but we might get lucky. Supposing we do, the next problem we'll face is how to access their archived records, especially those as far back as sixteen years ago.'

'They'd be computerised, wouldn't they?' Graymond asked. He was still catching up with certain aspects of the twenty-first century, but Alicia was becoming accustomed to the occasional naive questions that he asked from time to time.

'Yes,' Alicia nodded, 'the clinic will most likely have its own closed computer network system of records and my remote hacking skills aren't up to much.'

'Mine don't exist,' Graymond replied, 'but I know how to insert a flash drive into a computer and transfer a bunch of files if that helps?'

'It does,' she said slowly, 'but we'd need to physically have access to the computers in order to do that. You're not suggesting breaking and entering into private clinics up and down Harley Street, surely? You've only just made it out of prison, Gray.'

'Don't remind me,' Graymond said grimly. 'I wasn't thinking of breaking and entering into anywhere; it was more of a thought that one of us could go to the clinic in opening hours, as a legitimate client…'

'You're not thinking of getting a facelift, are you?' Alicia looked horrified.

'No, but you might be,' Graymond gave her a mischievous smile.

'Funny,' Alicia replied sarcastically, but at the same time the realisation of Graymond's idea slowly dawned on her face and her eyes sparkled as a game plan formed in her mind.

'Only problem is I don't have the first clue as to how to access a password protected file,' Graymond added.

'Don't worry, Gray,' Alicia replied, 'I've got a friend who'll take care of that little obstacle; a mini tutorial with Alexander and you'll be an expert hacker in no time.'

'You're sure?' Graymond wasn't entirely convinced.

'Absolutely.'

'This is a ridiculous idea, isn't it?' Graymond said.

'Yes, it is a ridiculous idea,' Alicia replied, 'and it would take an insane amount of planning and preparation, but if there's a chance that the clinic still exists, and we can find it, there's also a chance that we may just be able to pull it off.'

They briefly discussed the possibility of attempting to trace other aspects of the killer's paper trail, but they had conflicting ideas as to exactly what his actions would have been after the night of August 14. They did however, agree that he would have had to have laid low for a while, in light of the fact that he'd been badly burned as a result of the aircraft explosion and fire, the scars from which surely could not have been part of his original plan.

It was likely that he would have needed some medical attention and burns treatment, but Graymond and Alicia couldn't decide whether he would have risked showing up at the Emergency Department of a general hospital. He couldn't take the chance that he may be linked in some way to the Blackdeane Airfield murders. If his burns were severe, most Emergency Departments would have transferred him to the nearest specialist burns centre, which again would generate more paperwork. Too dangerous, Graymond had surmised. Too much risk of exposure and people asking questions as to how the burns were sustained, and thus easier, although not necessarily safer, to obtain treatment from elsewhere. There were too many unknowns and the net would have to be cast too wide to trace the initial path of the elusive killer, but, assuming Borja was as authentic as his art collection in the first room, the Harley Street clinic (or one close by) seemed like the logical next step in Graymond's quest for the truth. In spite of their initial enthusiasm for the plan however, the more they discussed it, the more overwhelming and ambitious it began to feel.

'There'd be a serious amount of data to transfer,' Graymond remarked sombrely, 'and not a whole lot of time in which to do it. Assuming we're able to successfully obtain it, it'd take weeks to trawl through everything, with the very slim chance that we'll actually find anything useful. Supposing he used a false name?'

'He almost certainly used a false name,' Alicia replied. 'We need to make sure we get pictures: before and after shots; although we know it can be done, a face isn't quite as easy to change as a name.'

'D'you think this is a crazy idea?' Graymond said again.

'Totally,' Alicia said, 'but I also think that we'll only find the true killer if we follow his path. We need to start thinking like he thought, going where he went, doing what he did, until one day we finally catch up with him. And one other thing Gray: we must *never* get caught in the process. We need to cover our tracks as well as he did.'

They were quiet for the rest of the journey home. The bright city lights had merged into darkened country lanes with the occasional street-lit village or town along the way. The snowfall had been heavier here than in London during the evening, and the surrounding fields and front gardens lay under about an inch of a fresh layer of white. As the Bentley's headlights shone on the snow-covered wrought iron gates of Blackdeane House, mounted on their tall red-brick pillars, Alicia was reminded of one of those traditional Christmas card scenes. The car purred up the long gravel driveway, parking outside the front of the house, where they were instantly bathed in the brilliant glare from the security lights. Graymond stopped the engine and turned to look at Alicia. Her face was in shadow as she faced him. The diamond necklace sparkled in the dim light of the car.

'Thanks for this evening,' Graymond said, 'for arranging it with Kam and getting us the invitations and everything. I know I don't show it very well but I seriously appreciate it.'

'I know,' Alicia replied, 'and it was my pleasure, Gray. You know I want to find the killer as much as you do.'

'I hope you get the story you want after all of this,' Graymond said. He gazed into Alicia's dark eyes, almost mesmerised.

'It was once just about the story,' Alicia began slowly, 'but now — I don't know — perhaps it's about something more.'

'What d'you mean?' Graymond's heart skipped in his chest and he felt an unexpected wave of ecstasy as he looked towards Alicia. He didn't stop himself from fixing his gaze on her; he couldn't stop himself. To his surprise, and delight, she returned the gaze with the same intensity. He leaned across to her a little. He was breathing faster than normal.

'Can't you tell?' Alicia said quietly. Her gaze shifted fleetingly to Graymond's mouth before she met his eyes again. Graymond shook slightly; it was the first time he had been this close to a woman for over seventeen years and he had forgotten the feelings and the emotions that came with being in such a position. Alicia didn't pull away; she moved a little closer towards him.

'Alicia,' Graymond said softly, 'I want to dare to believe that you feel the same about me as I feel about you, but I — well, it's been a while — if you do, I think I need to hear it from you.'

He swallowed hard. It wasn't easy to talk about his feelings, especially to someone like Alicia. Almost immediately, he regretted what he had just said. Alicia reached out and held Graymond's face in her hand. She leaned forward towards him and gently pulled his head closer to hers. She closed her eyes and her lips touched Graymond's. Suddenly there was a harsh ringing noise and they were jolted out of the moment as they both jumped back in their seats in surprise. In a daze, Alicia reached for her clutch bag containing her cell phone, which became louder as she pulled it out.

'Damn,' she said under her breath, closing her eyes for a moment, 'it's one of the junior reporters, there must've been a development in the jewellery case. I guess I'd better get this.'

Graymond sat back in his seat and took a ragged breath. His mind was in turmoil and his heart was racing. He wanted Alicia so much just then. The feelings of desire that had been crushed throughout the last seventeen years of a desolate landscape of emotion, had risen to the surface of his being, like the hot, intense lava of a volcano before being suddenly decompressed. And just as suddenly, the single moment of passion had been arrested by Alicia's cell phone. Graymond wanted to snatch it from her, hurl it far out of the window and then crush her mouth with the deepest, hardest kiss. Alicia was speaking, but Graymond didn't hear any words as he wrestled with his feelings and wrenched them back under the surface in order to maintain some form of composure. As an owl swooped low over the garden from a branch of a magnificent cedar tree, Alicia's conversation ended and she placed her cell phone back in her bag.

'Gray?' she said softly. 'I'm so sorry about that, it was pretty bad timing.'

'Yeah, it was,' Graymond replied awkwardly, without turning back to face her. 'Don't worry about it.'

'Something urgent's come up with the story,' Alicia said apologetically, 'I've got to go home and sort a few things before the morning.'

She touched Graymond's arm but he pulled away, opening the door of the car and getting out.

'Sure, you've got to go,' he muttered under his breath.

'Gray, I'm sorry, I don't have a choice.' Alicia slid out of the passenger seat and stood on the driveway where she shivered in the icy, night air.

'It's fine,' Graymond said flatly. 'Go and do what you've got to do.'

He had walked round the back of the car to Alicia and stood facing her. He studied her face coldly and saw the disappointment in her eyes. Without touching her, he turned and walked to the front steps of his house.

'I'll call you,' he said over his shoulder. He let himself in and shut the front door firmly.

Alicia stood motionless on the driveway outside, watching a light come on in one of the downstairs rooms before she composed herself and walked silently to her car, parked behind the Bentley. As she drove away from Blackdeane House, she focused on the road and tried to forget about Graymond. She told herself it was a mistake to become involved with a man who had served a life sentence for murder, whether he was guilty or not. A relationship with Graymond Sharkey was bound to be messy and complicated and was destined for disaster. Better to stick with the original plan of getting the truth, and the sensational story, before leaving him to the sad, lonely life that he was gradually carving for himself.

CHAPTER TWENTY-ONE

Graymond rose early the next morning following a sleepless night. After a run, a shower, four cups of coffee and three Sunday newspapers, he was still debating whether or not to call Alicia and apologise. His pride was getting in the way, however, and he was still resentful of the fact that it was *her* cell phone that had spoiled the moment, and *her* job that had prevented them from taking things further in Graymond's bedroom, or the back seat of the Bentley for that matter. His feelings were a confused mixture of frustration, resentment and disappointment, along with a desperate need to see Alicia again, to hold her and kiss her and release all the repressed desire and emotions he had for her. He glanced at his cell phone every few minutes, checking for any missed calls. There were none. Alicia was busy, or not awake yet, or speaking to one of her damned junior reporters, or just plain ignoring him.

Pouring a fifth cup of coffee, Graymond pulled his laptop towards him and tapped a key. The screen came to life and he entered his password with two index fingers. In the internet browser, he typed in the words *cosmetic clinics harley street london*. He was a little shocked and surprised to see the vast number of search results that were displayed. An accompanying map of Harley Street in London was covered with a disheartening number of red dots, each indicating a private clinic offering a variety of cosmetic services ranging from tummy tucks to nose jobs. There was a plethora of treatments which Graymond couldn't even begin to envisage what they might consist of. His imagination conjured up all sorts of possibilities of what cosmetic gynaecology might entail, and he winced at the uncomfortable thought of how much pain might accompany a microdermabrasion treatment where "an abrasive instrument is used to gently sand the skin on your face," according to one web site. The word "gently" wasn't terribly comforting.

Most alarming of all, however, was the number of clinics that were situated on Harley Street, let alone on streets nearby; he counted over fifty in total. He sincerely hoped they hadn't all been there since 2000 or before; it would render their plan useless as they could never hope to acquire the archived records of all of them. He looked back at the screen again, and realised that the count had included all the dental surgeries, which he eliminated, along with a handful of laser hair removal clinics, bringing the number to below forty. *Still too many*, he thought to himself, but how many had been there for any length of time? He considered the most efficient way to check this information out. A few of the "About Us" sections of the individual web sites had a paragraph informing the reader of the date the clinic had been established, but many of them gave no clue as to how long they had been in existence.

After a further internet search with a few inventive terms and phrases, Graymond gave up and wondered if there was a way to obtain a directory list from the year 2000; perhaps the library had an archive the same way it did with newspapers. He checked his cell phone one more time. No missed calls or messages. Closing the laptop, he decided he'd head to his office at the airfield and catch up with more paperwork. It was overcast and windy, not suitable for flying light aircraft; there would be few private pilots there. It was also a Sunday which meant that the majority of the flight engineers would not be working, especially in light of the fact that the Gulfstreams were currently grounded and awaiting renewal of their maintenance contracts. It was a good day to work uninterrupted.

Alicia's call came late that evening. Graymond had brought some work home with him and was sprawled across his bed with his laptop. There was so much more documentation online than when Graymond was at the helm of GS Executive Aviation the first time around; he was still learning how to navigate the world of the internet with everything from instructions for the latest aircraft GPS equipment to online banking. Alicia's name was displayed on the screen of his cell phone as it began to ring. He picked it up and took a deep breath before answering it.

'Gray, hi, it's Alicia.'

'Hi,' Graymond replied shortly.

'How was your day?'

'Fine. Yours?'

'Also fine.'

'Great.'

After a silence, Alicia spoke.

'Listen Gray, I'm sorry about last night. It didn't end in the way I was hoping it would, let's put it that way.'

'How did you hope it would end?' Graymond asked. He attempted to speak with a bored tone, as if he hadn't given it a moment's thought.

'I think you know the answer to that,' Alicia answered, 'but let's not go there; if we're going to work together to solve this murder mystery I think we need to put any feelings that might have developed to one side.'

'You mean just forget them?' Graymond's heart sank.

'Exactly that,' Alicia replied firmly. 'I think we should keep this strictly as a working relationship, otherwise things'll get complicated and we'll lose focus. What's our priority here, Gray? It's exonerating you from a crime you didn't commit and clearing your name forever. We can't allow anything to get in the way of that.'

It was a bitter pill to swallow, but she was right and Graymond knew it.

'Did you call just to tell me that?' he asked coldly.

'No, I called to let you know I've been doing a bit of research on private clinics that have been based in Harley Street since before the year two thousand,' Alicia replied.

'It's a waste of time,' Graymond said abruptly. 'There are too many of them.'

'On the contrary,' Alicia replied. 'I've spent the day going through all sorts of records and making a few calls; I'm pretty confident that our guy had treatment at one of three Harley Street clinics that are still there. It's just a case of getting access to their records.'

'Only the three?' Graymond queried. How did Alicia do it? He knew he needed her; he couldn't do this alone. He would have to get over his feelings for her. Somehow.

'I've also researched the medical directors of each clinic and got some background on them; their personal computers will likely contain the archived information and therefore their offices should be the ones we target when we visit the clinics. We'll need to do a bit more digging on each of them before we put our plan into action, but I thought we could discuss that tonight. We can then get started with a little undercover surveillance mission next week. What d'you think?'

'I'm listening,' Graymond replied. He sat up on his bed, and slid a pencil and paper towards him in order to take notes.

In succinct detail, Alicia outlined the three clinics which, according to various sources, were in existence in 2000 and which would have been a likely choice for someone seeking cosmetic treatment where the utmost discretion was required and, of course, where money was no object. There had been a few other clinics at the time which would also have been contenders, but they no longer existed and therefore access to their records was not possible. In general, there was far less choice in 2000 than in 2016 and Alicia was confident that one of the clinics would have the information they were looking for.

Graymond wrote down the name of each clinic and underneath, the name of the respective medical director. Alicia assigned one medical director to Graymond and said she would investigate the other two herself.

'We need to get as much information as we can on the daily routine of each one,' she said. 'Where do they buy morning coffee? Which underground station do they pick up the Evening Standard from? Or do they take a cab? Perhaps they drive? Where do they eat their lunch and with whom? On which days do they hold clinics? Any regular weekly meetings? The sixty-million dollar question is whether there is a similar time each week when their offices are unattended. Which is when you and I will visit that particular clinic.'

Undercover surveillance work was something that Alicia was probably all too familiar with. Graymond, however, wasn't quite sure how he would go about this particular task, but did his best to sound confident and upbeat about the whole idea. He conducted an online search as Alicia talked. The medical director assigned to him for the background checks worked at a clinic called The Ward Centre for Plastic Surgery. She was an attractive woman with blonde, wavy hair called Dr. H. Elizabeth Ward. She was probably approaching fifty, but looked much younger, such were the demands of the cosmetic industry. It wasn't clear what the "H" stood for. She reminded Graymond of one of the prison guards. He debated in his mind whether to request another medical director to surveil, but decided against it.

'Are you happy with the plan, Gray?' Alicia was saying.

'Yeah, I think so.'

'Good; any problems, call me, otherwise we'll catch up at the end of the week.'

'Sounds great,' Graymond tried to sound confident.

'And there's one other thing Gray.'

'What?'

'Don't get caught.'

Graymond smiled to himself. That was one mistake he wasn't about to make a second time.

CHAPTER TWENTY-TWO

Dressed in a dark jacket, pale blue jeans, Ray Bans and a New York Yankees baseball cap, Graymond hoped he'd blend into the scenery as he leant against a tree, hiding behind the day's edition of the Metro. Harley Street wasn't the easiest place in the world to blend in, as it was lined with town houses, many of which had been converted into clinics and medical practices. There were no coffee places or shops to loiter in to observe people coming and going. The street was busy however, even at the early hour of seven a.m., and Graymond reminded himself that this was London, a city whose residents and employees kept themselves to themselves. He guessed he'd be largely ignored and he was right. He kept half an eye on the front door of The Ward Centre for the imminent arrival of its Medical Director, hoping that she wasn't on vacation or had taken a day off. A large delivery lorry pulled up next to the entrance; the driver jumped out of the cab and began unloading supplies from the back of the lorry as a man dressed in a navy uniform came out of a side door to help him.

Graymond changed position slightly to ensure a good view of the main entrance and glanced at the picture he had printed out of Dr. H. Elizabeth Ward, which was concealed in the newspaper. She had piercing blue eyes and the hint of a smile, which turned into a sneer the more Graymond looked at it. He had read her biography on the web site of the clinic; she had a whole alphabet of letters after her name relating to various academic qualifications, and the description of the many titles that she held was an impressive menu of specialist roles and responsibilities, as well as being an authority on just about everything in the industry.

At precisely 9:02 a.m., Graymond spotted Dr. Ward approaching from the North on the same side of the street. She wore a light tan trench coat and navy court shoes. With a Starbucks coffee cup in one hand and a large black briefcase in the other, she walked purposefully towards The Ward Centre. As she passed Graymond, he dipped his head below his newspaper and she swept on by, up the steps into the front entrance. Graymond watched through the glass doors as she spoke briefly to one of the receptionists and disappeared through a door to the right. Graymond wasn't sure what to do next. Supposing she didn't emerge until later that evening. Was he expected to stand around outside the clinic all day? Surely he would eventually arouse suspicion; he had already counted at least five cameras strategically positioned at various points along the street. Aside from that, the temperature was below freezing and Graymond wasn't keen on the cold.

He made the executive decision to go into the reception area of The Ward Centre. He folded The Metro and tucked it under his arm; he had read it four times already and wanted to toss it into the trash, but it was part of his undercover disguise. He wondered if these were the kinds of problems private detectives encountered in their daily work, not to mention the tedium of standing around waiting. He was less than three hours into his surveillance mission and already fed up of it.

The reception area of The Ward Centre was very plush with a space age feel to it. Most of the furniture was made of brushed aluminium and chrome. The floor was grey tiled and the walls were white, with the back wall behind the brushed aluminium reception desk displaying heavily photoshopped photographs of the staff members who worked at the clinic. They were grouped according to profession with individual sections for doctors, nurses, dermatologists, nutritionists, psychologists and administrative staff. Graymond spotted Dr. Ward's picture; it was the same one that was displayed on the web site. He also spotted two dome security cameras embedded in the ceiling at each side of the reception area, which probably covered the entire room, including every entrance and exit without any blind spots. Graymond kept his face down.

Avoiding eye contact with either of the two receptionists who were busy with other clients, he picked up a glossy brochure and turned a few pages studiously, as if he were seriously considering some form of treatment. He was suddenly aware of someone behind him.

'Can I help you sir?'

A young attractive woman, in her mid twenties, dressed in a smart, grey trouser suit was at his side. She smiled politely at him. The badge that was pinned to one of her lapels stated that her name was Georgina Randall.

Graymond dropped the brochure back onto the table as if he were a teenager shoplifting a bag of sweets, who had just been accosted by a security guard. He hastily removed his sunglasses, but decided the baseball cap would have to remain. If he was planning on returning with Alicia at some point in the near future, he didn't need anybody recognising him.

'Hi,' Graymond stuttered.

'My name's George Randall, I'm the Practice Manager for The Ward Centre,' the attractive young woman was still smiling. 'Is there anything I can help you with today, sir? Any information you require?'

'I'm — er — my girlfriend's thinking about having one of those — er — hand makeovers,' Graymond said, 'the one with the laser.'

It was the first thing he could think of that he had seen in the brochure.

'I was wondering if I could — er — pick up some information for her.'

'Of course, sir,' George, still smiling, picked up the brochure and turned to the page containing details of the hand makeover.

'We'd be very happy to discuss the procedure with your girlfriend if she'd like to come in for a free consultation. We can answer any questions she might have and help decide whether the procedure is the right one for her. Would you like to make an appointment for her today?'

'Oh, I really don't know her schedule,' Graymond replied quickly, 'she's incredibly busy. Could you tell me, does Dr. Ward do this particular procedure?'

'Dr. Ward? No, she doesn't personally do the hand makeover. That would be Dr. Patel. Did your girlfriend specifically want to request Dr. Ward for any reason?'

'Only that I understand she's a renowned cosmetic surgeon. I've heard she's the best in her field.'

'Well, that's definitely true,' George replied.

'My girlfriend might be interested in other procedures too. Does Dr. Ward operate on any specific days?'

'Yes, her clinic days are every Monday, all day, so that's where she'll be today. And her operating days are Wednesdays and Thursdays, but obviously she can be flexible if required.'

If she's paid an obscene amount of money by a celebrity diva, Graymond thought.

'Is there anything else I can assist you with?' George asked.

'No, you've been most helpful,' Graymond replied, grateful to be able to escape. 'Thanks for the brochure, I'm sure my girlfriend will be in touch.'

'My pleasure,' George said.

Graymond headed for the door, relieved to have been able to escape, attempting once more to keep his face away from the cameras. He felt a blast of icy air as he stepped back outside onto the pavement and weighed up his options. Dr. Ward's office was vacant on Mondays, Wednesdays and Thursdays, due to her treatment schedule. Surely this was all the information they needed; as long as they chose to hit The Ward Centre on one of those days, it was pretty much guaranteed that they would be able to access her office without her being anywhere nearby. It was almost too easy. In addition, Graymond was cold and hungry and keen to get to his office at the airfield.

He thought back to Alicia's instructions. *We need to get as much information as we can on the daily routine of each one*. Reluctantly, he decided that a little more research probably wouldn't hurt, with the hope that he could obtain a bit more information on Dr. Ward's daily routine. He wondered if it was safe to leave his post outside The Ward Centre to grab some coffee. If Dr. Ward was in clinic all morning and then again all afternoon, surely he could take a break from his surveillance duties until late morning. He would then resume his post outside the entrance once more, should the good doctor choose to head out for her lunch. He had completed a brief reconnaissance mission of the premises earlier that morning and was pretty certain that the only way in or out was through the front entrance. This had been confirmed by the truck delivering medical supplies, which had been unloaded through the door to the side of the main door. There was therefore only one entrance that needed to be watched.

Graymond was back at his lookout point at 11:45. He was only just in time as ten minutes later, Dr. Ward suddenly emerged from the entrance of the clinic and hurried across the pavement to a navy BMW, which had pulled up to the kerb at the same time Graymond had arrived. She slid into the passenger seat and closed the door. Through the back window, Graymond watched her lean across to the driver where there was a lingering embrace before the BMW pulled away from the kerb.

Graymond swore under his breath and looked around desperately for a cab. He should have been prepared for the fact that his subject may not be traveling to her lunch destination on foot. A black cab was approaching with its light switched on. Graymond hurriedly waved it down and ran towards it.

'Follow that car up ahead,' he said urgently through the passenger window to the cab driver, before climbing into the back. The cab sped after the BMW which had been held up by a car attempting to parallel park into a space half its size. Graymond slouched low in his seat and said nothing. The cab driver focussed on the BMW and also said nothing.

Thirteen minutes, two miles, and a ride alongside Hyde Park later, the BMW pulled into the parking bay of a small hotel at the southern end of Park Lane. The cab swung into a drop-off zone outside the entrance to the hotel and Graymond quickly paid the driver and jumped out, just as Dr. Ward and her lunch companion approached. Graymond dropped to his knees to tie a shoelace that was already done up and watched as they entered the hotel through a door held open by a man in uniform.

Graymond, a small distance behind, followed another couple through the entrance into a brightly lit lobby with a magnificent crystal chandelier hanging from the ceiling, a small, curved reception desk in one corner and a group of ornate cocktail chairs in the other. Large brass letters in a baroque font stretched across the entire length of the back wall, proclaiming the name of the establishment to be L'Hotel Chateau.

Nice place, Graymond thought, but where the hell is Dr. Ward and her companion? He glanced frantically around the busy reception area before he spotted them getting into an elevator next to the reception desk. Pushing past a small group of American tourists he made it to the elevator just as the doors began closing. Dr. Ward's companion, a handsome young man much younger than H. Elizabeth herself, quickly pressed a button and the doors sprung back open.

'Thanks,' Graymond nodded, stepping into the elevator. The button for the twelfth floor was lit up; Graymond pressed the button for the fifteenth and took a small step back. The doors closed and the elevator began its smooth ascent.

'So Jeremy, are you saying you can't do next Monday lunchtime?' Dr. Ward spoke in hushed tones to the handsome young man. They huddled close together.

'That's right, my wife's got some wretched charity do she wants me to attend,' came an equally hushed reply from Jeremy. Graymond stared straight ahead and upwards, watching the number of each floor light up as they passed it.

'A charity do?'

'Yeah, a real inconvenience all round to be honest, but I'm not sure I can get out of this one.'

'What about our Paris weekend?'

'Oh don't worry, I told her it was a business trip.'

'And she bought it?'

'Totally.'

A brief pause before Jeremy spoke again.

'Are you free next Tuesday at noon?'

'Depends.'

'On what?'

'How you're planning on making it up to me.'

Graymond wasn't sure he was entirely comfortable with where this conversation was going. They were passing the tenth floor.

'Next Tuesday it is,' Jeremy confirmed. 'I'll book the room on our way out.'

The elevator hit the twelfth floor and the doors opened. Graymond nodded once more at Dr. Ward and Jeremy as they got out and the doors slid shut. On the fifteenth floor, Graymond hurried out and followed the signs to the stairs. He ran down two flights (there was no floor thirteen) to the twelfth floor and let himself through a door with a twelve on it into a corridor lined with identical doors. It was empty. He hastily removed his cap and jacket, tucking them under his arm, and jogged along until he came to the end where there was a T-junction with another corridor going from left to right. The one to his left was empty. Further down on the one to his right there was a couple entering one of the rooms; it was Dr. Ward and Jeremy. Graymond waited until the door had closed and then sauntered casually past. A business meeting this was not. He wondered how long these lunchtime liaisons lasted for, bearing in mind there was a clinic scheduled at The Ward Centre in the afternoon. He decided to wait downstairs in the lobby to find out.

An hour later, Dr. Ward and Jeremy reappeared, looking revitalised and with a renewed healthy glow. Young Jeremy looked as though he had dressed rather hastily, with a crooked tie and partially tucked-in shirt. The same man in uniform held open the door for them and bid them a good day. Neither of them noticed the man in the dark jacket and Yankees baseball cap observing them carefully from a corner of the lobby. A few minutes later, Graymond stood outside L'Hotel Chateau and wondered what to do next. The bay where the navy BMW had been parked was empty; Dr. H. Elizabeth Ward was being chauffeured back to the Harley

Street clinic where she would spend the afternoon seeing patients. Graymond was doubtful that he would learn any other useful information about her routine for the rest of the day. He had ascertained that she would be safely away from her desk next Tuesday at noon for at least an hour; his mission was accomplished.

CHAPTER TWENTY-THREE

Alicia arrived with the findings from her own surveillance operations and an extra large thin-crust pizza with extra pepperoni and extra cheese. It was late on Thursday night and a heavy rain storm beat relentlessly on the leaded windows as they tucked into the pizza, along with onion rings and nachos. They set to work immediately. Graymond began by summarising his stakeout of The Ward Centre which ended with the clandestine rendezvous at L'Hotel Chateau.

'I thought we could head over to The Ward Centre to inquire about getting you some Botox treatments at twelve noon next Tuesday,' he concluded, with a mouth full of pizza.

'Botox, thanks Gray, I'll look forward to it. And good work, by the way,' Alicia laughed. She had also managed to successfully obtain some information about her two surveillance subjects. The first was a Dr. Abadiya Khan, medical director of The Platinum Cosmetic Clinic who left work early every Tuesday afternoon for a personal training session.

'I think we should pay the clinic a visit next Tuesday at four p.m. to ask about some ear reshaping surgery for you,' Alicia said, adding 'we'll have to move fast after we've finished at The Ward Centre.'

'Ear reshaping surgery?' Graymond raised his eyebrows. 'Really Alicia? Is that the best you could do? You could at least have booked me in for something with a bit of credibility.'

'What did you have in mind?' Alicia asked. 'A male chest reduction or something?'

Graymond pulled out his brochure from The Ward Centre and flicked through some pages listing treatment options for men.

'You actually picked up a brochure?' Alicia said, sounding amused.

'I was on a covert surveillance mission,' Graymond replied indignantly. He pulled another slice of pizza from the box. 'It was a necessity in order to maintain my cover.'

'I'm impressed at the extent to which you got into character,' Alicia laughed. She outlined the third and final medical director, a Dr. Tony Lusardi of The Cosmetic Artistry Clinic, who apparently hit the golf course every Wednesday afternoon, rain or shine.

'Who's having treatment next Wednesday?' Graymond asked curiously.

'Nobody.'

'Nobody? What's our cover story then?'

Alicia reached into her laptop bag and produced two name badges with a logo on them that Graymond wasn't familiar with.

'We're inspectors for the CQC; it stands for Care Quality Commission. It's an independent regulating body of health and social care in England,' Alicia explained. 'The role of CQC personnel is to carry out inspections of healthcare providers such as hospitals and care homes, general practice surgeries and clinics — whether public or private — and make a report depending on what they find. They inspect everything from cleanliness to how staff treat their patients. It's generally a pretty terrifying experience for an establishment to receive notice of a visit from the CQC, and, of course, the media are all over the reports at either extreme of the scale.'

'I'm not sure I can impersonate a CQC inspector,' Graymond said doubtfully, 'unless they operate like prison guards. Can't we just book another consultation, same as for the other two clinics?'

'No,' Alicia replied firmly. 'We need to mix things up a bit, just in case someone gets suspicious. Don't worry, Gray, I'll do all the talking; you can do the hacking.'

'Yeah, about that,' Graymond interjected.

'Let me know when you're free this weekend and my expert hacker friend Alexander will come and spend an hour or two with you, talk you through what to do.'

'Got lots of friends with shady jobs, haven't you?'

'Comes with the territory,' Alicia replied diplomatically and with a grin, added, 'you're hardly Mr. Sweet and Innocent yourself, Gray.'

'Touche' Graymond laughed. 'Tell Alexander I'm free any time this weekend thanks to my crazy social life. Get him to come here; I don't want anyone at the airfield asking questions. What car does he drive? Just so I know what to expect when I let him through the gates.'

'He's got a little white Hyundai,' Alicia replied. 'I'll give him a call and get back to you. Right, what else? Oh, the unannounced CQC inspection at The Artistry's going down at two p.m. next Wednesday when Dr. Lusardi will be busy perfecting his backswing on a golf course somewhere.'

'Is it a common thing for the people from the CQC to just show up?' Graymond asked.

'Oh no, they're always supposed to give notice of when they'll be coming,' Alicia smiled, 'but by the time the clinic has made some calls and found out we're not the real deal, we'll be long gone.'

'And what about security at the two clinics you checked out?' Graymond guessed he already knew the answer to this question.

'Cameras everywhere. Security guards not visible but they'll be there and we need to be aware of that.'

'Perfect. Just what I wanted to hear.'

'We'll be fine, Gray,' Alicia said reassuringly. 'All we need is some Oscar-winning acting and disguises all round, with the sole aim of getting out with what we want as quickly as possible, without getting caught, obviously.'

'You make it sound so easy.'

'It will be. Trust me.'

In keeping with Alicia's description of an expert hacker, Alexander proved to be just that. He arrived at Blackdeane House at eight o'clock sharp the following evening, as agreed, and within a couple of hours Graymond was beginning to feel vaguely confident that he might just be in with a chance of successfully hacking a range of computer systems and bypassing all manner of complex pass-word-protected files. Alexander was a patient tutor, allowing for the fact that Graymond was still catching up with twenty-first century technology. He was clear and concise and somehow managed to make a potentially complex task sound relatively simple.

By midnight, he was happy with Graymond's progress and said goodnight, advising his pupil to practice regularly over the weekend and to call him if any further tutelage was required. The important thing about practicing, he had stressed more than once, was to gain familiarity with the keyboard in order to complete the task as confidently and quickly as possible each time. Graymond thanked Alexander and promised to call him with any questions that arose, before returning to the computer for another hour to consolidate his new skills. Graymond would be a master hacker before the weekend was through.

Over the next couple of days, Graymond and Alicia discussed their forthcoming plans by telephone. Graymond was concerned that the mystery man who had received the cosmetic surgery could be someone he didn't know, in which case he would be unrecognis-able in both the before and after pictures. Alicia had insisted that their undercover mission was still worth the risk, as it may produce even the smallest clue which could lead to the identity of the ac-complice, even if not to the man himself. She also doubted that there would have been many clients seeking extensive cosmetic intervention as a result of severe burns, and suspected that most would simply have been individuals who were unhappy with an as-pect of their appearance. The search could therefore be narrowed considerably. All they needed was a face, a name and some contact details. Even if these were a long time out of date, people could be traced.

Another point for discussion raised by Graymond was the fact that Mrs Davidson had called him a number of times, insisting that he stop by for morning coffee or afternoon tea. He had run out of excuses and felt that he ought to make some kind of effort to visit, partly as he owed it to her for her unwavering loyalty throughout his time in prison, but mainly to get her off his back and to leave him alone. Alicia was still keen to accompany Graymond on his visit to the elderly lady in light of the fact that she may know the whereabouts of the elusive Caleb Fonteyne, the final suspect that they had been unable to track down. Graymond was a little uneasy about bringing up the past with the Sharkey family's former cleaning lady, and wasn't entirely reassured by Alicia's insistence that she would be discreet. There was no way around this, however, and Graymond hoped they would be able to obtain the information they needed with as little probing as possible.

Coffee at ten o'clock on Monday morning at Mrs Davidson's home was agreed by all parties, with Mrs Davidson expressing her excitement at the prospect of being introduced to Graymond's young lady friend. Graymond's insistence that Alicia was "just a good friend" appeared to fall on deaf ears, and when the subject of marriage was broached he was ready to hang up on the old lady. Alicia could fend off the awkward questions, he decided, after saying a firm goodbye. He went back to his computer screen and studied Alexander's instructions, wondering if he'd been through the hacking sequence enough times to memorise it.

CHAPTER TWENTY-FOUR

Graymond and Alicia arrived at the Davidson residence a few minutes after ten o'clock. It was the second time Graymond had walked up the garden path of Blacksmith's Cottage since his release from prison, the first time being when he arrived to collect the keys to his home. Most of the snow had melted to a dirty, wet slush and the little cottage, with the pale, wintry sky behind it, looked like a scene from a Charles Dickens novel. As Graymond pressed the doorbell, a high-pitched ring came from somewhere inside. He stepped back and wiped sweaty palms on his trousers. He decided he was grateful for Alicia's presence after all.

Mrs Davidson was ready for them, and so was a rather spectacular selection of freshly baked chocolate chip cookies and mince pies. The coffee, which was almost as weak as the stuff Graymond had become accustomed to in prison, was served in large porcelain mugs decorated with bunches of holly and mistletoe. According to Mrs Davidson, they were special Christmas mugs. Graymond felt this was a fairly redundant statement as she would hardly be serving drinks in Christmas-themed porcelain in July, but he kept this opinion to himself. She herself was not partaking of the coffee, which was why she had no idea how dreadful it tasted. Instead, she was drinking what she had loudly announced was a lemon squash, although Graymond suspected that it had been diluted with something a little stronger than water. She had always been fond of a drink.

They were seated in a small but cosy living room on a well-worn sofa covered with a pale lavender throw. Mrs Davidson sat in a chair next to a roaring coal fire which gave plenty of warmth to the room. A small collection of early Christmas cards had been carefully placed on the walnut mantlepiece above. A rather pathetic-looking Christmas tree with large gaps between its spindly branches occupied one corner. It was laden with gaudy decorations and coloured tinsel which seemed to emphasise the sad lack of foliage. The only thing the tree appeared to compliment was the array of Christmas decorations hanging from various points of the Artex ceiling, which looked like something out of a 1980s village hall Christmas party.

The other corner housed a large television, resembling a monster-sized black hole which looked as though it was about to swallow up the rest of the furniture in the room. Mrs Davidson explained somewhat apologetically that Roy, her husband, had purchased it the previous year in order to watch the sport. Graymond and Alicia nodded with complete understanding.

The dark maroon carpet was threadbare, except for the area underneath the large glass coffee table in the centre of the room. As Graymond looked around, he realised the place hadn't changed in seventeen years except for one thing: a large, poster-size aerial photograph of the Davidson's tiny cottage and the surrounding fields, including an area which formed part of Blackdeane Airfield. The photograph was set in a cheap frame and hung above the mantlepiece. Graymond couldn't remember what had previously hung in its place, but the aerial picture he had not seen before, he was certain of it.

'That's a lovely photograph, Mrs. D,' he commented, taking a bite of a mince pie and nodding in the direction of the fireplace.

'Oh that,' Mrs Davidson glanced at the picture. 'It was a gift.'

'It's very nice,' Graymond said.

'So tell me how the two of you met,' Mrs Davidson leaned forward eagerly, primed for a juicy narrative of a whirlwind romance.

'Well, we kind of…' Graymond looked desperately at Alicia who was ready with an answer.

'We're old friends. We go back a long way, Gray and I. I'm in the aviation business. We were introduced through a mutual associate.'

'Oh how wonderful. What do you do in the aviation business my dear? Are you a pilot?'

'Yes, I'm a qualified pilot. I've also got my own aviation engineering company.' The lies kept on coming. Mrs Davidson was taking it all in.

'Actually, there's something you may be able to help me with,' Alicia said suddenly.

'Oh I don't know the first thing about aviation,' Mrs Davidson replied. 'You'll need to speak to Landon, my son. He's very good at that sort of thing. He should be home any time now; it's his day off today, he just popped out to the bank.'

'Is Landon still working nights at the local supermarket?' Graymond asked.

'Yes, he's still there. I keep telling him it's about time he went for a promotion, but he's not bothered. Says it'd be too much work. He's not like you, Gray; he's never been one for hard work. Anyway dear,' Mrs Davidson turned to Alicia, 'what was it you wanted to ask me?'

'I'm looking for one of Gray's former employees, Caleb Fonteyne,' Alicia replied. 'He was a particularly skilled mechanic, according to Gray, and I'm looking for someone to replace my chief flight engineer who's retiring. Apparently, Caleb comes highly recommended but Gray has, for obvious reasons, lost touch with him over the years, and I was wondering if you knew of his whereabouts.'

'Oh yes, Caleb,' Mrs Davidson scratched the side of her head thoughtfully. 'Yes, I remember him. Landon knew him, but I don't think they were friends, particularly. Well, now let's see, the last I heard I think he'd moved abroad somewhere.'

'Any idea where?' Alicia asked hopefully.

'I — I'm not sure...' Mrs Davidson hesitated and a strange look came over her face. Her eyes met Alicia's.

'Mrs Davidson?' Alicia asked gently. 'Do you know where he is now?'

'No,' replied the old lady. She placed her glass of lemon drink on the table in front of her. 'Why are you asking about him again?'

'I'd like to talk to him,' Alicia replied.

'About the mechanic's job?'

Alicia was puzzled. Mrs Davidson was fishing and she didn't know why.

'Yes. And — other things,' Alicia said slowly. *What did Mrs Davidson know?*

'You were there, weren't you?'

'I'm sorry?' The question took Alicia by surprise.

'You were there, in the courtroom, all those years ago,' Mrs Davidson said. 'I remember you now. At the end of every day when I left the courtroom at Gray's trial, I saw you. You always had the same seat in the back row, and you were always writing your notes. You were there.' Her voice quivered as the memories of Graymond's trial came flooding back. It had clearly been an emotional time for the old lady. Alicia wasn't sure how to reply. She had been prepared with numerous lies and cover stories for as many conversational threads as she could imagine, but not this one. Mrs Davidson may have been elderly, but her memory was apparently still perfectly intact.

Alicia looked at Graymond who nodded. *Tell the truth.*

'I was there,' Alicia said solemnly. 'And I'm not in the aviation business; I'm a reporter. I covered the events at Blackdeane Airfield seventeen years ago. I'm sorry I lied to you, Mrs Davidson, but I'm trying to find Caleb Fonteyne because...'

'Because you think he may have had something to do with what happened there?' Mrs Davidson interrupted.

'Yes,' Alicia couldn't hide her surprise. This she was not expecting. She was speechless for a moment.

'What makes you think Caleb was involved?' Mrs Davidson asked quizzically.

'We're not absolutely certain he was,' Alicia continued.

'Do you suspect anyone else?'

Graymond was surprised and intrigued at Mrs Davidson's reaction to Alicia's confession and at the notion that she knew more than she had ever admitted to in the times she had visited him in prison. He had appreciated her visits; it had been a lot for her to make the journey and even more to step inside the walls of an institution which housed some notorious criminals, but she had remained faithful to the end, both with the visits and her firm belief that Graymond was innocent. Their conversations had always been innocuous for the most part, however, and had dwelt on the weather, inoffensive village gossip and other bland items of news. Not for one moment had he thought that she knew anything more than what she had learned in the courtroom or read in the newspapers. If Mrs Davidson knew something, it raised the question of who else may have concealed information over the years. What about her husband, Roy? Or her son, Landon?

'There are a few others we'd like to catch up with,' Alicia was saying, 'in particular someone who may have been burned in the aircraft explosion. We think he had treatment for the burns and some facial reconstruction work done at a clinic in London some time after August in ninety-nine. Do you know who this might be?'

Mrs Davidson thought for a moment and shook her head firmly. She had no knowledge of anyone who had received cosmetic surgery for burns at any time. Graymond knew she was telling the truth. There was silence as they sipped coffee and lemon, and ate their mince pies. Alicia's eyes fell to the sugar bowl which was not in keeping with the rest of the Christmas crockery. It had on it a small printed picture of a beach with palm trees. Underneath was a place name: Negril, Jamaica. It was an odd item to belong to an elderly lady who had never travelled and probably did not even own a passport.

'What a cute little sugar bowl,' Alicia remarked. 'Have you been to Jamaica, Mrs Davidson?'

Their host shifted uncomfortably in her chair and drained the contents of her glass. She looked mournfully into the bottom of it.

'I'll just get myself another lemon squash,' she said, getting up from her chair. 'Help yourselves to more coffee.'

Graymond and Alicia exchanged glances as she left the room. No one helped themselves to more coffee.

'She knows something,' Alicia said. 'What is it?'

'I don't know,' Graymond replied, 'but whatever it is, it's a secret she's been keeping for a very long time.'

The old lady was back. She settled herself into her chair again and took a long sip from the fresh glass containing the lemon-coloured liquid.

'What were we saying?' she asked.

You know exactly what, Graymond thought to himself.

'Jamaica,' Alicia prompted. 'You were about to tell us…'

'Oh yes, if I'd been. No, I haven't, the sugar bowl was a gift.'

'From whom?'

'Oh I don't remember now; it was a long time ago.'

Another sip of the lemon. Graymond and Alicia waited. Neither of them believed that she had forgotten who gave her the sugar bowl, although they let it pass. It seemed an odd thing to lie about, however.

'I'm not one for travel,' Mrs Davidson volunteered, 'I'm just as happy on a coach tour round the West country. Have you ever been to Cornwall, Alicia?'

'Once. I was a teenager. But you were telling us about Jamaica.'

'So I was.'

Another pause. She seemed to suddenly make up her mind about something, perhaps aided by the lemon squash.

'I don't know where Caleb Fonteyne is,' she began, 'but if I was you, I might go on a holiday to Jamaica. It's a popular place; Reese and Julia Coraini had their honeymoon there. And I don't know what's become of Alisdair Brooks, who used to manage your clubhouse at the airfield, Gray, but he spent some time sailing around the Caribbean working as a restaurant manager or something on a cruise ship.'

She looked at Graymond and Alicia. They had heard and understood.

'Is there anyone else you can think of, who may have a connection with Jamaica?' Alicia asked.

Mrs Davidson leaned forward in her seat. There was more to tell.

'I don't know much more than that.' She spoke uneasily, but she appeared to be on the cusp of deciding whether or not to reveal some other piece of information. She needed a little encouragement.

'Tell us what you do know,' Graymond said gently, but with a note of urgency in his voice.

Mrs Davidson took a deep breath.

'There is one other thing,' she began hesitantly. 'On that night at the airfield when Rory and Jimmy were — murdered — there's something that I never told anyone, but I — Gray, I think it's time I... I don't want to live with this anymore.'

'I'm listening, Mrs D,' Graymond edged forwards. 'What is it?'

'I've been wanting to tell you for some time. But there's never been a good moment.'

The old lady appeared to become distressed. Her hand shook as she held her glass. Her eyes began to water.

'Tell me what it is,' Graymond said.

'It was that night, at about midnight...'

Mrs Davidson was suddenly interrupted by the sound of the front door opening and closing, and male voices. Her husband Roy's face appeared round the door frame of the living room, followed by another face, which Graymond remembered belonged to one of the police officers who had been first on the scene in the control room on the night of August 14. He had since retired and was apparently the golfing companion of Roy Davidson, from his sports attire which was visible under an all-weather jacket.

'Well, well, well, if it isn't Graymond Sharkey, back in Blackdeane after all this time,' Roy exclaimed in a jovial tone. He had aged well for seventeen years, Graymond thought; it must be thanks to a life of retirement on the golf course.

'Heard you got out, Gray,' Roy went on. 'How's life on the outside?'

'Pretty good thanks, Mr. Davidson,' Graymond replied curtly. Roy Davidson had never been his favourite person.

'Got yourself a woman already, have you?' he nodded hello to Alicia, who nodded back without smiling. 'Good work, Gray!'

Leave it, Graymond told himself.

'You remember Kev Mason, don't you Gray?' Roy was introducing his companion.

'How could I forget him?' Graymond muttered.

'I'm sure that's mutual,' Roy chuckled, in apparent ignorance that this was probably a sensitive issue for both men. Kevin had been the one who had checked Rory for signs of life, who had noticed Jimmy lying fatally wounded next to the Cessna, who had alerted his co-worker Tango Four to the casualty on the tarmac, who had called the paramedics, and who was in the tower with the rest of his team and Graymond when the aircraft exploded. Kevin had given evidence in court stating that he, as one of the first on scene, was convinced that Graymond had murdered both of his friends and had rigged the Cessna to explode. Kevin gave a small nod in acknowledgement of Graymond and looked away. He appeared somewhat taken aback and certainly unwilling to extend a hand of friendliness in any way.

'I've still got the scars from the explosion,' he said coldly.

'Where's Landon? Is he back from the bank yet?' Roy asked, changing the subject to everyone's relief. 'Dora, let him know we'll be at the Coach and Horses if he wants to join us.'

'Are you having lunch there?' his wife asked, without turning around to face him.

'Nah, we'll be back for lunch,' came the reply. Roy and Kevin disappeared simultaneously from the door frame.

Graymond was about to resume the conversation, when more loud voices could be heard in the hallway. This time it was Landon's head who peered round the door frame. He was easily recognisable as he was one of a few of Graymond's former acquaintances who had aged reasonably well. His face lit up into a bright smile and he entered the room. He was tall and good looking and appeared to have relinquished the nerd-like air he had once possessed.

'Gray! How wonderful to see you, and how kind of you to visit mother,' he said, leaning over to shake Graymond's hand. He turned to Alicia and beamed.

'And who is this beautiful young lady you've brought with you?'

'Landon, meet Alicia, a good friend of mine,' Graymond replied. He felt suddenly proud to be able to call Alicia a friend.

'Wow, how amazing to see you after all this time,' Landon said, perching on an arm of the sofa. 'Tell me what you've been up to since you've been home, Gray. Oh and if you need any help with getting that airfield of yours back to how it once was, just give me a shout; I'll be glad to lend a hand in any way I can. I saw what an awful mess your cousin Paul made of it.'

'Thanks, Landon,' Graymond replied.

Although eager to know what Mrs Davidson had been about to say, Graymond decided it was safer not to probe any further for now and to pay her another visit another day in the near future when he could be sure the rest of her family were safely out of the way. Landon provided a welcome lift to the current mood of the conversation, and even managed to produce some laughs with memories of their days as teenagers and the fact that he was so bad at flying, his flying instructor wouldn't send him solo for six months.

'I was never cut out to be a pilot,' he smiled, with a faint note of sadness in his voice. Graymond was impressed with him; he was far from the Landon that Graymond had once known; perhaps he had judged him too harshly back then.

CHAPTER TWENTY-FIVE

It was gone one o'clock when Graymond and Alicia thanked Mrs Davidson and Landon for such a lovely morning, and promised to return for another visit as soon as they could. Although Blacksmith's Cottage was in walking distance of Graymond's home, they had ridden in the truck. As they sped off in the direction of Blackdeane House, Graymond suggested they go somewhere for lunch.

'Anywhere but the Coach and Horses,' Alicia said with a smile.

They settled for a small bistro in a nearby town which served excellent home-cooked food and offered the privacy of small, intimate booths, instead of tables. Graymond and Alicia could reflect on the morning spent at the Davidson's without risk of being overheard.

'Thoughts?' Graymond asked as they tucked into two extra large chicken Caesar salads.

'Too many croutons and not enough anchovies, for a start,' Alicia replied. Business was slow and the bistro was empty, except for a young couple, deep in conversation, on the other side of the room.

'You want me to complain prison-style?' Graymond asked jokingly, shovelling a fork full of lettuce and chicken into his mouth.

'Now that would be very amusing,' Alicia grinned. 'But not today, Gray; I'll put up with the abundance of croutons; we've got too much to discuss.'

'Not going to argue with that,' Graymond said. 'I'd like to raise the first point in that you, Alicia Clayton, are one of the most flagrant liars I've ever known, and I've known many.'

'What're you implying, Gray?'

'You even went so far as to say you've got a pilot's licence,' Graymond protested.

'Well, I have.'

'Come on, Alicia.'

'No Gray, really, I have. I needed an excuse to hang around Blackdeane Airfield and sneak about without looking suspicious, so I saved like crazy to pay for some flying lessons and ended up going all the way and getting my private pilot's licence.'

'You're serious?' Graymond was stunned, not for the first time that day.

'Deadly. I've kept my flying skills current since then too — you never know when they might come in useful — I try to go flying once every week or so.'

'Why didn't you tell me? D'you fly from Blackdeane? I've never seen you there.'

'I guess it just hasn't come up in conversation. No, I don't fly from Blackdeane anymore; I wanted to distance myself from the place after a while, so now I fly from one of the other local airfields.'

A server passed by the table to check everything was okay with the food. They both nodded yes, everything was perfect, thanks, and the server was gone.

'What, or who, d'you think is in Jamaica?' Graymond asked.

'I don't know, but one of us needs to go there to find out.'

'It'll have to be you; it's going to take me weeks to get a passport organised.'

'Really? Fine, Gray, just give me all the worst jobs to do, why don't you,' Alicia grinned. 'It's a bit of a needle-in-a-haystack task, though. I mean, I've got no idea who I'm looking for, or where on earth to start searching when I get there.'

'Should we forget our visits to the Harley Street clinics for now, and just focus on the lead in Jamaica?' Graymond asked.

Alicia shook her head, no. She finished her mouthful before speaking.

'Jamaica's a bit of a game-changer, but I still think we should pursue the clinics avenue too; hell, even that retired police officer said he had some scars from that night; I'm assuming he meant physical ones. Is there any chance he could be involved in some other way? And what about Roy or Landon?'

'I guess we can't rule anyone out, but I'm pretty sure that Roy and Kevin aren't involved. What would their motive be? I can't think of one. As for Landon, I just don't think he'd have what it takes to overpower and kill two men, and then set an aircraft alight. And again, he doesn't have a motive.'

'Jealousy?' Alicia asked.

'He was never the jealous type; you've seen how he is now: happy to still be doing the same job he's always done and living at home with his parents with no thought of a promotion or getting his own place.'

'In that case, I think we should visit Mrs Davidson again, as soon as possible, to find out what it was she was about to tell us; we need to speak to her alone,' Alicia said, 'and next week we'll hit the clinics as planned. You can then start trawling through the records from the clinic databases and I'll take a little vacation in the Caribbean; I've hardly taken any leave from work this year, so I'm sure it won't be a problem to get the time off.'

'Does that mean you'll be away for Christmas?' Graymond asked. He surprised himself. Since when had he started to care about how she was spending Christmas and with whom?

Alicia smiled at this unexpected remark; she enjoyed the rare moments when she caught him off-guard.

'I'll be back by then, Gray. The case will be solved, we'll have the real killer and the truth, and the only thing you'll have to worry about will be the size of my Christmas present.'

CHAPTER TWENTY-SIX

It was a number he had dialled twice in the last sixteen years. He had received strict instructions to call only in case of emergency. He considered this to be an emergency. He waited impatiently as the single dialling tone sounded, separated by long pauses; it was different to the UK dialling tone. Finally, a voice answered.

'Hello?'

'It's me.'

There was a pause, followed by: 'What do you want? This had better be important.'

'It is. Gray's out of prison; he's snooping around with some nosey reporter girl who covered the trial back in two thousand. They're asking too many questions.'

'What do they know?'

'I'm not sure exactly. We do have one major problem though.'

The voice on the end of the line listened quietly as the caller elaborated.

'What do you want me to do?'

'Take care of it,' the voice on the end of the line replied.

'I thought so.'

'Well, what are you calling me for then? Get on with it.'

'Right. I will.' The caller sounded uneasy.

'What's the problem?'

'Nothing. Everything's cool. I'll handle it.'

'Good. I'm sure there won't be any complications.'

'There won't be.'

The voice on the end of the line hung up. The caller took a deep breath and felt sick at the thought of the problem he needed to take care of.

It was late afternoon by the time Graymond and Alicia returned to Blackdeane House. They had taken a detour via an electronics store where Graymond had purchased a twenty-seven inch iMac with Retina Display, which the store assistant informed them was in a class of its own with regard to accuracy, brightness and clarity. With great enthusiasm, he also explained that, thanks to the revolutionary Retina Display, every photo and video appeared even more true to life. True to life photographs were exactly what Graymond needed when it came to the task he would be faced with following their clinic database heists. Once the new iMac was set up in Graymond's study, Alicia suggested they check out a few online pictures to see if the quality of the images was everything the store assistant had said it would be. She keyed "negril, jamaica" into the search box and pressed return.

'You know how to torture a man, don't you?' Graymond remarked.

'It's called research, Gray,' Alicia replied, 'and has nothing to do with the fact that I want to remind you that in less than a week's time, I'll be lying on a white-sand beach and swimming in the crystal clear waters of the Caribbean Sea while you're battling with the cold and rain of England.'

'Bitch,' Graymond murmured with a faint smile.

'I'm doing this for you, Gray.'

'That's what makes it harder to swallow.'

Once Alicia had decided that they had reviewed enough stock photographs of the Caribbean, they inserted a flash drive into the iMac that had been passed to them by Alexander. It contained detailed schematics of three Harley Street cosmetic surgery clinics: The Platinum Cosmetic Clinic, The Ward Centre and The Cosmetic Artistry Clinic.

'He's a genius,' Graymond said, in awe. 'How did he get hold of these?'

'I don't ask and he doesn't tell,' Alicia replied.

'Can't he just hack into the computer networks of each of these places and save us the job of getting caught?'

'I've already asked him that. He says it's possible to do remotely, but it would take some time as the computer systems of most of the private clinics are closed and pretty secure, what with patient confidentiality and personal medical records and stuff, and money is obviously no object for the biggest and best cybersecurity. He said if he was after that kind of information and wanted it fast, he'd probably do it the way we're doing it and make it an inside job.'

'Just what I wanted to hear,' Graymond replied, sounding disappointed. He focussed on the diagrams displayed on the screen in front of him. It was a blueprint of the ground floor of The Platinum Cosmetic Clinic, which was where the office of the Medical Director Dr. Abadiya Khan was situated. A door requiring a passcode, which had been conveniently marked on the blueprints, separated the reception area from the corridor which led to the Medical Director's office. If everything went according to plan, it would be a straightforward job.

The last time he had murdered anyone was seventeen years ago. At least, he had hoped it would be the last, because he wasn't cut out to be a killer. It was hard enough then, but it had to be done, as it had to be done now. He had decided he couldn't face any more stabbings; they were brutal and there was so much blood. He had never liked the sight of blood. And it took so long to wash it all off afterwards. But getting rid of physical stains was the easy part. He felt he understood Lady MacBeth's psychological demons when she spoke of ridding herself of the "damn'd spot" and was haunted by his own from that sultry August night at Blackdeane Airfield. He'd considered strangulation, but had dismissed it almost immediately; he didn't know if he'd have the strength to see it through. The thought of a half-strangled body lying in front of him, and the grit to finish the job prevented by a conscience which paralysed him to the core, didn't bear thinking about. At the very least, it forced him to admit to himself that he was a weak, pathetic coward.

The method he had finally decided upon would be easier, calmer and much, much cleaner. The downside was that he'd had to involve someone else in process. Third parties were always risky, although admittedly, this particular third party potentially had more at stake than he himself did, should the truth ever float to the surface of the murky cesspool he was trying to bury it in. Third parties were also expensive, but he had the cash — plenty of it — and every man has his price. For a grossly inflated fee, the third party handed over the necessary meds, which had been slipped into the pocket of his theatre scrubs a few hours earlier, following the desperate telephone call from someone he preferred to refer to as an acquaintance.

The fee may have been steep, but it was worth every penny: the sleeping tablets that he had ground into powder and slipped into a hot drink earlier that evening had clearly taken effect; the victim appeared to be heavily drugged and would feel nothing. He crept quietly into the bedroom. The victim was lying on the bed, breathing heavily. As he approached, he eased out of his pocket a syringe with a hypodermic needle attached. It contained a large dose of rocuronium, a muscle relaxant. He moved slowly and precisely as he came closer to the bed. Breathing heavily himself, he tried to steady his hand as he carefully rolled up the sleeve of one of his victim's arms to just above the elbow. In the dim light, he could make out a prominent bluish vein in the left arm; it would be easy to inject the drug into.

Beads of sweat formed on his forehead as he gently pulled the skin taut around the vein, in order to hold it still while he inserted the hypodermic needle with the other hand. The needle seemed to slide into the vein with ease and he hoped he was in the right place, before he pressed the plunger firmly. The contents of the syringe were injected into the circulatory system of his victim. The muscle relaxant would take a matter of minutes to take effect: after about ninety-seconds the victim's effort of breathing would fade. Between three and five minutes, respiration would stop completely as the muscles involved in the work of breathing became paralysed. The victim would suffocate to death. Removing the hypodermic needle with care, he stepped back and stood quietly watching his victim. A trickle of blood began to ooze out of the vein and he pressed on it hard with a tissue for a few moments. After five minutes the breathing had stopped completely. He felt for a pulse; there wasn't one. Without looking back, he turned and left the room. The problem was no longer a problem.

At six o'clock, the alarm awoke Graymond from a pleasant dream where he and Alicia were swimming in a clear, turquoise sea, surrounded by white-sand beaches and palm trees. He turned over in a daze, half expecting — hoping — to see Alicia lying beside him, before he remembered that she had left sometime before midnight the previous evening. The shrill alarm on his cell phone continued to sound. He reached over to his bedside chest of drawers and grabbed it, switching it off. It was still dark, but sunrise in England in December wouldn't be happening for another two hours, such was the latitudinal position of the United Kingdom on the globe. Graymond wanted to turn over and go back to sleep; mornings weren't his thing. He put this down to seventeen years of having to rise at the same early hour in his gloomy prison cell, no matter what day it was. There was no such thing as a lie-in in prison. A knot in his stomach formed as Graymond remembered why he had set his alarm for such an objectionable hour. He had planned to spend a couple of hours revising his newly acquired hacking skills in preparation for the undercover operations that would unfold later that day.

A few minutes later in the kitchen, Graymond poured himself a freshly brewed cup of coffee, pulled his laptop towards him and commenced his carefully memorised hacking routine. He noticed he was getting faster at it, having also memorised and practiced a number of basic keyboard shortcuts over the weekend. For the second time that morning, his cell phone made him jump. This time it was the ring tone. The caller ID stated that it was Oliver Jacobs. He answered it reluctantly; it was the first time they had spoken since Oliver had stormed out of the Mexican restaurant.

'Gray! How're things?' Oliver spoke with a slurred voice. He was probably drunk, Graymond thought.

'Good thanks. You?'

'Oh never better, Gray, never better.' The line was faint and crackled a little; it sounded like a long distance call. Suddenly,

Graymond remembered that Oliver had said he would be heading out to one of the Caribbean Islands.

'Where are you?' Graymond asked curiously.

'Oh you don't want to know, Gray. Somewhere beautiful, exotic, hot, just like the girls out here.' It was followed by loud laughter.

'Are you in Jamaica?'

'But of course; working, naturally. You know how it is, Gray. I only wish you were here with me to enjoy the — scenery.'

'Where in Jamaica?' Graymond asked.

'I'm at my condo in Montego Bay. Why? Thinking of joining me? I can arrange a ride from the airport if you like.'

More laughter.

It wasn't Negril, but it was the same side of the island, with about an hour and a half's drive between the two locations.

'I won't be joining you,' Graymond replied. 'Why are you calling me now? What time is it there? It must be gone midnight.'

'It is.' Oliver's voice took on a solemn note, as the alcohol spurred him on into a deep and meaningful soliloquy.

'I'm calling to apologise, Gray. I was out of line the other night. It's not like me, as you know; I put it down to stress. This trip's been a complete tonic; I'm a new man, Gray. What d'you say to meeting up for drinks when I get back in a few days?'

'I'm pretty busy right now, Oliver. I'll have to get back to you on that.'

'Sure, no problem. Let me know when you're free. I just wanted to check that we're cool after what happened?'

'Yeah, we're cool,' Graymond replied, barely listening. He hung up and switched his cell phone off; he didn't need any more interruptions that morning. He also didn't need his location to be traceable. He was tempted to leave the phone at home. The fact that Oliver was in Jamaica played on his mind. It was more than a coincidence, surely, that Mrs Davidson should mention the very same island. But to his knowledge, they had never met and didn't even know about each other. He decided he would ask Mrs Davidson about Oliver the next time he saw her. For now, it would have to wait; there was work to be done.

CHAPTER TWENTY-SEVEN

Alicia was late, which was very unlike her. Where was she? Graymond fidgeted as he stood waiting on the corner of Harley Street and Devonshire Street, partly due to the icy December wind which lowered the temperature to below freezing, and partly due to the fact that he was nervous about the role he was about to play. His disguise was immaculate and had been carefully planned by Alicia. Of course, it had also meant that Graymond had had to part with more money for an outfit he would likely wear only once, which in his mind, was a complete waste. This time, however, he had managed to acquire a suit off the peg, rather than one that was made to measure, which was both quicker and cheaper. It was navy pin-striped and he rather liked it. He wore a woollen short trench coat on top of the suit, also navy, and a maroon silk scarf around his neck. He was wearing a pair of designer spectacles, chosen by Alicia, and looked like the tycoon business man he was supposed to be. He glanced at his watch impatiently. Where the hell was she? He was about to switch on his cell phone to call her, when he caught sight of her hurrying along Devonshire Street.

'Gray, I'm so sorry I'm late,' she caught her breath, 'the door on the carriage of the underground train I was on got stuck; no one could get in or out for fifteen minutes. Typical, huh?'

'It's fine,' Graymond replied, sounding relieved.

'Are you ready for this?' Alicia asked, as they made their way, side by side, towards The Ward Centre.

'Not really. Alicia, something weird came up this morning.'

'What d'you mean?'

'Oliver Jacobs called me. Guess where he was calling from?'

Alicia shook her head. No idea.

'Jamaica.' Graymond let the word sink in for a minute or two.

'That's got alarm bells and red flags all over it,' Alicia said finally. 'We need to go back and talk to Mrs Davidson.'

'My thoughts exactly,' Graymond agreed. They approached The Ward Centre. It was nearly twelve o'clock. Graymond spotted Dr. H. Elizabeth Ward who was just getting into Jeremy's navy BMW. There was the customary embrace, as before, and then Jeremy pulled away from the kerb. The usual routine, Graymond thought.

'That's her,' he nodded towards the disappearing car, 'she's safely out of the way.'

'Time to go,' Alicia glanced at Graymond as they faced The Ward Centre, 'and don't forget, Gray: don't get caught.' They walked up the steps, hand in hand.

The young couple approached the reception desk where a lone receptionist sat juggling paperwork, telephone calls, an electronic appointments diary and the client in front, who had a complaint of some kind. With the exception of an elderly lady who sat reading a magazine in the small waiting area to the side, it appeared to be a quiet day for The Ward Centre. George Randall, the Practice Manager, was nowhere to be seen, for which Graymond was grateful since there was a small chance she may recognise him. He stood patiently with Alicia next to him before they were called forward by the receptionist who, like George Randall, was attractive and in her mid-twenties. She was wearing a name badge attached to her lapel with the name Nikki Davey.

'Good afternoon, how can I help you?' She forced a smile, but it was clear she was under pressure and inundated with work. There had been two receptionists when Graymond had visited the previous week.

'Hi,' Graymond flashed a dazzling smile. 'We'd like to speak to someone about a consultation for Botox treatment for my girlfriend; her name's Melissa Quant.'

'Certainly sir; I'll just check to see if someone's available.' Nikki tapped a few keys on her computer screen.

'*Botox*?' Alicia suddenly said in disgust. 'I'm not here for a Botox consultation. I want to speak to somebody about having that facial rejuvenation with the fat cell transfer procedure.'

'Darling, I thought we discussed this,' Graymond looked perplexed, 'and we decided that you weren't going to go for that particular treatment.'

'I've changed my mind,' Alicia snapped, 'Candice has it all the time in Los Angeles; *I* want it done too.'

'Well, that's no problem,' Nikki began, 'I'm sure I can arrange…'

'Don't tell *me* what treatments to have done,' Alicia shouted angrily at Graymond, interrupting Nikki.

'Well, as I happen to be paying for them, I think I have every right to,' Graymond retorted.

'How *dare* you?' Alicia snarled and hit Graymond's chest hard with both hands. She was pretty tough, he thought to himself, somewhat amused. By now they had a small audience including the elderly lady in the corner, and three more clients who had entered the reception area.

'Calm down, Melissa,' Graymond said loudly. He looked across at Nikki apologetically. 'I'm very sorry about this.'

Nikki gave him a look of mock sympathy; this was one spoiled girlfriend and it was probably his fault. Alicia started crying hysterically.

'How could you *do* this to me?' she shouted at Graymond. 'You *promised* me I could have it done. And now you're telling me I can only have Botox. I don't *want* Botox; it's so last year. I want the fat transfer procedure.'

She began hyperventilating between sobs as tears streamed down her cheeks.

'Sweetheart, this is very embarrassing.' Graymond was trying his best to pacify her, with little success.

'Could we go somewhere a little more private, do you think?' he asked Nikki in a stage whisper, glancing round at the small audience. Nikki stood up and walked around the reception desk.

'Come with me,' she said shortly, clearly not impressed with Melissa's behaviour. As she led them through a secure door to the right of the reception, accessible only with a key card which she wore around her neck, Alicia continued to sob and hyperventilate.

They were in a wide corridor with cream walls and expensive cream carpet. The surroundings were plush but with a clinical feel. Graymond knew from the schematics that there was a seating area ahead on the right. Further along was a small restroom and beyond that was the sizeable office of Dr. H. Elizabeth Ward. Sure enough, Nikki directed the distressed couple into the seating area and motioned for them to sit down. Alicia refused and continued to stand, on the verge of a full-blown panic attack if she didn't receive the consultation she wanted.

'Please wait here and someone will be with you shortly,' Nikki said. 'Can I get you anything, madam? A glass of water perhaps?'

'Where's the ladies' room?' Alicia asked, through breaths and sobs.

'Just along the hallway, the first room on your right,' Nikki replied, and disappeared.

There was a dome security camera in the seating area, which prevented Graymond and Alicia from coming out of character, even briefly. They exchanged eye contact: so far, so good. Graymond checked his watch as Alicia retreated down the corridor in the direction of the ladies' room; she would only have a few minutes. He took a seat and absentmindedly picked up a magazine, which he flicked through without paying attention to it. He supposed it wouldn't be too out of character for him to appear nervous and fidgety in light of the drama he was providing the supporting act for.

Nikki was back with some good news: one of the doctors would be with them in about ten minutes to discuss treatment options for Melissa.

'Thank-you, I'll let her know as soon as she's back from the ladies' room,' Graymond said and went back to his magazine. After five minutes he checked his watch; there was still no sign of Alicia and he hoped she had not run into trouble. Alexander had provided them each with their own flash drive with super-fast file transfer speeds and the maximum amount of storage available, the Rolls Royce of flash drives, he had explained. Nine minutes had passed when Graymond heard footsteps approaching from the direction of the reception. A tall, middle-aged man wearing a white coat over a set of blue theatre scrubs appeared.

'Hello there,' he said, smiling, 'are you the companion of the young lady requesting a consultation for some cosmetic treatments?'

'Er — yes, that's me.' Graymond stood up uneasily. 'Sorry my girlfriend's just in the...'

'I've changed my mind,' came a voice from the corridor. The man raised an enquiring eyebrow at Graymond who nodded. He tried to hide a look of relief as Alicia appeared, her face flushed and tear-stained.

'I'm very happy to answer any questions you may have,' the man said politely. 'My name's Dr...'

'I said I've changed my mind,' Alicia interrupted rudely. She looked at Graymond. 'If I can't have the treatments I want...'

'Darling, of course you can,' Graymond replied, taking her arm gently. 'Why don't you have a chat with this doctor and...'

'We're leaving,' Alicia said abruptly, shaking her arm free. She pushed past the two men and strutted to the door leading to the reception area, wrenching it open. Graymond followed her, smiling apologetically at the doctor who had clearly seen it all before. Alicia stormed through the reception, out of the entrance doors and down the steps into the street.

'Melissa, wait for me,' Graymond tried to sound as though he were desperately trying to gain control of the situation for the benefit of any curious onlookers. He caught up with her on the street and they continued to walk quickly, side by side, without talking, until they reached New Cavendish Street where they took a left. The fast walk gradually slowed and after a few minutes, it felt safe to talk.

Alicia looked at Graymond, her eyes sparkling with excitement. She pulled the small silver flash drive from her coat pocket and held it in front of them.

'Everything's here,' she said excitedly. 'Every client who ever walked into The Ward Centre between the years two thousand and two thousand and two.'

'Good work,' Graymond replied, almost in disbelief at their success. 'Do you think two years' worth of records is going to be enough?'

'More than enough,' Alicia said, slipping the flash drive back into her pocket. 'We don't need to go further back than two thousand, and if he had more work done after the initial surgery, two years should easily cover that. We'll just end up with far too much data to wade through if we expand the file transfer to include more years.'

'I guess you're right.'

'You're the one who's going to have to go through all this information, don't forget,' Alicia added. 'I'll be sunbathing on a beach in Jamaica.'

'Don't remind me,' Graymond replied. He looked at his watch. 'We've got just over three hours before Dr. Khan leaves The Platinum Clinic for his personal training session. Let's grab some coffee.'

Alicia was in agreement; it would enable them to synchronise their plans for the next data heist.

At precisely 4:04 p.m., two minutes after Dr. Abadiya Khan had walked out of The Platinum Cosmetic Clinic in a bright purple tracksuit, ready for an afternoon of power skipping and burpees, Alicia walked through the revolving glass door at the main entrance and took a seat in the waiting area.

'I'm waiting to meet my mother,' she replied, when the receptionist, a pleasant young man called Pete, asked if she needed any help, 'she wants to make an appointment to see someone about weight loss management; she just wanted me to be here with her.'

The amiable Pete understood completely, many daughters accompanied their mothers to such appointments, and vice versa, of course, and would Alicia care for a tea or coffee while she waited?

'Thank you, that would be lovely,' Alicia smiled. She looked brightly around the room and extended the smile to the other people in the waiting area; she counted eight in all which was very useful.

A few minutes later, Graymond entered. He was dressed in slightly more casual attire and had ditched the trendy specs for some nerdy ones. He approached Pete who had just reseated himself behind the reception desk after delivering a cup of coffee to Alicia. A telephone was ringing which Pete ignored and another receptionist answered. Pete was the man in charge. He looked up at Graymond and his professional gaze wavered for just a second as he caught sight of Graymond's ears before recovering himself and re-focussing on his face.

'Good afternoon sir, can I help you?' Pete said pleasantly.

'Yeah, I hope so. I'd like to see someone about my ears.'

'Your ears?' Pete asked innocently. His poker face was exemplary after the initial shock. Graymond and Alicia had just spent the last forty-five minutes in a public restroom applying spirit gum and flesh-coloured Scar Wax to the back of Graymond's ears, with the alarming but delightful end result of two distinctly protruding ears.

'Come on man,' Graymond replied in an agitated tone, 'don't pretend they look normal. I've lived with them all my life; I can't take this any more. I want to see someone, have something done about them.'

'I understand sir,' Pete said, tapping a few keys on his computer, 'let's have a look...' More tapping. 'Dr. Ellis is available for a consultation tomorrow morning at nine thirty.' He looked up at Graymond.

'I'd like to see someone today, if possible. I don't mind waiting.'

Pete looked back at his screen.

'Dr. Janowski has had a cancellation this evening at five o'clock. Would that be of any help sir?'

'Yeah I'll take that one.'

'Perfect, I'll get you all booked in. Can I take your name please sir?'

'It's Miles Jones.'

'Thank you. If you'd like to take a seat in the waiting area over there sir?'

Graymond nodded, ambled over to where Pete was pointing and sat down immediately opposite Alicia who was engrossed in a book. A few people glanced at his ears after overhearing the conversation with Pete, immediately looking away again before staring covertly; Alicia's stage make-up skills gave a whole new meaning to the term "bat ears". For a moment, Graymond imagined how he would feel if the ears were real. He considered the shallow, judgemental attitude of society towards someone who didn't fit in, whether it was due to a physical characteristic or some other reason. It was a cruel world. He sat staring at the floor for a few minutes until he decided it was time for Act Two. He looked up and caught Alicia's eye. He scowled.

'What?' he asked, sullenly.

Alicia ignored him and went back to her book.

'What're you looking at?' he asked again. How many times had a violent fight in prison started with these petty words, he thought with amusement.

'I wasn't looking at anything,' Alicia replied, frowning.

'The hell, you were; you were looking at my ears,' Graymond said, raising his voice.

A few people glanced in his direction, including Pete.

'I wasn't, jerk.'

'What did you just call me?'

'Nothing. Go and sit somewhere else.'

'*You* go and sit somewhere else, you stuck-up...'

Pete was suddenly on hand to diffuse the rapidly escalating situation.

'Excuse me sir, I'm very sorry, but if you're disturbing other clients who are also waiting, I'm afraid I'm going to have to politely ask you to leave.'

'Sorry,' Graymond said apologetically, 'I'm just a bit paranoid about my ears; I've been through a lot, you see. It's a sensitive issue for me.'

'I'm sure it is sir,' Pete replied patiently.

'Is there anywhere... private that I could sit and wait?' Graymond asked suddenly.

Pete seemed to debate this for a moment. Reluctantly, he said: 'Come with me sir.'

Graymond followed Pete through a door with a combination lock which led into a wide hallway. According to Alexander's schematics, a number of offices and clinic rooms were accessed via the hallway, including Dr. Abadiya Khan's. Graymond knew it was three doors down on the right. Pete led him towards it, stopping at the second door on the left, which he opened and ushered Graymond in.

'This is a small additional office that we sometimes use for clients requiring a little more privacy; you're very welcome to wait in here,' he said. 'If you need anything in the meantime, I'll be in the reception. I'll let Dr. Janowski know where you are.'

'Thanks, I really appreciate this,' Graymond said in a grateful voice, 'I'm just so conscious about my ears, I...'

'No problem at all, sir,' Pete smiled reassuringly and disappeared.

Graymond waited until he heard the door leading back into the reception area click shut before stepping out of the office. He checked the hallway; further along a nurse in scrubs was walking his way. She disappeared through another door to her left before she got to him. He checked for cameras; there was one above the reception door which panned along the entire hallway, covering all the office doorways. He doubted there was anyone watching live surveillance monitors; he would have to take his chances. He headed towards Dr. Khan's office, which was almost immediately opposite, and tried the door handle as discreetly as he could. It was locked.

Checking the hallway once more, Graymond knelt down and discreetly pulled two small tools from his pocket: the first was a piece of thin rectangular metal with a ninety degree bend on either side which he inserted into the bottom of the lock. With the longer section of the tool hanging down to one side, he gently applied a small amount of rotational pressure. He then slid another rectangle of metal with a serrated edge at one end into the lock just above the instrument applying the tension, the serrated edge on top. Carefully working the second piece of metal back and forth, Graymond located each lock pin, one by one, until all five had popped into an unlocked position, in alignment with the shear line inside the lock.

Feeling pressure on the tension wrench, Graymond gently turned the handle of the door; it was unlocked in less than a few seconds and Graymond was inside. Prison hadn't been a complete waste of time, he thought perversely. Closing the door behind him, he walked around Dr. Khan's desk, switched on the computer and sat down in a comfortable office chair. The desk was immaculate, with every item at right angles to its neighbour, from the stapler to a framed photograph of a rather attractive middle-aged woman; the doctor's wife perhaps, Graymond thought, who would have access to all the cosmetic surgery she could ever wish for. He was careful not to touch anything as he inserted the flash drive and rapidly keyed in Alexander's instructions, now consigned to memory. After a few minutes of circumventing passwords and accessing various files, he located the archived records of all clients who had received treatment at the clinic between 2000 and 2002 and watched anxiously as the file transfer began.

A minute ticked by slowly. Two minutes. Fifty-four percent of the transfer was complete when there was a knock at the door. Graymond froze. What to do? He couldn't remove the flash drive before the transfer was complete or he would forfeit all the data and would have to start over, but neither could he risk being caught. Someone tried the door handle. He knew it would open; he should have locked it behind him. Cursing his oversight, he dropped to his knees and slid into the small space underneath the desk where he was concealed by its wooden back. He heard the door open and soft footsteps on the thick pile carpet. He held his breath and waited. It sounded as though something was placed on the desk and then the footsteps retreated to the door which clicked shut.

Graymond waited for a few moments before levering himself out of his hiding place and back up into Dr. Khan's chair. He noticed a brown file on the edge of the desk which had not been there before. It was not at right angles to the rest of the desk furniture, something which Graymond was sure Dr. Khan would be quick to rectify. Suddenly, there was a chime sound indicating that the file transfer was complete. Graymond surveyed the screen and tapped a few keys before ejecting the flash drive. He shut down the computer, checked the hallway was clear before exiting Dr. Khan's office, closing the door behind him, and made his way back to the reception area. Alicia was already gone.

Pete finished speaking on the telephone and looked up at Graymond.

'Is everything okay sir?'

'Yeah, something's come up and I don't think I can wait until five o'clock for the appointment. Sorry about that.'

'No problem sir, would you like to reschedule?'

'Not right now; I'll call back later this week.'

'That's fine sir, have a good day.'

'Thanks. You too.'

Graymond breathed a sigh of relief as he departed the clinic through the revolving door. It was almost dark outside and the wind was cold. He scanned the street for Alicia but there was no sign of her; he guessed she was already on her way back to his truck which was parked a few streets away. Graymond walked quickly, keeping to the shadows, although he wasn't sure why. He held the little silver flash drive tightly in his pocket and wondered if it contained a secret that had been hidden for sixteen years.

CHAPTER TWENTY-EIGHT

The journey home to Blackdeane House in Graymond's truck was a slow one as they joined the rush hour traffic, a winding snake of red tail lights heading out of the City at the end of another working day. In spite of this, the mood inside the truck was jubilant as Graymond and Alicia celebrated their success in obtaining the archived files from The Ward Centre and The Platinum Cosmetic Clinic.

'Two down, one to go,' Graymond remarked.

They laughed about the stares their characters had received from a number of people in the waiting areas and complimented each other on their sterling acting abilities.

'Seriously, Gray,' Alicia said, 'it was all I could do not to laugh when you tried to pick a fight with me for looking at your ears.'

'I'm pretty sure I've got some fractured ribs from where you hit me,' Graymond replied, putting his hand over parts of his chest.

'I can't wait to download those files,' Alicia said. 'I really hope we find something.'

'So do I,' Graymond replied wistfully.

They had not been back at Blackdeane House for long before Graymond remembered that his cell phone had been switched off for most of the day.

'I'd better check for messages,' he remarked to Alicia, 'I haven't been to the airfield all day and I'm expecting a call to confirm that all the paperwork for the Gulfstream jets has been completed.'

'That will be good news,' Alicia replied, opening the door of Graymond's refrigerator. She stepped back with a look of disgust. 'Seriously, Gray? Half a can of tomato soup and an item of food so covered in mould that it's beyond identification?' She held up something that had once resembled a block of cheese, but was now a medium for a fluffy grey-green fungus, the growth of which had clearly not been hampered by the cooler temperature of Graymond's refrigerator.

'I've been busy,' he protested, examining the screen on his cell phone, 'I haven't had time to stock up. Why don't you call for a takeaway or something?'

Alicia didn't need to be told twice.

'Chinese, Indian or Thai?' she asked Graymond, but he didn't reply. He wasn't listening; he was staring at his cell phone with a puzzled look.

'That's odd,' he said slowly.

'What?'

'Mrs Davidson's been calling all day; I must have over fifty missed calls from her. I hope she's okay, I'd better call her back.' He put the phone to his ear and waited. 'Is that Landon? Hi Landon, it's Graymond Sharkey. I've got like a million missed calls from this number; is everything…'

'Gray, oh thank goodness, I've been trying to reach you all day; something terrible's happened.' Landon sounded distraught.

'Landon, what the hell's the matter?' Graymond asked.

'It's mother,' Landon began sobbing uncontrollably at the other end of the line, 'she's dead.'

'*What?*' Graymond froze in shock. All he could think of was the information that she had been about to tell them, before they were interrupted by Roy and Kevin.

'But *how?*' Graymond asked.

'Last night,' Landon managed to say, 'we've had the doctor here… and some paramedics…'

'Are you okay? Is your dad okay?'

'Dad's in shock; he's the one who found her when he took her morning cup of tea to her; they sleep in separate rooms, you see,' Landon said weakly, 'and no, I'm not okay.'

'Is there anything I can do?' Graymond asked. 'Shall I come over?'

'Would you mind? I think dad and I would both appreciate that. I know mother thought a lot of you.'

'No problem, Landon, I'll be round as soon as I can,' Graymond replied. He hung up. Alicia was looking at him expectantly; she knew something was up.

'Mrs Davidson's dead.' The words sounded harsh and unbelievable.

'How? When?'

'Don't know how. It happened sometime last night.'

'Damn. We should have gone back yesterday to see her. We should never have left it. We've just got her killed, Gray.'

Graymond stood still at the sudden realisation of Alicia's words.

'But Landon didn't say anything about…'

'No, but it's too much of a coincidence,' Alicia replied. 'Someone murdered her, Gray, and unless there was someone else at the cottage yesterday that we don't know about, then there are potentially three people who are involved in this.'

Graymond thought back to the moment Mrs Davidson had been about to reveal what she knew; it was at that moment that Roy and Kevin had interrupted them.

'Gray, I think you should be careful,' Alicia warned. 'Something is really not right here. One of those three men could be a murderer and you may be walking into a trap.'

'What d'you mean?'

'You could be about to be framed or implicated in her death, just by being at her house. You could also be in danger yourself.'

Graymond laughed scornfully.

'Alicia, I've survived seventeen years in a maximum security prison; I'll take my chances.' He picked up the keys to his truck. 'I'm going to the Davidsons'.'

'Then I'm coming with you,' Alicia said firmly.

Graymond knew there was little point in arguing.

The truck pulled up outside the Davidsons' cottage behind a brand new Range Rover Sport. A cold damp mist had descended in the still night air. As Graymond and Alicia walked towards the cottage, they could see lights on in the downstairs rooms, the pale yellow beams illuminating the gloomy darkness of the garden outside. An owl hooted and there was a flapping of wings in the trees above.

Alicia knocked on the front door which was opened by Landon, still very distraught. He beckoned them inside, reiterating how thankful he was that they had come. He offered them cups of tea, which they declined, and led them through to the living room, where his father Roy sat, apparently in a state of shock. Kevin Mason and his wife were also there, along with a few other close friends including, to Graymond's surprise, Reese and Julia Coraini. They had insisted on driving over as soon as they received Landon's call. They had been there for most of the afternoon.

'Gray, good to see you,' Reese extended his hand which Graymond ignored. 'Julia and I were just heading home.' Reese retracted his hand.

'Good. Is that new Range Rover yours? I think I might have blocked you in,' Graymond replied curtly.

'The white one? Yes, that's ours.'

'Then I'll move my truck.' Graymond retreated towards the front door; anything to expedite the departure of Reese and Julia. They followed behind.

'Terrible news, isn't it?' Reese had another attempt at making conversation with Graymond as they walked.

'It's just so — so sad and unexpected,' Julia added.

'Yes, very unexpected, wasn't it?' Graymond replied.

'Landon says they don't know the cause of death yet,' Julia went on, 'and there's going to be a post mortem.'

'I'm sure we'll all be interested in the outcome of that,' Graymond said dryly. He reached his truck. Reese and Julia were hovering.

'Gray, now may not be the best time to ask, but Reese and I would love it if you'd join us for dinner sometime,' Julia said, a little hesitantly, 'and your — er — friend would be most welcome too. How about tomorrow evening?'

'Thanks but things are pretty busy right now, I'm afraid I'll have to decline.' Graymond could think of nothing worse than dinner with his ex-girlfriend and her husband.

'Then maybe we could catch up in a few weeks' time?' Julia suggested.

Like a dog that won't let go of a stick, Graymond thought to himself.

'Yeah, maybe,' Graymond replied, climbing into his truck.

'We'll swing by the airfield sometime and set up a date,' Reese called out as Graymond slammed the truck door shut and started the engine with a deliberate roar. Reese and Julia retreated to the Range Rover in front while Graymond reversed. He watched Reese pull away from the side of the road rather cautiously before parking the truck once more.

Nice vehicle, he thought to himself, *where d'you get the money to pay for it, Reese?*

Back inside the Davidsons' cottage, Landon was describing to Alicia and a captive audience of family friends the drama that had unfolded earlier that morning, in between broken sobs and deep breaths. Roy remained silent, with a stunned expression, and was being comforted by Kevin and Mrs Mason.

'So we called an ambulance but — it was too late,' Landon was saying, 'sh — she was already dead you see.'

He paused to blow his nose.

'The doctor said the time of death would have been before midnight. Dad and I were at a dinner at the golf club last night until late; we didn't get home until gone twelve and we just went straight to bed. But she was already dead, and we didn't know. No one knew, no one went to check in on her, maybe we could have done something if we had?'

An elderly lady whom Graymond thought may have been a friend of Mrs Davidson's from the church choir put her arm gently on Landon's arm.

'Don't be upset with yourself, dear,' she said, 'I'm sure there's nothing you could have done.'

'But if only we'd been at home last night, instead of at the golf club,' Landon collapsed into a fresh burst of sobs, 'mother might still be alive.'

'You don't know that, dear,' the lady consoled him patiently.

There was little else that could be said or done at such a solemn hour. Graymond and Alicia stayed a little while longer to express their support and sympathy to the grieving family, before they said their goodnights and departed, with Landon promising to inform them of any further news.

Graymond was quiet on the journey home and Alicia left him alone with his thoughts. She acknowledged that Mrs Davidson was the last person who had truly had some kind of connection to Graymond's parents and brother. As the Sharkey family's former cleaning lady, she was the last person who could have shared in the distant memories of his childhood and of happier times. Graymond didn't say anything, and Alicia guessed he would probably prefer to shed any tears for his elderly friend in private. She also guessed that the feelings of loss and sadness would be accompanied by an impression of guilt. Although the cause of death had not yet been determined, she was certain that natural causes could be safely ruled out. Which meant that the old lady had been murdered. But why?

Because she knew something, Alicia thought, *and she was about to tell us what it was that she knew.* Alicia tried to remember Mrs Davidson's exact words during their visit. She had certainly appeared to be disturbed at the mention of Caleb Fonteyne but had been adamant that she had no knowledge of his whereabouts. Then again, she had appeared surprised at the idea of Caleb being involved in the airfield murders and had vehemently denied knowing anyone who had received burns treatments or cosmetic work of any kind. The lightbulb moment appeared to be at the mention of Jamaica, prompted by Alicia's observation of the sugar bowl from Negril. Did Mrs Davidson deliberately get out the sugar bowl in order that she might draw attention to the place? If so, why? What was the connection? Alicia had wanted to ask Landon if he knew who had given his mother the sugar bowl, but felt it may have been a little insensitive in light of the circumstances. And finally, Mrs David-son had been about to reveal something that had happened on the night of August 14, 1999, at around midnight, that she knew about but probably shouldn't have, before they were interrupted by Roy her husband and his golfing buddy, Kevin.

It was this interruption that interested Alicia. How very timely it was. She wasn't one for coincidences and wondered how long they may have been listening to the conversation before they had no choice but to rapidly bring it to a halt. But then they were faced with a problem: damage control. The old lady had to be silenced, and quickly, before she talked. Alicia wondered if Kevin was really at the cottage that evening to offer his condolences, or if he was there to ensure Roy kept his mouth shut. And now, of course, the killer knew that Graymond and Alicia were searching for the truth.

Graymond slid the truck to a halt outside Blackdeane House in the glare of the security lights. He switched off the engine and stared straight ahead.

'Reese and Julia invited us for dinner, by the way,' he said suddenly.

'What did you say?'

'I said no. Why d'you think they invited us?' Graymond was suddenly suspicious of everyone. Alicia knew he was thinking the same things as her.

'I don't know. Perhaps they were just being friendly,' she replied, unconvincingly. 'The one thing I do know is that there is a killer at large; perhaps the same killer who murdered your two friends and framed you for it.'

CHAPTER TWENTY-NINE

Fay Dayton, the Practice Manager of The Cosmetic Artistry Clinic had had her coffee break interrupted by the timid receptionist who annoyed her, and she had received no advanced warning from the CQC team regarding their visit. In addition, the clinic had been fully inspected only a few months before, receiving outstanding ratings in almost every area; it was unprecedented that they should return so soon. She supposed the receptionist had made a mistake, which was not quite so unprecedented.

She forced a sickly smile as she approached the couple in reception who were dressed in smart business suits and wearing name badges bearing the unmistakeable CQC logo, attached to CQC lanyards.

'Good morning, can I help you?' Fay adopted an efficient tone of voice.

Graymond and Alicia introduced themselves as Norman Flynn and Kiera Moran, on behalf of the CQC. Alicia wore a blonde wig, and Graymond had on a pair of designer glasses with tortoiseshell rims and tinted lenses.

'But you guys were only here three months ago,' Fay said, with a puzzled expression, 'you gave us an outstanding.'

Yes, absolutely, Mr. Flynn and Ms. Moran were fully aware of the recent inspection but there were just a couple of issues that needed clarification. Alicia nodded to a thick bundle of official-looking paperwork with CQC logos on it that she was carrying and Graymond held up a large black briefcase.

'What kind of issues?' Fay asked.

According to Mr. Flynn and Ms. Moran, the issues were IT-related, and it would be most helpful if they could have access to a computer.

'I haven't received any information from the CQC about this,' Fay said, hesitantly, 'aren't you supposed to tell us if you're coming?'

Mr. Flynn and Ms. Moran assured her notice of their visit had been given to the medical director of the clinic, at which point Fay rolled her eyes and gave a weary sigh.

'Typical,' she said. 'That explains everything. I apologise to you both about this misunderstanding. Dr. Lusardi can sometimes be a little — er — unreliable in passing on important information such as a visit from the CQC.'

'Is he here to confirm that?' Graymond asked hopefully, knowing full well that Dr. Lusardi was, at that moment, happily working his way around eighteen holes of golf with no prior knowledge of the CQC's return. Fay shook her head, no.

'He has every Wednesday afternoon off,' she said, 'however, you're more than welcome to use his office if you need access to a computer.'

'That would be most helpful,' Alicia beamed.

Fay showed them to the medical director's office and left them to it. She was a busy lady and had already been summoned back to the reception area to deal with another matter.

'Let me know if you need anything else,' she said on her way out.

Alicia took a seat behind the desk and set to work. She was a little quicker at transferring the files than Graymond, so while she pecked at the keyboard, Graymond perched on the desk and busied himself with some paperwork, for the benefit of any security cameras that may be running. He leaned over to look at the computer screen; the transfer was in progress with sixty-two percent complete. Suddenly, there were footsteps outside and the door opened. Fay strode into the office with an angry expression.

'I've just called the CQC,' she began. 'It seems that nobody there has any record of a planned visit taking place at this clinic today.' She looked accusingly at Graymond and Alicia. 'Perhaps you'd like to explain yourselves?'

Graymond slid off the desk; he felt a wave of panic. What could they do? He glanced around and spotted his cell phone lying in top of the briefcase. He picked it up.

'That's strange,' he said, with a confused look, 'let me check my calendar.' He pulled up the calendar on his cell phone which contained precious little engagements. He frowned and glanced at Alicia while Fay stood impatiently, with her hands on her hips. Alicia shook her head; the file transfer was still not complete.

'Just get the right date,' Graymond in an unhurried voice, 'here we are… Wednesday, December the fourteenth…' Another glance at Alicia; this time she nodded, the file transfer was complete.

'This is The Platinum Cosmetic Clinic, isn't it?' Graymond said, stepping between Fay and Alicia to obstruct Fay's line of sight towards the computer in order for Alicia to remove the flash drive.

'It's The Cosmetic Artistry Clinic,' Fay said frowning.

'Ah, then I think we might have the reason why you weren't expecting us,' Graymond replied brightly, pocketing his cell phone.

'You mean you've come to the wrong clinic?' Fay asked, incredulously.

'It would appear that way,' Graymond said, 'I apologise for the misunderstanding.'

Fay rolled her eyes again. It was something she appeared to do a lot. She watched as Graymond and Alicia picked up their papers and briefcase and escorted them back to the reception area where they apologised, once again, for the silly mistake, and hurried out of the clinic. Once outside, they walked south towards Cavendish Square Gardens. They were now in possession of the archived files from all three clinics.

Alicia's flight to Sangster International Airport, Montego Bay, Jamaica, left London Gatwick at eleven o'clock the following morning. Graymond had insisted on driving her to the airport. After Alicia had checked her bag in, they bought coffee and sat down in a small seating area. It was the start of the Christmas holidays and the airport was busy. It was the first time Graymond had been in a major airport for nearly twenty years and he was enjoying the activity and the people-watching: there were lone business travellers, couples, families with parents frantically trying to keep their excited children under control, airport employees dressed in high-visibility vests driving golf-carts, and uniformed pilots and cabin crew pulling their carry-on cases behind them. Graymond watched joyful hellos and emotional goodbyes; he was fascinated with it all, and felt as though he could stay all day and never get bored.

'Gray, I just asked you for your thoughts on Kevin Mason,' Alicia asked, waving a hand in front of his eyes.

'Sorry,' he replied, blinking, 'what did you say?'

'I think Kevin looks good for the murder of Mrs Davidson,' Alicia said in a low voice, 'or he at least orchestrated it. He's got burns scars too. And I think Roy's in on it as well, they were both right there when she was about to tell us what she knew. We know Roy was at the golf club with Landon that night; find out if Kevin was there too. Keep an eye on them Gray, and be careful.'

'Alicia, I'll be fine; I can protect myself.'

'And as for the other suspects,' Alicia said, ignoring him, 'we still haven't found Caleb Fonteyne yet. Oliver Jacobs is in Jamaica, in his condo in Montego Bay and not coming home for a few more days, Alisdair Brooks is still in London — I checked last night — and as for Reese and Julia, they've been close by the whole time. Whoever it is, they're watching us; they're watching our every move.'

Graymond suddenly remembered the night he was released from prison, as he walked along the lane beside Blackdeane Airfield; the rustling in the long grass on the other side of the fence. He had dismissed it as a night animal, or his own paranoia, but now he wasn't so sure. Was he being watched after all, as he walked to his home? If so, by whom?

'I'd better go,' Alicia said, checking the time on a nearby departures board and downing the remains of her coffee. She pulled on the handle of her carry-on and stood up. Graymond walked with her to security control where he could go no further. She turned to face him.

'I'll bet you didn't imagine this would include a last minute Christmas mini-break in the Caribbean,' Graymond said with a smile.

'I'll put up with it,' Alicia replied jokingly. Suddenly she was serious. She looked up into his eyes for a long moment. 'I wish you were coming.'

'What? Really? No teasing, Alicia,' Graymond stammered, unsure of how to reply.

'I'm not, Gray. It's not about the story any more; it's about...'

'Yes?' Graymond looked earnestly into her eyes, searching for confirmation of what she was saying.

'It's a bad time to be doing this, isn't it?' Alicia said.

'Yes — I mean, no! It's never a bad time. Tell me you mean it,' Graymond almost shouted.

Alicia didn't reply. Instead she tilted her head up and kissed him quickly on the mouth. 'Take care, Gray, and trust no one.'

'You too, Alicia. Call me when you get there.'

'I will,' she said over her shoulder as she disappeared into the melee of travellers headed for security control. Graymond watched as she presented her passport to the officer at the entrance and was quickly ushered through. He turned and made his way back to the car park. He tried to focus on the day ahead, the work to be done at the airfield, the files from the clinics to be looked over, but the only thing he could think of was Alicia's kiss. He wanted to run back into the terminal, push through the crowds, force his way past the security control officer and find her, to hold her and kiss her, deeply and passionately. The more he thought about it, the more he believed he might just do it. Forcing common sense to prevail, he got into his truck and headed to the exit, the roar of the engine echoing around the concrete walls. He thought about Alicia's words. The conversation would be continued.

CHAPTER THIRTY

The Boeing seven four seven touched down on the runway at Montego Bay and taxied to the gate. The passengers disembarked onto the tarmac in the blazing Jamaican sunshine and were directed to an air-conditioned terminal for passport control and baggage reclaim. It was late afternoon and a number of flights had landed within a short space of time; Alicia waited patiently in a long arrivals line as the laid-back Jamaican authorities stamped passports in island time. Once she had collected her case, she made her way outside the airport where a car was waiting to transport her to Negril. The cab driver chatted animatedly throughout the hour and a half journey, recommending various places on the island that were well worth a visit.

'Yuh traveling alone?' the cab driver asked.

'I'm meeting someone in Negril,' Alicia replied, smiling. At least she hoped she was meeting someone, although who it might be, she had no idea. The route from Montego Bay to Negril followed the coastline for much of the way and Alicia gazed out of the window, admiring the crystal clear water of the Caribbean Sea, a bright hue of aquamarine which slowly became a deep shade of azure blue as it neared the horizon. The fiery ball of the orange sun to the West had begun its descent against a darkening sky. The tropical scene was a far cry from the dreary grey of the British winter and Alicia wished once more that Graymond was with her. In view of his past, she had tried to reason with herself, to no avail, that a relationship would most likely be complicated, but she couldn't deny the feelings that she had for him, which were only reinforced each time they were together. Her words at the airport had been unexpected and impulsive, but something about them had felt right, and Alicia knew in her heart that if she was to remain true to these feelings, there was only one way this thing could go.

It was dark by the time they reached Negril and bright stars twinkled in the night sky like brilliantly cut diamonds. Alicia tipped the driver and checked into a cheap motel overlooking a parking lot. It wasn't the greatest two star place she had ever stayed in, but her second floor room was clean if not exceptionally comfortable and would suffice as an undercover surveillance base for as long as she needed it. After she had unpacked her few belongings, she showered, changed into a light cotton dress and stepped outside. Palm trees swayed gently in the warm breeze and she could hear the waves lapping lazily on the beach a few steps away. It was a paradise, but Alicia knew that in the midst of such beauty, a dark secret was hidden. Her only clue as to what this might be, or to whom it may lead, was in the words of an elderly lady who had been murdered because of what she knew, and who had ultimately taken the secret to her grave.

Alicia found a small diner on the beachfront where she ordered jerk chicken and a cold beer. A live reggae band playing an eclectic mix of past and present hits from Bob Marley to Rihanna had drawn a small crowd to the sandy dance floor. The chicken arrived and Alicia walked the room with her eyes as she ate. The diner was clearly a popular place with tourists, although the locals had a presence too; it was this group that interested her the most. While nothing and nobody was off-limits, she wasn't expecting to obtain anything interesting from the tourist angle. If the key to the airfield murders was indeed to be found on this tropical island, it was more likely to be found in a beach condo belonging to Oliver Jacobs or a bar where Alisdair Brooks may have moonlighted. A name or a face would come in handy right now. She wondered if Graymond had had a chance to start looking through the clinic files. She had called him upon her arrival but her message had gone straight through to voice mail. She hoped it was because he was caught up with work. She knew he could look after himself, but there was still a killer at large who knew that Graymond had been asking questions.

The jerk chicken tasted good and, when dinner was over, Alicia took a seat at the bar where she ordered a cocktail. The barman insisted she try his own version of a rum punch, which was suddenly on the house when she informed him that she was a freelance travel journalist. She thanked him and left a generous tip anyway. The bar was loud and busy and there was little opportunity to talk, but she sat patiently.

In between serving customers, the barman returned to Alicia, interested to know if she would be writing a review on the diner and bar. Absolutely, she replied. She was here for a number of days, writing a piece on Negril for a travel journal and a guide book, and wanted to sample as much of the place as she could. The barman offered his services as a tour guide by day if required. Alicia was grateful and, since he had been so kind, she wondered if he knew a good friend of hers, also a barman, who had spent some time in Negril; his name was Alisdair Brooks. Alicia held up a photograph which she had printed from Alisdair's Facebook page. Both the name and the picture were met with a blank look. How about his friend, Oliver Jacobs, Alicia asked, offering up another Facebook profile picture. Another shake of the head. The barman was sorry, neither man was familiar.

At midnight, Alicia walked back to her motel room, exhausted from travelling and pleasantly tipsy from the rum punch. The pungent scent of marijuana lingered along the beach and the distant beat of the reggae band echoed in the sultry night air. She had achieved nothing, but tomorrow was another day.

As Alicia drifted to sleep listening to the rhythmic sound of crickets chirping outside, Graymond awoke, aching and cold, from where he was slumped at his desk in front of the twenty-seven inch iMac screen. It was five-thirty in the morning and not yet light. Graymond blinked in the darkness and tried to work out what he was doing, sitting at his desk in his study. What had happened? Why was he not in bed? He hit the mouse and the iMac screen came to life with a glare, causing Graymond to shield his tired eyes. He was staring at a before and after shot of a client who had had some rather drastic facial cosmetic work undertaken in November 2000 at The Ward Centre. Graymond made an attempt to focus on the pictures and the personal details of the client written alongside. He remembered this as one of the last photographs he had been looking at before he fell asleep a couple of hours earlier. As his eyes became more accustomed to the pictures on the screen, he studied them more closely. He scrutinised the photographs — both the before and after shots — and read through the personal details beside them: name, date of birth, contact details, allergies and some medical terms which Graymond didn't understand. Nothing stood out, there was nothing familiar about any of it and he clicked to the next client. He was working his way through surnames in alphabetical order and was currently up to D. Progress was slow.

He yawned and stretched and pushed his chair back from the desk. This wasn't going to be productive without a long, hot shower to wake him up, followed by a few generous shots of caffeine to keep him awake. He checked his cell phone on his way to the bathroom. There was a missed call from one of the engineers working on one of the Robin HR 200 aircraft at the airfield, no message, and a voicemail from Alicia: she had arrived safely and was just checking in with him, as promised. She hoped he was okay and would call again soon. He listened to it a second time, just to hear her voice, before hanging up. He debated whether to call her back straight away, but remembered that Jamaica time was five hours behind the UK; he should probably wait until at least eleven o'clock before returning her call.

Back at his desk, with a large cup of coffee and a renewed enthusiasm for the task of examining the clinic records, one by one, Graymond clicked to the next set of photographs. This was definitely a contender for the prize for the most tedious job, along with folding jumpsuits in the prison laundry. Boredom aside, Graymond was as careful and methodical as possible with what needed to be done. There was a great deal of information to work through, and no shortcut. It could potentially take hours, even days. He tried to pay particular attention to white males in their mid-twenties, who had undergone treatment and surgery related to burns injuries, and who had had any facial reconstruction work done. He decided to spend a couple of hours looking through more photographs before he headed over to his office at the airfield for a nine o'clock meeting. He tried not to think about how he would feel if he discovered nothing useful after scrutinising all three databases.

It was close to midday before he had an opportunity to call Alicia. She answered her cell after the second ring.

'Alicia, how are things? No wait, don't tell me, I don't want to hear about tropical beaches and palm trees while I'm freezing my ass off back here in Blighty. Tell me you've solved the case and you've coming home.'

'No to both of those,' Alicia replied. 'How about you? Have you come across any leads from any of the databases? Found any familiar faces? I could really do with a bit of help right now; my search radius covers seven long miles of the most beautiful white-sand beach you've ever seen.'

'I'd much rather be sitting in front of a computer trawling through endless mugshots of some of the ugliest faces you've ever seen, anyway,' Graymond said, 'and at the rate I'm going it could take months.'

'I'll take my time out here then.'

'Oh you're hilarious, aren't you,' Graymond said with a dry tone. 'Listen, I've got to go, my flight engineer's just arrived, the biz jets are back in action so I'm going to take a look round them with him.'

'Great news, we'll catch up later, and Gray?'

'What?'

'I miss you.'

Graymond paused. The flight engineer stood at the door within earshot.

'Yeah, whatever,' he replied casually, and hung up.

Alicia stared at her cell phone in disappointment. Was Graymond angry at her for what she had said to him at the airport? If he wanted to play it that way, then she was fine with it. Annoyed at how he had made her feel, she pulled her running shoes on and set out for the beach, trying to convince herself that she was doing this for a sensational story and nothing more.

The next few days brought nothing in the way of progress on either side of the Atlantic. By day, Graymond juggled meetings with flight engineers, pilots, accountants, financial advisors, airfield staff and his trusted lawyer Avery Sherwood-Johnson; by night he laboriously worked his way through the clinic databases. The Ward Centre and The Platinum Cosmetic Clinic revealed nothing useful, and on Monday night of the week leading up to Christmas, he made himself a fresh pot of strong coffee and opened up the files retrieved from The Cosmetic Artistry Clinic in preparation for a long night ahead. The first set of photographs belonging to a man about his own age flashed up on the screen. The layout of the databases varied from clinic to clinic but essentially contained the same information. Graymond studied the before and after shots of the man staring back at him, a Thomas Abbott who had undergone a simple rhinoplasty, which by now, Graymond had learned was a nose job. Neither the name or the face bore any resemblance to anyone from Graymond's past, and it was the wrong kind of surgery anyway, with no reference to burns or major facial reconstruction work. Graymond clicked on. He wondered what Alicia was doing. They had not spoken directly since their initial conversation following Alicia's arrival in Negril, partly due to the different time zones and partly due to preoccupation with work and undercover activities.

Messages had been left on each other's cell phones; Graymond's daily text remained unchanged: "Progress: none, interesting updates: none, exciting developments: none, the will to live: almost none." Alicia's messages had borne similar sentiments, with the exception of her most recent text, which stated that she was following up on a potential lead, although it was too soon to say if it was going anywhere and she'd keep him informed.

CHAPTER THIRTY-ONE

Alicia's third morning in Negril had commenced with an early run along the beach, much the same as the previous two. Each day, on the way back to her motel, she would stop at a different beach bar for a drink and a chat with the locals. During the chat, the mention of some old friends she was trying to track down in the area would come up, along with names and photographs of faces. At this point in the conversation, the response would always be the same: a blank look, a shrug of the shoulders, a shake of the head. Nobody recognised Oliver Jacobs, Alisdair Brooks, Reese Coraini or Julia Tripp, whose photograph was thrown in for good measure. There was also a seventeen year old picture of Caleb Fonteyne — the only one Alicia had been able to find — which nobody recognised either. She was becoming increasingly despondent; was the journey, the time and the effort all a complete waste? She knew Graymond was getting nowhere with the clinic databases either. They couldn't fail. Not now.

It was Sunday morning. The mercury had already hit ninety degrees by eleven o'clock and Alicia stopped at a beachfront bar called Alpen's Beach Shack. It had a verandah sheltered by a roof made of dried palm leaves and a reggae version of Little Donkey boomed over the loud speakers which were balanced precariously on two tall wooden crates. It wasn't yet midday but Alicia asked for a Red Stripe beer anyway, and sat waiting to engage the bartender in conversation after he finished serving two Australians. A few benign pleasantries later, and Alicia's photographs were out on the countertop. Did the bartender recognise anyone here? He studied the faces carefully before giving the same response that Alicia had become accustomed to. Sorry, nobody looked familiar. None of the names rang any bells either. Alicia sighed.

'Are you English?' It was an Australian accent. Alicia glanced along the bar to where the young couple, a man and a woman, sat further down.

'Yes, I am,' she replied, 'and you're all the way from Australia?'

'That's right,' the woman replied. She introduced herself as Angie; she was travelling with her fiancé Tim. 'I didn't mean to interrupt you, but I overheard you were searching for an old friend?'

'Yeah, I am. Without much luck so far, sadly.'

'There's an Englishman who runs a water-sports outfit just down the beach,' Angie said pointing, 'I went waterskiing there yesterday and I'm hoping to do a bit of sailing this arvo. It might be worth checking him out, see if he knows anyone you're looking for.'

'What's his name?' Alicia asked. It was worth a shot.

'Sam Leeburne. He's the owner of Leeburne's Water-sports.'

At this, the bartender stiffened and muttered something under his breath.

'Do you know him?' Alicia asked, turning back to him.

'Me no like dat man; him a ginnal,' the bartender replied with a scowl. He moved to the other side of the bar to serve an American family who had just entered. Alicia looked across at Angie again who shrugged and said casually: 'he seemed all right to me.'

'Thanks,' Alicia replied, finishing her beer, 'I'll go check him out some time.' She stood up, gave a little wave to the barman and made her way outside. Perhaps Sam Leeburne would recognise someone from her stash of mugshots. She also considered the bartender's reaction at the mention of his name, and decided that it should be followed up another time. She jogged gently along the beach in the direction that Angie had indicated, trying to recall if she had spotted Leeburne's Water-sports on a previous occasion. There were a number of small outfits renting kayaks, sailboats and catamarans along the beach, mostly by the locals. Some were attached to resorts and hotels; others were independently owned. She guessed Leeburne's Water-sports settled into the latter category.

Alicia had run about two miles before she spotted a blue and white sign with a picture of a rainbow coloured Hobie cat sail on it, advertising Leeburne's Water-sports. She slowed to a walk and approached a small wooden cabin surrounded by a number of sailing craft, pulled up high on the beach, away from the water's edge. At the back of the cabin, a range of life jackets of varying colours and sizes hung on metal coat hangers.

'Wahgwan!' said a voice. Alicia glanced around and spotted a young Jamaican man, dressed in a pair of faded shorts and a t-shirt, knelt down behind one of the Hobie cats; he looked as though he were fixing the sail on it.

'I'm looking for Sam Leeburne,' Alicia replied, 'you know where I might find him?'

'Sam? He soon come back.' The young man nodded in the direction of the sea, where Alicia saw a motorboat towing a waterskier, rapidly approaching the shore. 'Can I help you?' asked the young man.

'Oh er, thanks but it's actually Sam I need to speak to,' Alicia smiled.

'No problem.' He returned to the Hobie cat sail.

Alicia watched as a man, roughly her own age, expertly manoeuvred a powerful Bayliner with an inboard motor which destroyed the tranquility of the beach, onto the sand. It slid to a halt and was followed by the waterskier who appeared to be reasonably competent. The man leapt out of the boat holding a piece of frayed rope which he tied to a sturdy wooden post. He then turned to the waterskier who had detached himself from the waterskis and they walked up the beach together, towards the small hut.

'Great skiing today, Leon,' Alicia heard the boat driver say to his companion.

'Thanks Sam,' Leon replied. 'Same time tomorrow? I think I've nailed this now.'

'You sure have,' Sam grinned. 'I'll see you then. Have a great day.'

'You too, Sam,' Leon said, handing Sam his lifejacket. They shook hands and Leon set off along the beach.

Alicia approached Sam as he busied himself hanging Leon's lifejacket up in the back of the hut and placed the waterskis carefully in an upright container.

'Sam,' the young Jamaican called over to him, 'the pretty lady wan tak to yuh.' He motioned to Alicia. Sam looked up and smiled. He walked over to Alicia with a wide grin.

'Hi there,' he said cheerfully, 'what can I do for you, pretty lady?'

It was unmistakably an English accent, with perhaps a hint of American thrown in. Sam Leeburne was about the same age as Graymond, handsome, tanned and with a gorgeous smile, Alicia thought. He wore a sun-bleached pair of Bermuda shorts and a long-sleeved rash vest. Alicia was about to show him the photographs, when she stopped herself. Since arriving in Jamaica she had done nothing but try to track down Graymond's suspects, with no luck, and had not even taken any time out to enjoy a piece of island life. The photographs could wait, she thought to herself. She could come back tomorrow and get Sam to examine them then. Graymond wasn't exactly making much progress himself. One day wouldn't make any difference. She deserved a bit of fun as well as trying to track down people from Graymond's past.

'I see you have a ski boat; any chance of doing a bit of water-skiing this afternoon?' Alicia asked.

'Sure, no problem! We can go now if you're free?'

Alicia had no plans and, after Sam sized her up for a life-jacket, complimenting her on her perfect figure, he untied the motorboat and jumped in, offering Alicia his hand even though she was perfectly capable of getting in herself. As they sped away from the beach, lightly bouncing over the motion of the waves, Alicia felt the warm breeze in her hair and shielded her eyes as she gazed out to sea. Sam steered the boat expertly and they were soon in deep enough water for Alicia to slide over the side of the boat with her skis attached. Sam threw her the ski rope and slowly manoeuvred the boat away from her until the rope was just taut. At Alicia's signal, he smoothly opened up the throttle and the boat surged forward. Alicia had spent many childhood summers waterskiing behind her cousin's motorboat in the UK and remembered the technique as if it was only yesterday.

She felt the warm water of the Caribbean Sea splashing up at her as she skied expertly back and forth along the shoreline. Looking back towards the beach, she admired the tropical beauty of the coast and forgot about Graymond and the murders, the cursed airfield and the suspects, and everything else to do with his macabre world. When at last it was time to return to shore, Alicia skied straight up onto the beach, behind the motorboat.

'You're pretty good,' Sam remarked, as he tied the boat to the wooden post.

'Thanks!' Alicia replied happily, stepping out of the skis and carrying them to the wooden hut, walking beside Sam. She pulled some dollars out of her bag.

'Tell you what,' Sam said, giving her a wide smile as he gently removed her lifejacket, 'this was on me if you promise to come back and see me tomorrow.'

'Wow! That's very kind of you,' Alicia beamed. 'If you're sure, then I'd love to.'

'Another waterskiing session first thing tomorrow, say about ten o'clock?'

'You're on!' Alicia grinned.

'I'll see you tomorrow,' Sam replied.

Alicia felt elated as she strolled back along the beach to her motel, partly due to the excitement of waterskiing in the crystal clear waters of the Caribbean, but mostly due to the charms of the gorgeous Sam Leeburne. She remembered the barman's reaction to his name and dismissed it; it was probably nothing, she would return to the bar another day, if she thought it was worth the time. Back in her motel room, she checked her cell phone. Among other messages, there was one from Gray: the usual. She sent a short reply, informing him of her potential lead, before she showered and changed for dinner.

CHAPTER THIRTY-TWO

Dressed in the same Bermuda shorts and rash vest, Sam was waiting for Alicia when she arrived at Leeburne's Water-sports at ten the following morning. She hadn't intended to forget the photographs, but in her excitement over another waterskiing session with Sam, she had left them back in her motel room. She debated whether or not to ask him if he recognised any of the names, but from the moment that she set eyes on him, Sam kept her engaged in charming and witty conversation, and all thoughts of Graymond's suspects were forgotten.

It was another beautiful morning, the breeze was light and the sea was warm. Alicia had gained more confidence with her skiing the second time around and Sam was impressed.

'Have you ever tried the little Hobie cat?' he asked.

Alicia admitted she didn't have much sailing experience.

'How about I give you a few lessons? Once you've picked up the basics, it's a lot of fun, and you'll be able to take the craft out yourself.'

'Sure, why not?'

'Are you here alone?' Sam asked suddenly.

Alicia hesitated. She wasn't entirely comfortable with the question, but what the hell.

'Yeah, I'm out here by myself for a few days,' she replied, 'I'm a travel journalist, doing some research on the island for a couple of travel magazines and a guide book, covering everything from accommodation to places to eat, things to see and do, and water-sports on the beach, of course.'

'What do I have to do to get a good review?' Sam asked jokingly. Alicia couldn't help but smile at the loaded question.

'How about I take you to dinner tomorrow evening?' Sam asked. 'I happen to own this great little place just along the beach; you'd love it. What d'you say?'

'You own a restaurant?' Alicia asked. She had been hesitant about taking him up on his offer, having only just met him, but his reputability was suddenly heightened at the mention of the ownership of a restaurant.

'Sure do,' Sam grinned. 'I own quite a few bars and diners in and around the area. I hope you'll be kind enough to review a couple of them?'

'I'd be delighted to,' Alicia smiled.

'That's settled then,' Sam replied. 'I'll see you tomorrow.'

Alicia bought a carton of coconut water and found a shady spot on the beach under a palm tree where she called Graymond. It was one p.m. in the Caribbean and six p.m. in the UK.

'I'm glad you've called.' Graymond sounded unusually bright.

'You've found something in the clinic records?' Alicia asked hopefully.

'No, not exactly. To be honest, I haven't had much time to look through those over the last day or so, but I do have exciting news: I'm back in business with the two Gulfstreams. The flight engineer's happy and both jets have been professionally valeted inside and out. I've already got some charter flight bookings set up for the new year, so it's all looking good.'

'That's great news, Gray.' Alicia was happy for him.

'How are things with you?' Graymond asked.

'Ever heard of a Sam Leeburne?'

There was silence at the other end of the line as Graymond considered the question.

'No, that name doesn't sound familiar. *Should* I know him?'

'Not necessarily,' Alicia replied. 'To be honest, I'm not sure he has anything to do with your case at all. It's just that he's British.'

'Have you asked him where he's from in England?'

'Not yet, but I will when I get the right moment.'

'I'll let you know if I think of anything.'

'Okay, fine. Any update on Mrs Davidson's killer?'

'Not that I've heard. I called Landon yesterday but there was no reply. I guess they'll have completed the post mortem by now, but I've no idea what they found. I saw a couple of police cars outside the Davidson's cottage last night, but as you know, I'm not exactly in with the village gossip. I'll call if I hear anything.'

'Just keep your eyes open and be safe, Gray.'

'You too.'

'Talk to you tomorrow.'

'Bye Alicia.'

Alicia placed her cell phone beside her and looked out to sea. If Graymond didn't recognise the name, then Sam Leeburne was likely to be yet another dead end. Above the sound of the waves, she heard another familiar noise. Looking into the cloudless sky she spotted a small aircraft, the buzz of its engine a noise she was very familiar with. She watched it for some time. It was flying south and appeared to be making a gentle descent before it dipped below the horizon to a landing spot.

It was an angle of the case she hadn't considered, but it made perfect sense to search for information at an airfield. Back at the motel, she spoke to the desk clerk on duty who told her that there was a small aerodrome in Negril, a few minutes' walk from the motel. Its main purpose was to serve the tourist resorts in the area and had a scheduled passenger service provided by an American company, the name of which the desk clerk could not recall. In response to Alicia's further questioning, the clerk thought that scenic flights around the island were also available and there may be small aircraft based there for private pilots to rent for themselves. Alicia set off for the aerodrome with a tourist map with directions drawn on by the helpful clerk.

Negril Aerodrome was situated at the end of a gravel road and consisted of a tarmac runway and a smart wooden hut which served as the passenger terminal. A number of aircraft were parked beside the runway, from small passenger jets to two-seater aircraft, much like the one Alicia had learned to fly in. Next to the passenger terminal hut was a smaller one with a bright yellow sign across the front, which had "Island Flying: Light Aircraft Rental" painted on it. The door was open and Alicia went inside. An elderly man dressed in khaki shorts and t-shirt sat behind a battered wooden counter

'Help you, ma'am?' he asked, slowly getting to his feet.

'Yeah, I think so,' Alicia paused, not entirely sure what to ask for. 'Do you rent out small aircraft to private pilots?'

'Sure, we got a Cessna one five two, a one seven two and a Piper Cherokee. Rental prices are per hour an' start at two twenty dollars for the one five two. They go up to two sixty for the Cherokee, fuel and landing fees all in. We just need to see your licence and some ID, a passport or somethin'. You from the UK?'

'Yeah,' Alicia replied. She had learned to fly in a low wing aircraft and thought she'd be more comfortable in the Piper. 'You got someone who can fly a couple of circuits with me, just to make sure I'm happy with everything?'

'Hal's not here right now. You want to book a flight in the Piper?' He leafed through a tatty-looking diary. 'Hal will be in tomorrow afternoon.'

Alicia thought about her plans with Sam and shook her head.

'I can't do tomorrow; what about Wednesday?'

The man took his time finding a page in the diary that apparently corresponded to the day after.

'Wednesday mornin'?' he asked after examining what appeared to Alicia to be a blank page.

'Sounds good,' Alicia replied. She gave her name and contact details which were painstakingly written into the diary.

'Mind if I take a look at the Cherokee now?' Alicia asked. She had spotted it on one corner of the apron next to the runway.

'Go right ahead,' the elderly man replied, levering himself back into his chair.

As Alicia walked across the apron to the aircraft, she watched a small passenger jet carrying about twelve people land on the runway, in a northwesterly direction, towards the sea. The Piper Cherokee looked in reasonable condition from a distance. It was a four seater, single engine piston aircraft with low-mounted wings and a tricycle landing gear. She had learned to fly in something very similar. Up close, she walked round it, inspecting the control surfaces and general condition of the aircraft. It was apparently well-maintained and looked as though it would fly well. It was a little extravagant perhaps, she thought to herself as she walked back along the road leading away from the aerodrome, but it was important to explore every angle in the search for something relating to the Blackdeane murders, especially perhaps with a link to aviation. There was also a potential link to stolen artwork that should be investigated, however, short of the many paintings being touted by the myriad of beach vendors, Alicia wasn't sure how easy that particular task would be.

She took a route back to the motel along the beach, where the sun, a glowing ball of orange, was beginning to set. In contrast to a UK winter sunset, which could take half an evening, a sunset in the Caribbean was over in a few minutes. It was dark by seven o'clock and, on arriving back at her motel room, Alicia felt it may be too late to call Graymond. Instead she left him a message informing him of her visit to Negril Aerodrome and of her plans to rent a light aircraft to go flying on Wednesday morning, while continuing with her search for information on their suspects.

Graymond had sent a short reply back at some time during the night acknowledging Alicia's message and expressing excitement at the thought of doing some flying in Jamaica. He promised to check out the web site of Negril Aerodrome and wished her a safe flight. He himself had had no luck with his database search and was up to surnames beginning with J on The Cosmetic Artistry Clinic records. He had a busy day planned at the airfield with meetings all day, and therefore would probably not be able to resume the search until later that evening. There were no updates on Mrs Davidson's post mortem and Roy and Landon Davidson remained unreachable. No news of possible murder suspects for her death either.

After a lazy morning on the beach, reading and re-reading the notes she had carefully entered into a journal on the progress of Graymond's case in preparation for her sensational news story, Alicia returned the journal to the small safe in her motel room and set off to Leeburne's Water-sports, tucking her room key and cell phone into a waterproof pouch that was attached to her arm. Sam had the Hobie cat ready and together they pushed it off the beach into the water before jumping onto the mesh trampoline area, stretched across the hull of the craft. Demonstrating expert nautical skills as before, he set a southerly course and soon they were travelling at some speed, bouncing across the waves, the spray of salty water deliciously cooling from the heat of the Jamaican sun.

Alicia glanced over in the direction of the aerodrome. She decided to ask Sam about it.

'It's mostly for tourists,' he said, ducking under the mast as he changed direction. They switched sides. 'I've lived on the island for fifteen years and I've never been there to be honest. Not really into flying; I'm a seafaring man myself. Love the water. Could be out here all day.'

'Where were you based in England before you came to Jamaica?' Alicia asked.

'London. I was in insurance. One day I decided I'd had enough of the rat race. Quit my job, came out here, got a job in a bar which I ended up buying, bought myself a little sail boat which turned into Leeburne's Water-sports, and the rest is history as they say.'

'What a great story,' Alicia said dreamily, 'and pretty brave to just up and leave.'

'Well, I've got no family,' Sam said, 'it just seemed like a fun thing to do at the time, and here I am, fifteen years later. Life couldn't be better.'

Alicia laughed. She admired his attitude and sense of adventure. They fell silent, listening to the waves slapping against the side of the little Hobie cat and surveying the white sand of the beach which seemed to stretch the entire length of the coastline. Suddenly, the perfection of the moment was interrupted by the roar of a motorboat which sped past close to them, its wake rocking the Hobie cat violently. The driver of the boat was apparently oblivious to the small sailing craft and intent on impressing his three passengers who were yelling and cheering in delight. The boat turned sharply and headed back in the direction of Sam and Alicia.

'What the hell does he think he's doing?' Sam said furiously. He attempted to steer away, but their speed was no match for the horsepower of the approaching motorboat. It roared past them.

'Hold tight,' Sam shouted over the sound of the engine.

Alicia gripped the edge of the trampoline mesh of the Hobie cat as the boat's wake tossed them violently in all directions. Suddenly, she felt her hands slip and as a wave crashed against the side of the catamaran, she lost her grip and went tumbling backwards into the sea. When she resurfaced, Sam was peering anxiously into the water. He immediately stretched out a hand and helped her back up onto the catamaran.

'Alicia, I'm so sorry,' he said with a look of concern. 'Are you okay?'

'It's not your fault,' Alicia replied with a grin, wringing sea water out of her hair, 'and yes, I'm fine thanks, just wasn't expecting to be swimming as well as sailing today.'

Sam laughed.

'Shall we head back now? The wind should dry you off a bit.'

Alicia nodded and they swapped sides again. As they changed positions, Alicia happened to glance across at Sam. His rash vest had risen up his body a little, after he had stretched out his arm to help her back onto the Hobie cat. Because it was wet, it had stuck to his body, revealing an exposed piece of skin on the side of his back between his shorts and the vest. The skin was badly scarred with what looked like the aftermath of severe burns. Alicia froze and looked away quickly as Sam took up his new position. He looked at her.

'You sure you're okay Alicia? You look a bit shaken up.'

'I'm absolutely fine,' Alicia replied quickly. She would call Graymond as soon as they reached the shore. She looked down at the waterproof pouch attached to her arm and realised in horror that it had split open with the force of falling into the water. Her cell phone and room key were gone. Sam looked over at her.

'I just lost my phone and room key,' Alicia said with annoyance.

'You want me to dive down and look for them?' Sam asked.

'No point,' Alicia replied, 'the phone will be useless and the motel is sure to have a spare key. Let's get back to the shore.'

The mood was somewhat subdued when they pulled the catamaran up on the beach, level with Sam's hut. Sam apologised again and offered to drive Alicia into town to pick up a new cell phone.

'Thanks Sam, but that won't be necessary,' Alicia forced a smile, 'I'll figure something out.'

'You know where I am if you change your mind,' Sam replied kindly, 'and I hope you're still happy to have dinner with me tonight?'

'Oh yes, absolutely,' Alicia said.

'Great. Shall I meet you here at seven-thirty and we can walk along the beach together to my restaurant?'

'Sounds perfect.'

As Sam turned to hang up her lifejacket, Alicia studied the back of his neck and ears above the collar of his rash vest, where she noticed small but visible scars. Although they were faint, perhaps having faded over time, they were distinctive enough and looked as though they may have been the result of some past facial reconstruction work. Alicia swallowed hard.

'I'll see you tonight,' she said, and set out along the beach in the direction of the motel.

CHAPTER THIRTY-THREE

For the grand total of twenty-five dollars, Alicia was issued with a new room key by the desk clerk at the motel. She had also purchased a prepaid cell phone from a local corner store along the street, but was still unable to contact Graymond as her only record of his number had been lost at sea with her cell phone. She kicked herself for not making a note of it on paper in the event of an emergency such as this, but the whole Jamaica trip had been rushed and she had not had time to thoroughly prepare. Her best bet was to locate his contact details from the Blackdeane Airfield website, which presented another problem in the form of internet access. The prepaid cell from the corner store was a cheap model from way back in time when cell phones were used for making calls and sending texts and precious little else. The officious desk clerk at the motel on duty that day was less than helpful, and unwilling to allow the use of the sole computer in the establishment, even when Alicia offered what she felt was a generous bribe. According to the desk clerk, the computer was not for guest use and the nearest internet cafe was in the town which was a fifteen minute taxi-ride away.

Alicia checked her watch. She needed to shower and change for dinner, before walking back along the beach to Sam's hut; there wasn't time. She would have to abandon the idea of contacting Graymond for now and focus on a much more puzzling problem: who was Sam Leeburne and was he connected in some way to the Blackdeane murders?

Sam sat perched on the side of his waterski boat as Alicia approached. He was wearing a pair of beige chino trousers and a white shirt with the sleeves rolled up. The exposed parts of his arms were free of scars. Catching sight of Alicia, he stood up and walked towards her. The light of the full moon shone on his tanned face and as he smiled at Alicia and kissed her lightly on the cheek, she wondered what cosmetic secrets lay behind his handsome looks.

'You look beautiful,' Sam whispered to her, taking her arm. They walked side by side along the beach. 'Were you able to replace your cell phone and room key?' he asked in a concerned voice.

'The room key was easy to sort,' Alicia replied, 'my cell phone, not quite as straight forward I'm afraid.'

'If you need to borrow mine at any time, all you need to do is ask.'

'Thanks, but there's really no one I'm desperate to get in contact with,' Alicia replied. The very last thing she wanted was to add Blackdeane Airfield to the search history in Sam's cell phone.

A few minutes later, Sam pointed to a brightly lit restaurant which was elevated on raised decking, overlooking the beach.

'Welcome to The Leeburne Room,' Sam announced, guiding Alicia up some steps leading from the beach. A waiter showed them to a table by the window and presented them with menus attached to slate boards. Alicia noticed it was the last table left in the otherwise full restaurant.

'It's a popular place,' Sam smiled. He turned his attention to the menu. 'Now then, I absolutely insist you have the surf'n'turf with sweet potato fries and local vegetables. The lobster is locally sourced; you won't have tasted anything like it before.'

'Whatever you recommend,' Alicia replied. She tried to appear calm and relaxed, although she felt far from either. She bitterly regretted the loss of her cell phone and was uneasy about the fact that she had been unable to communicate with Graymond.

Sam ordered a bottle of wine to accompany their food; the most expensive on the menu, and raised a toast to Alicia's travel journal and guide book. A reggae band took to the stage at the back of the busy restaurant and began their set with a version of "Killing Me Softly".

'They're amazing, aren't they?' Sam beamed. 'They play nightly here and in another of my bars in downtown Negril.'

'How many bars and restaurants do you own?' Alicia asked.

'Oh, one or two,' Sam grinned, feigning modesty.

The steak and lobster arrived and Alicia had to agree it was excellent. Sam's choice of wine complimented the food perfectly and Alicia found herself relaxing in his amiable company. He had many interesting stories to tell, along with a few anecdotes about rescuing stranded tourists from perils at sea to amusing tales of beach wedding disasters. Towards the end of the meal, Alicia found herself wondering if she had imagined the burns and facelift scars. Sam was so unbelievably friendly and charming, how could he be anything but the fun-loving person he claimed to be.

'Now Alicia,' he said with his elfish grin, his green eyes sparkling in the light from the candle on their table, 'while the after dinner cocktails here are superb, I can recommend something even better and in a much more — intimate setting. How about you come back to my beach house and we'll finish our evening there?'

Alicia hesitated.

'No pressure and no strings attached,' Sam said, holding up his hands, 'just two friends enjoying each other's company on a secluded balcony with an unrivalled view of the beach and the sea in the moonlight.'

'I guess I can't refuse, can I?' Alicia smiled weakly.

'Absolutely not,' Sam grinned.

They thanked the waiting staff and said goodnight as they left their table. Sam took Alicia's hand and led her down the wooden steps to the beach. As they walked along, the sound of the waves on the shore blending rhythmically with the reggae band's tuneful rendition of an island song in the background, Alicia's thoughts drifted to Graymond. She wasn't sure that she was in love with him, but she missed him and wished he were there with her now. It wasn't even that he would know what to do or say; hell, he'd probably opt for completely the wrong thing altogether, but ultimately Alicia knew she felt something for him that wouldn't go away. She promised herself she'd tell him straight the next time they were face to face.

'Here we are,' Sam said. He keyed in a four-digit security code to a key-pad which unlocked a metal gate and beckoned Alicia through. 'Home sweet home.'

Sam's beach house was an impressive place, a wooden chalet-style construction overlooking the sea, surrounded by palm trees and lush, tropical gardens. Sam switched on lights and soft music simultaneously with a remote control, and led Alicia onto a balcony from a large, open-plan kitchen and living room. There were comfortable wicker chairs arranged around a table and Sam motioned for her to take a seat.

'How does a Leeburne mojito sound?' he asked. In the kitchen behind her, Alicia heard him opening cupboards and blending mojito ingredients. She stared out to sea and watched the silhouette of small boat bob up and down, a long way out. Closer to the shore, a brightly lit party boat sailed by, accompanied by a dance beat and drunken cheers of revellers.

Sam reappeared with two highball glasses filled with ice, mint and lime wedges immersed in white rum, soda water and lime juice. He placed the drinks on the table in front of them and sat down next to Alicia, placing his arm on the back of the chair behind her. He followed her gaze out to sea.

'You can't beat it, can you?' he said. 'I tell myself the same thing every day; I'm a lucky sonofabitch to lead this kind of a lifestyle.'

'I agree with you,' Alicia replied, 'you're very lucky.'

'Very,' Sam reached for his cocktail. The ice clinked in the glass as he picked it up. 'So, my beautiful travel journalist, what did you think of The Leeburne Room? Favourable reviews all round?'

'Oh absolutely. The highest compliments of the day.'

'I thought you'd love the place,' he grinned, leaning in towards Alicia. She took a sip of the mojito. Sam was a little too close for comfort.

'Can I use your bathroom?' she asked suddenly, placing her glass back on the table.

'Go ahead. It's through the kitchen, turn right and at the end of the hallway.'

'I'll be back in a minute,' Alicia said, standing up.

'Take your time babe.'

Beyond the kitchen, Alicia found herself in a wide hallway as Sam had directed. She could see the bathroom through the door at the end. There was a door to the left that opened into a bedroom. Quickly checking that Sam was still out on the balcony enjoying the view, Alicia slipped quietly through the door. The room was fairly minimalist, with a large bed facing a set of French doors which opened out onto a patio area surrounded by tropical gardens. Aside from the bed, the only other piece of furniture in the room was a Georgian-style bureau made of mahogany. Alicia walked over to it and gently pulled at the fold-down desk; it was locked. She slid open one of the drawers which contained a few clothes. She stood up; there was probably nothing here of interest. She turned back towards to the door and as she did so, she caught sight of the wall behind her. It wasn't the wall that made her gasp in astonishment; it was what was hanging on it. She recognised it instantly. At first she assumed it must be a copy, but on closer inspection and re-calling Kam's guidance on determining whether a painting was the genuine article, she was certain this was the real thing.

Alicia had memorised every single one of the seven paintings in the Blackdeane Airfield art heist so carefully that the images were ingrained on the retinas of her eyes. In amongst the more famous paintings that had disappeared that night was a lesser known one, but still of considerable worth. At the time it was stolen from a private home in Europe, it had been valued at thirty-million dollars. The painting was by a relatively unknown artist called Kleid Kaufman, a German-Jewish immigrant whose family had settled in the southwestern United States at the turn of the twentieth century. His oil on canvas masterpiece was painted in 1905 and depicted a small town in the Sonoran Desert in Arizona. Alicia had always liked this particular piece of art; it was an emotive picture, blending the colours of the desert, hues of a golden orange, with blue-grey mountains in the distance and a stormy sky with swirling, angry clouds above. The outline of a small town in the centre of the painting lay in the shadow of tall cacti and desert plants in the foreground. The painting was called Desert Town. It was one of the two pieces of art that had not passed through Borja Moreno-Fernandez's hands and remained undiscovered. It had not been burned; it was hanging on the bedroom wall of a beach house in Jamaica.

Face to face with the stolen painting that had been missing for over seventeen years, suddenly Alicia knew exactly how Sam Leeburne was connected to the Blackdeane murders and who he was. She also knew why he had chosen to keep this painting more than all the others, instead of selling it. A picture paints a thousand words, and this one told her everything. She stood stunned, rooted to the spot, unable to move, her eyes fixed on the vibrant colours of Desert Town. How could she prove what she had just discovered? An outright confession would be impossible to obtain. Or would it? As she returned to rejoin Sam on the balcony, she thought quickly and a plan began to come together in her mind.

For the remainder of the evening, Alicia employed her greatest acting skills in playing it cool, although inside she was in turmoil over the secret she had stumbled upon and what it meant.

'What are your plans for tomorrow?' Sam asked, slurring his words. He was on his second mojito and it showed; he was clearly not used to the consumption of anything more than a small amount of alcohol which Alicia realised she could use to her advantage.

'I'm going flying tomorrow morning.'

'Flying? What, like a scenic flight around the island?'

'Sort of. I'll be flying myself though, after a check flight with a pilot here.'

'Flying *yourself*? Don't tell me you're a pilot as well as the most beautiful travel writer I've ever set eyes on?' Sam was impressed.

'I've got a private pilot's licence,' Alicia replied casually.

'Wow, you're amazing,' Sam said leaning even closer to her. 'As you know, I'm more of a nautical man myself, but it must be something to be able to fly. Are you renting an aircraft from the little aerodrome here in Negril?'

'That's the one,' Alicia nodded. She took a deep breath. 'Sam, you've been so kind to me over these last few days, how about I take you for a flight, sort of as a thank-you?'

Sam hesitated.

'I don't know,' he said uncertainly, 'I'm not really one for small aircraft.'

He was drunk. She had to persuade him. She placed a hand on his arm and looked into his eyes, leaning her face in towards his.

'Come on Sam, I think you'll love it.'

He was taking the bait. She leaned in closer still and brushed his lips with hers. Sam needed no further invitation and Alicia suddenly found herself locked in a deep kiss. When she had managed to disentangle herself, she caught his gaze.

'How about Thursday?'

'Okay Alicia, as it's you asking,' Sam smiled. 'I'm free in the afternoon from three-thirty.'

'Perfect,' Alicia beamed, 'I'll book the aircraft for four o'clock. Let's meet at your water-sports hut and walk up to the aerodrome together.'

'I can't wait,' Sam replied, nuzzling his face into her neck, which he began gently kissing. Alicia's hands found the buttons on his shirt and she began to undo them, one by one. She felt him stiffen before he continued kissing her neck. Soon, the shirt was undone and Alicia slid it off his shoulders before bringing her hands back to his chest and the front of his body. She felt his skin carefully, pretending to caress it. Sure enough, her fingers touched rough, raised scars, the kind one would expect from partial and full thickness burns that had healed with skin grafts and time. She pulled back gently and looked at his body in the candlelight. He clearly took care of himself; he was toned and muscular, but underneath the rash vest by day and the shirt by night, were hidden the scars from what had once been horrific burns.

Realising Alicia had discovered the disfigurement that he worked hard to hide, Sam pulled back.

'I had a diving accident many years ago,' he explained. 'The boat I was diving from had an electrical fault which caused a fire. I wasn't able to get my oxygen cylinder away from me quick enough and it burst into flames.'

'That's terrible,' Alicia said, shocked, 'were you okay?'

'I was burned quite badly — full thickness on some parts of my body — ended up needing surgery to have skin grafts taken from my legs, but I guess I'm lucky to be alive.'

'You are,' Alicia replied, 'and I'm lucky you're alive too.' Sam smiled, half-relieved and kissed her again.

'Shall we take this inside?' he murmured. Alicia pulled away gently. She glanced at her watch and feigned astonishment and alarm at the time.

'Sam, there's nothing I'd rather do more, but I need to be getting back otherwise I'll be falling asleep at the controls of the aircraft tomorrow morning.'

'I completely understand,' Sam replied, 'we can't have that, can we? What about dinner tomorrow night? I'll take you to one of my restaurants downtown.'

'Oh Sam, I'd love to, but my editor has arranged for me to dine at another place along the beach that he's desperate to include in the travel journal.'

Sam appeared genuinely disappointed.

'Why don't we have dinner on Thursday evening, after our flight?' Alicia suggested.

'You're on,' Sam replied enthusiastically, 'I'll look forward to it. And the flight as well, of course.'

'Great.' Alicia kissed him on the cheek and stood up. It was time to go. Sam walked her back to the beach and they said goodnight. As she made her way back to the motel, Alicia's mind was in turmoil. She had set the stage for a daring plan in order to discover the truth behind the Blackdeane murders, but her ability to successfully pull it off was another matter.

CHAPTER THIRTY-FOUR

While Alicia was eating steak and lobster with Sam at a nice restaurant overlooking a tropical beach and the Caribbean sea, Graymond fished the last slice of a pepperoni pizza, which had gone cold hours before, out of a greasy cardboard box. It was nearly one a.m. and Graymond shivered; his study felt colder than a meat locker. The temperature outside had dipped below zero and Graymond's heating wasn't programmed to run overnight. He took a bite of the pizza slice and threw the rest back into the box. His eyes were sore and red; he had been examining before and after pictures on his iMac from The Cosmetic Artistry Clinic for the last four hours and he was still only up to surnames beginning with the letter L. Wiping grease-covered fingers on his jeans, he clicked the mouse to move onto the next client in the database. He sighed and looked wearily at the screen, and then he froze.

A cold chill enveloped him, but not because of the ambient temperature of his study. It was an icy chill, which seemed to go right through him, as a November fog does the man who has arisen before the dawn to set off on some long journey. Graymond's hand shook as he held the mouse, not daring to let go lest the photographs and name in front of him should disappear in some way. He felt sick and he couldn't breathe as he stared at the screen in disbelief.

It can't be, he said out loud. *I don't understand. There must be some mistake.* But there was no mistake and Graymond knew that Alicia was in grave danger. He quickly saved the file, backing it up to his hard drive and the cloud, and picked up his cell phone. He took a picture of the iMac screen in front of him and then checked the call and message logs. There were no missed calls, no voice mails and no messages from Alicia. He dialled her number; it went straight to voice mail without even ringing. There was no point leaving a message, she wasn't picking up. If something had happened to her, he would never forgive himself for letting her go to Jamaica alone. She had gone for *him*, dammit. She was investigating the murders *he* had been framed for, and he believed her when she said it was no longer just about a sensational news story. He tried to stay calm, he tried to think clearly and logically, but he was reeling from the shock of what The Cosmetic Artistry database records had revealed and fearful about what might have happened to Alicia.

Graymond knew there was only one thing to do, but the risks were huge and there was so much at stake. Reluctantly, he dialled a number that he knew by heart. After three rings a male voice answered.

'Hello?'

'It's Gray Sharkey.'

'Gray? What *the* Gray Sharkey? No way! This is an unexpected pleasure. You still doing time or did they finally let you out?'

'They let me out. I'll fill you in with the details later, but right now I need a favour — and I need it fast.'

'It'll cost you.'

'I know that. And I'll pay.'

'Then I'm listening. What d'you need?'

The conversation lasted less than a minute. When it was over, Graymond took himself off to bed. He needed to get some rest before dawn.

Alicia arrived at Negril Aerodrome at nine o'clock sharp the following morning where she met Hal, the pilot with whom she would go for a brief check flight before being allowed to take the Piper Cherokee off by herself. It was a perfect flying day with clear skies and light winds and Hal was friendly enough. Once he was satisfied with the validity of Alicia's private pilot's licence and medical certificate, they collected their headsets from the flying club and checked out the aircraft together before climbing in. With Alicia in the left hand seat, Hal went through the cockpit checklist with her, making a few useful points specific to the aircraft. Throughout each stage of the start-up, taxy and take-off, Hal prompted Alicia with hints and tips regarding local information, such as the direction and height of the circuit pattern, certain instructions to expect from the air traffic control officer and how to respond, and areas to avoid overflying. When Alicia informed him that she would be taking a friend flying the following afternoon, he suggested a popular scenic route that she might like to consider, highlighting various waypoints on the paper chart and the GPS.

The check flight was a success. Alicia carried out a text book landing on returning to the aerodrome and Hal was happy that she was a safe and competent pilot who handled the aircraft well. It was time for her to take the Cherokee for a flight by herself. She felt nervous, but excited. As she took off from the runway for a second time, she reminded herself that the scenic flight she had originally planned would now be more of a reconnaissance mission. On the page on her kneeboard where she had made a note of the takeoff time, the pressure setting, and the wind speed and direction, she now made careful notes on the location of populated areas, fields, open spaces, roads and other significant infrastructure. She would borrow an aviation chart from the flying club which she would study that evening, cross-referencing it with the notes she had made during the flight. Nothing could be left to chance.

When she was happy with the information she had gathered, she returned to the aerodrome, joining the circuit pattern behind two other light aircraft. She lined up on final approach and informed the air traffic controller of her position. When the aircraft in front of her had vacated the runway, she was cleared for landing. It was another perfect touchdown and she taxied the aircraft to a parking spot between a Cessna 152 and a Piper Warrior. She climbed out and attached the pitot cover to the pitot head to prevent any insects from crawling inside and blocking its tiny tube. Hal had informed her that it would not be necessary to replace the aircraft cover which had shrunk over time from exposure to the sun and ultraviolet rays and no longer fitted the aircraft properly anyway. It was slung over the back seats.

Alicia walked to the Island Flying hut, with its bright yellow sign, in order to hand back the aircraft key to the man she had spoken to on her first visit to the aerodrome. His name was Mack, according to Hal.

'Enjoy yuh flight?' Mack asked, placing the key in a small lock box containing other aircraft keys.

'It's beautiful up there,' Alicia replied, 'I'll see you tomorrow at four.'

'See yuh then,' Mack replied. Alicia left him slowly repositioning himself in his chair. She headed for the beach where she made her way to Alpen's Beach Shack. She needed to know what the bartender had on Sam Leeburne.

Business was slow at Alpen's Beach Shack that afternoon which meant that Denzel, the bartender, was bored and in the mood to talk. Alicia ordered a rum punch which Denzel took his time to prepare before sliding it over the counter.

'Yuh find the fren you lookin' for?' he asked casually, remembering the photographs Alicia had shown him a few days before.

'Sadly no,' Alicia replied, shaking her head, 'however, I did find Sam Leeburne.'

Denzel raised an eyebrow and pulled a face of disgust.

'Tell me about him,' Alicia coaxed.

'Mek me tell you, him is a tiefing rass,' Denzel said angrily. At first he seemed reluctant to elaborate on the reason for his dislike of Sam, but after a sizeable tip for the rum punch appeared, he opened up a little and began talking.

Alicia learned that Sam Leeburne had arrived in Negril around fifteen years ago — Denzel couldn't remember exactly, but it was something like that anyway — presumably from the UK as he spoke with a British accent, though nobody ever found out exactly. Although he didn't flash any cash around, he didn't seem to be short of money and gradually bought up a number of clubs, bars and restaurants all over the island, as well as setting up his water-sports business, with some pretty expensive sailing craft and equipment. So far, Alicia couldn't see what Sam had done wrong, other than putting a few noses out of joint by entering the competition, however, Denzel was only just getting warmed up.

A number of his friends had worked for Sam over the years and he was not renowned as a kind, generous employer. He certainly wasn't popular with the locals and had put many other small bars and restaurants out of business. In addition it was widely rumoured that he took advantage of tax loop holes and off-shore bank accounts elsewhere in the Caribbean to avoid paying any tax to the Jamaican authorities. But that's not all, Denzel added; he was on a vitriolic roll now. Sam was heavily involved in the illegal drug trade and was rumoured to have his finger in the pie in every drug trafficking operation that took place on the island and throughout the Caribbean.

'Why has he never been exposed?' Alicia asked curiously.

'He's clever,' Denzel shrugged, 'an' he tek care to not get caught.'

There was a brief silence before Alicia spoke.

'Denzel, supposing you and your friends were given a chance to change things going on around here, without being mentioned or implicated in any way; would you take that chance?'

Denzel nodded slowly, but needed clarification as to what Alicia was implying. He also needed reassurance that he wasn't being put up to some shady operation that he wanted no part of. Alicia explained carefully and persuasively, emphasising what was in it for Denzel and his friends. His nodding became more enthusiastic. He had a small role to play which, in his opinion, wouldn't be a problem if Alicia could guarantee to take care of the rest. By the time they had finalised their plans, Denzel had a large grin over his face. Some locals entered the bar and he took their drinks orders, leaving Alicia to finish her rum punch. Sliding off the bar stool, she waved goodbye to him.

'Me see yuh later!' he called out cheerily with a wink. Alicia stepped out of the bar onto the beach, squinting in the bright afternoon sunshine. On her way back to the motel, she bought a plate of freshly caught sea-food from one of the crab shacks on the beach. She would have dinner in her room that night while she studied the aviation chart in preparation for her flight the following day. She had decided she would leave the internet search for Graymond's number until she had some positive progress to report. He was unable to join her in Jamaica and she didn't want to prematurely raise his hopes with her potential lead on Sam Leeburne and the stolen painting; he would only feel helpless, especially if he had lucked out with the clinic databases. By this time tomorrow, she would know more and she would contact him with something concrete.

CHAPTER THIRTY-FIVE

Sam Leeburne was giving last minute instructions to his young assistant as Alicia arrived at the Leeburne's Water-sports hut at three-thirty the following afternoon. He gave Alicia a kiss on the cheek as she approached and nodded to the young man.

'Not exactly sure he was listening to any of that,' he said, rolling his eyes.

'He seems smart enough to me,' Alicia replied, 'and he certainly appears to work hard.'

'Looks can be deceiving,' Sam said with a shrug. He put his arm around Alicia's waist and pulled her gently to him. 'And anyway, this afternoon's not about him; it's about you and me.'

'Of course it is,' Alicia forced a smile. 'Shall we go?'

'Absolutely,' Sam replied, 'I'm looking forward to seeing your pilot skills, Captain Alicia, although you'll have to excuse my ignorance when it comes to flying; I've only ever flown in a light aircraft once before.'

'Oh that's not a problem Sam,' Alicia said reassuringly, 'I'll take the greatest care of you and I guarantee you'll enjoy it.'

At the aerodrome, Mack struggled up from his chair and retrieved the key to the Piper Cherokee from the lock box, which he signed out to Alicia along with two headsets. As they walked across the apron to where the small aircraft was parked, Alicia spotted Hal checking out a four-seater Robin DR 400. He waved at her before turning back to the Robin.

Sam stood watching other aircraft taking off and landing as he waited for Alicia to carry out the external pre-flight checks. When they were complete, she climbed into the cockpit — accessible only through a door on the passenger's side on the right of the aircraft — and instructed Sam to climb in after her, reminding him not to step on the flaps on the rear edge of the wing. Alicia plugged his headset in and helped him secure his safety harnesses before she fastened her own. She went through a short passenger briefing which included emergency procedures and the location of vomit bags, should they be required. She then explained to Sam that she had a few more checks to complete before they would be on their way. Sam listened carefully and nodded nervously. He was a nautical man himself, he reminded Alicia, but the briefing made sense, in fact there were even a few similarities. He watched casually as Alicia finished her checks, inserted the key and started the engine. It spluttered to life with a roar, and after confirming that she had good oil and fuel pressure, Alicia requested a radio check and taxy instructions from the control tower.

As directed by the air traffic controller, Alicia manoeuvred the Cherokee to holding point Bravo where she completed the pre-takeoff checks before informing the tower that she was ready for takeoff. Immediate clearance was given to enter the runway, followed by further clearance to takeoff. The little aircraft lifted off smoothly and Alicia retracted the flaps before turning north.

'I thought we'd head up the coastline; it's stunning from up here,' she said to Sam.

He was gazing out of the window as they climbed, admiring the vivid blue of the sea, the dazzling white sand of the beach and the patchwork of lush, tropical vegetation further inland.

'I can see why you enjoy it,' Sam said, glancing across at her, 'the view's breathtaking.'

'You feel as if you're in your own little universe up here,' Alicia smiled, 'away from the rest of the world, just for a bit.'

The visibility was crystal clear in the cloudless sky and the majestic coastline seemed to stretch for miles. Alicia carried out some brief inflight checks and leaned the fuel mixture for cruising.

'Would you like to take the controls for a bit,' she asked Sam, 'and see how it feels to fly one of these things?'

'I'll pass,' Sam replied. 'I'm just here to enjoy the view.'

'Sure thing. Let me know if you change your mind.'

They followed the coastline north for about fifty miles at an average air speed of one hundred and ten knots before Alicia changed course and turned the aircraft onto a southeasterly heading, the new track taking them slightly inland where there were more fields and open spaces.

'You can see how populated the area next to the beach is, along that main highway, can't you?' Sam remarked.

'The tourists go for the beach,' Alicia replied. She checked her chart and the GPS; she was right where she wanted to be. As Sam looked out of his window to the West into the sun, Alicia reached down to the fuel tap on the left hand side of her seat and turned it quickly to the off position. She waited, with one eye on a field in the distance. After about twenty-seconds, the engine spluttered and stopped completely. Sam looked round in alarm.

'What's going on?' he asked.

'Not sure,' Alicia replied, looking at the instruments in consternation, 'the engine's cut out; I don't know why. Everything was running fine.'

They were flying at an altitude of three thousand feet. Alicia quickly adopted a glide angle and trimmed the aircraft controls. She could see her emergency landing field ahead, but she hoped it wouldn't be needed.

'Can't you do something?' Sam asked anxiously, 'try re-starting the engine or something?'

As the needle on the altimeter began dropping, indicating that they were descending, Alicia made some half-hearted attempts to restart the aircraft, knowing that as long as the engine was starved of fuel, all apparent efforts would be in vain. She appeared hesitant and unsure of what she was doing. The Cherokee continued to descend. It was eerily quiet without the noise of the engine.

'Alicia, talk to me, what's going on?' Sam said in alarm. He turned to face her.

'I don't know,' Alicia raised her voice in a panic, 'I've never had an engine failure before.' The ground below was getting closer by the second. They were at two thousand feet and still descending, with the altimeter needle winding backwards, like a crazy, broken clock.

'Shouldn't we make a Mayday call?' Sam sounded desperate.

'Yeah, I guess we — oh Sam, I don't know what to do, I can't think properly.'

'Alicia, get a grip,' Sam almost shouted, 'find somewhere to land and get this damn aircraft on the ground.'

They were at one thousand feet, still descending, the ground getting closer with each moment.

'Sam, I don't think I can,' Alicia began to cry. 'Oh gosh, I can't do this...' She collapsed into a fit of uncontrollable sobbing. Sam looked nervously out of the window. The altimeter needle passed nine hundred feet, eight hundred, seven hundred. The ground was very close now, coming up at them fast; it looked as though they were going to crash. Through the tears Alicia watched Sam closely. She still had full control of the aircraft and in a matter of seconds she would have to resume her composure and carry out a forced landing, or switch the fuel tap on and restart the aircraft, but there was very little time to...

Suddenly Sam grabbed the stick and put his feet on the rudder.

'I have control,' he said firmly.

'What?' Alicia glanced at him quickly.

'I said I've got control of the aircraft.'

'But — you said you don't know anything about flying.'

'I lied. I do. I used to be a pilot and a flying instructor. Luckily for you. What were you hoping to achieve, losing it like that? You could've got us both killed.'

Alicia quickly reached down and twisted the fuel tap back on to one of the fuel tanks. As the aircraft approached four hundred feet and Sam prepared for an emergency landing in the field ahead of them, Alicia turned the key and waited as the engine spluttered for a second before roaring into life. They were almost at one hundred feet as Alicia opened the throttle to full power and firmly took the controls from Sam, re-trimming the aircraft to climb away. Sam looked at her in astonishment.

'What the hell just happened?' he asked.

'You just demonstrated that you *do* know how to fly an aircraft, and you just admitted to being a pilot, that's what happened,' Alicia replied.

Sam's eyes narrowed.

'What?' he asked, with a confused look. Alicia didn't answer for a moment, while she focussed on the instruments as they regained altitude. When she was happy that the aircraft was settled into a comfortable cruise climb back up to three thousand feet, she turned to Sam.

'You *can* fly, can't you?' she said. 'Because you're not Sam Leeburne; you're Jimmy Keyes.'

Although Sam remained calm, a look of disbelief came over his face. His usually tanned complexion turned a shade of white as Alicia's words sunk in.

'What're you talking about?' he asked, although Alicia could see faint signs of defeat. He knew he had just given away the secret he had kept hidden for seventeen years and there was no taking it back. He was a pilot; he could fly.

'Who *are* you?' he asked suddenly, suspicion in his eyes as he turned to Alicia.

'Someone you should really start telling the truth to, because I know who *you* are Sam, or should I say Jimmy?' Alicia looked him in the eyes and spoke coldly. 'I know you faked your own death and framed Graymond Sharkey for your murder and the murder of Rory Conway. I know you retrieved the stolen paintings from the Cessna and sold five of them on the black market. I know you torched the Cessna, but got caught in the explosion yourself. Those burns on your body aren't from a diving accident; they're from the aircraft explosion at Blackdeane Airfield. I know you needed skin grafts for the burns and you had a facial reconstruction in order to change your appearance so you could start your new life as Sam Leeburne.'

Sam turned away, fixing his gaze on a point on the Jamaican coastline. Alicia watched the look of astonishment change to one of realisation.

'You're that crime reporter bitch who's sleeping with Graymond Sharkey, aren't you?' Sam said suddenly.

It was Alicia's turn to show a look of surprise. It didn't go unnoticed.

'Yeah, that's right, you're not the only one who knows stuff,' Sam said with a sneer.

'Then you may as well fill me in,' Alicia replied coolly, 'because there are a few gaps in the story I'm still not clear on.'

For a moment Sam teetered on which way to provide a response, but realising Alicia knew too much and that there was no way he could refute his ability to fly an aircraft, he suddenly appeared to make up his mind to adopt a different approach.

'So how did you find me?' he asked.

'It was thanks to a sugar bowl.'

'A *sugar* bowl?'

'Yeah, Mrs Davidson's sugar bowl. It said Negril, Jamaica on it. Sent her a little "wish you were here" present did you?'

Sam sighed.

'I knew it was a mistake from the beginning to get Landon involved.'

'*Landon?*' Alicia asked in surprise.

'Landon Davidson. I couldn't pull the whole thing off on my own; I needed an accomplice, or in Landon's case, a gofer. He was desperate to become an airline pilot, not that he was ever going to make it as one; hell, he barely managed to get his private pilot's licence. Anyway, the Davidsons didn't have the money to pay for his airline training, so I promised Landon that if he worked with me, he could have a cut of the profit to pay for flight training school and fulfil his dream. Of course, he spent all the money paying for it, but was too stupid or lazy to actually get the qualification and succeed. I've no idea what he's doing now; probably still working night shifts at that supermarket.'

'So how did he get the sugar bowl?'

'He visited me here in Negril a few years afterwards. He must've picked it up from the airport or some gift shop and taken it home as a present for his mother. I wasn't keen on the idea of him coming over, but he assured me that everyone would just think it was a holiday. Once I got my new face and new name, I wanted to break away from everything to do with Blackdeane, but Landon wanted to stay in touch, just in case there was ever any fallout from that night. There wasn't, of course, until Gray was released from prison and you two started asking questions. Landon called me a few days ago in a panic; said his mother knew something and was about to spill everything. I've no idea what she knew, but Landon said he'd take care of her.'

'He killed his own mother,' Alicia gasped in horror.

'I told him to frame Gray for it,' Sam continued. 'It made sense as he'd just been released from prison; I like to think there's no such thing as a coincidence.' He gave Alicia a contorted grin.

'Why did you do it Jimmy?'

'Don't call me that,' Sam snapped. 'My name's Sam.'

'Okay Sam, why d'you do it?'

'To get what was rightfully mine, of course.'

'The paintings were stolen; how were they rightfully yours?'

'Well, yes obviously they weren't *my* paintings, but they weren't Gray's either. Sure, Rory and I got a cut of the pie, but Gray always took the biggest slice with the cherry on top. Which wasn't fair. *I* was the one who did all the flying; *I* was the one doing the dangerous work ferrying the artwork all the way from the Channel Islands while *he* sat in his cosy little control tower waiting to load it in his truck and take it to a warehouse somewhere. I knew I deserved a greater share of the money, so I decided to rectify that.'

'By faking your own death and framing Gray for your and Rory's murder?' Alicia asked in disgust.

'I didn't kill Rory,' Sam replied. 'That was Landon's job while Gray was driving out to the runway to see why I'd stopped in the Cessna.'

Alicia glanced at their position on the GPS and steered the aircraft slightly off course from their return track to the aerodrome. There were still some things in Sam's story she wasn't sure about and she needed more time to keep him talking.

'Tell me what happened,' she said. Sam hadn't noticed the subtle track deviation.

'Oh it was all too easy really,' he said with an air of arrogance. 'I landed the Cessna and Landon drove out to the runway where we quickly unloaded the bags of stolen art into his truck. He drove back to the control tower via a little unlit side road, as per the plan, while I got back in the Cessna and covered myself with fake blood. During the flight I'd already applied some knife wounds with a bit of stage makeup, to look as if I'd been brutally stabbed, and then when I saw Graymond come out of the control tower and get in his truck to drive over to me, I splashed the fake blood all round the cockpit. It was great fun. When he got to the Cessna, he fell for it completely. It was quite dark and the blood looked so realistic. I pretended to be barely alive; he got in a total panic and radioed to Rory who didn't answer because he was probably being stabbed by Landon at that moment, if he wasn't already dead.'

'You're evil,' Alicia said in disgust.

Sam laughed.

'I like to think of myself as *creative*,' he said. 'Anyway, when Gray couldn't get Rory to reply, he jumped into the cockpit of the Cessna to take it back to the tower; he nearly killed us both by slamming the wing of the aircraft into the cab of his truck when he was turning, which would have completely ruined the plan, of course. I'll give him credit though, he wasn't concerned about getting his hands on the artwork; all he focussed on was saving my life. It was touching.'

'It's also what got him framed for your murder, you sonofabitch,' Alicia said angrily.

'Yes, he did play his part rather well,' Sam said scornfully. 'Anyway, while he went into the control tower to see what had happened to Rory, I was busy soaking the Cessna with aviation gasoline in preparation for the big explosion, all ready for when the police arrived.'

'The anonymous 999 call?'

'That was Landon too; we had to give the police a bit of a head start, make sure they pitched up at the right time. As soon as they arrived, I set the Cessna alight, but it didn't go up in flames as quickly as I'd hoped.'

'Is that how you got the burns?'

'A minor setback in the plan, I'm afraid Alicia. I went back to the aircraft to try to pour more aviation gasoline over it and stoke up the fire a bit, but I got too close and when the thing finally exploded, I was caught in the blast. I was burning and had to dowse the flames out myself before I got Landon to drive me to a friend who was an Emergency Room doctor. He had to go and get a bunch of burns dressings and fluids from a nearby hospital. He practically saved my life. Obviously I had to pay him a lot of money to keep quiet. I then had the skin grafts done privately at a cosmetic surgery clinic in London.'

'And you changed your face?'

'That too. Miraculously, my face wasn't as badly burned as my body, but I needed a new look. To the rest of the world, Jimmy Keyes was dead; someone had signed my death certificate and I'd even had my own funeral. I needed a whole new identity, including a new face. I chose one of the Harley Street clinics which was renowned for dealing with celebrity clients with the utmost discretion.'

'Your body was found at the scene,' Alicia said, puzzled. 'It was badly burned but you were positively identified by your dental records. How did you do that?'

'I don't have to fill you in with *all* the details, do I?' Sam sneered. He shrugged his shoulders. 'What does it matter? You're not going to make it out of this aircraft alive anyway. To answer your question, I befriended a homeless guy, an addict, and persuaded him to see a dentist associate of mine for X-rays and some dental work under the guise that he was getting some free dental treatment. On the day of the art heist, I shot him up with enough heroin to kill a horse and stuck him in the back of the Cessna for a little cross-Channel trip; it's a shame he was too dead to enjoy it. When I set the aircraft on fire, I hung around just long enough to make sure his body was practically incinerated and would only be identifiable by dental records. It was one of the reasons I went back to pour more aviation gasoline on the aircraft. I paid my dentist buddy very handsomely to provide the medical examiner with the homeless guy's X-rays as my own dental records. He hasn't worked as a dentist since; retired on some desert island somewhere I believe. We never stayed in touch.'

'But your blood was on Gray's knife, the one that Rory was stabbed with,' Alicia said suddenly.

'Oh yes, the knife,' Sam grinned, 'I'd forgotten about the knife. That was easy too. I stole it from Gray's house a couple of weeks before and made sure it was contaminated with my blood before I gave it to Landon to stab Rory with. Obviously Gray's fingerprints were on the knife whether he touched it in the control tower or not. But I've answered enough of your questions, Alicia. Now answer one of mine: you found me, Sam Leeburne, thanks to that stupid sugar bowl, but what gave away my true identity, other than the fact that I can fly an aircraft?'

'The fact that you're really Jimmy Keyes?' Alicia asked. 'Two things: your burns scars and the stolen painting hanging on your bedroom wall. I knew that the man who sold the artwork from the heist on the black market had been badly burned from the aircraft explosion; when I discovered those scars on your body the other night, I realised it was you. But I still couldn't work out how you were connected to the murders, other than that you were at the airfield that night. It was the painting that gave it away; that was your one big mistake. The painting's called Desert Town, isn't it? It's of a small town in the Sonoran Desert in Arizona at the turn of the twentieth century; a place called Phoenix. I realised why you had chosen to keep *that* painting above all the others, because it described *you*. *You* were the phoenix, rising from the ashes to your new life.'

'I've always loved that painting,' Sam replied. 'Out of the seven, I quietly sold five of them and gave one to Landon as well as his cut of the money to pay for his airline training, but I couldn't part with this one. It's such an impassioned piece of art, I thought it was beautiful; I had a cheap frame made for it and hung it on my wall. I didn't think anyone would ever recognise it as the genuine article and I thought I was far enough away from Blackdeane — geographically and, as the years went by, chronologically — that it would never be discovered.'

'You took a lot of risks, Sam,' Alicia said, 'you didn't really think you'd get away with them in the end, did you?'

'Sure, the stakes were high, but they paid off, didn't they?' Sam replied. 'I've had sixteen years living on a beach in paradise while Graymond Sharkey has been rotting in prison.' Turning to face Alicia, he gave her a sadistic smile and brought his hand up to caress the back of her neck. 'Alicia, I'm sorry to have to do this because I quite like you, but now that you know everything, I'm afraid I'm going to have to make sure that you don't tell.'

With his right hand, he released his safety harness allowing him to turn unrestricted in his seat. He brought both hands up to Alicia's neck and began to squeeze tightly. Quickly, Alicia felt underneath her kneeboard, attached to her right thigh, where she had concealed a small switchblade. As Sam applied more pressure on her neck, she flicked open the knife, but Sam, noticing it, released his grip and grabbed her wrist. He wrenched the knife away from her, sending it clattering to the floor of the cockpit, out of reach.

'Oops,' he said sarcastically. He brought his hands back up to her neck; his eyes were angry and wild. Alicia glanced ahead; in the moments of distraction, she realised that the Cherokee had started to descend to the right.

'Sam, I need to reset the trim or we'll end up in a spiral dive.'

Sam did not respond but continued to squeeze her neck tighter, his fingers wrapping themselves all the way around until they met and applied more pressure.

'Sam — *stop*,' she tried to shout, but she could hardly breathe, he had almost completely occluded her windpipe. She pressed the push-to-talk button to call the air traffic controller to alert him to the fact she was in trouble, but could barely speak.

'*Sam*,' she tried again but no noise came out of her mouth. He squeezed tighter and tighter. With blurred vision, Alicia looked at the altimeter which was winding itself steadily backwards again; the aircraft was descending, but this time she wasn't in control. It was the last thing she saw before she closed her eyes.

CHAPTER THIRTY-SIX

'Alicia. Alicia. *Alicia — wake up. Wake up, dammit!*' It was a familiar voice, over the noise of the aircraft's engine. Alicia slowly opened her eyes and tried to focus. She put a hand to her neck which was painful and felt swollen. Her breathing was shallow and her chest felt tight. She felt sick and dizzy and closed her eyes again, allowing her head to roll down onto her chest.

'*Alicia, open your eyes.*' It was the voice again, a voice she knew well, but it must be a dream. How could he be here, with her now?

'*Alicia, it's Gray.* Listen to me, wake up. I need you to fly this aircraft.'

Fly the aircraft, thought Alicia. She remembered now; she was in an aircraft. She slowly opened her eyes and looked in front of her, at the instruments of the Piper Cherokee. The altimeter read two thousand feet, but the needle was haphazardly lurching up and down . Likewise, the turn coordinator instrument indicated that the aircraft was acutely out of balance.

'*Alicia,* can you hear me?'

Alicia turned her neck slowly and painfully to her right. She gasped in shock and surprise. Next to her sat Sam Leeburne; his eyes were partially closed and he appeared to be unconscious. His arms and body were taped to his seat with duct tape and he had a large red graze on the side of his forehead. Leaning over the seat, stretching between Sam and Alicia to reach the aircraft controls in front of Sam, was Graymond.

'Gray?' Alicia said in disbelief.

'Alicia, are you okay?' Graymond asked. He didn't look at her but kept his gaze forward and outside the cockpit window, occasionally glancing at the instruments as he tried to maintain a semblance of straight and level flight.

'Gray, what are you doing here?'

'No time for that,' Graymond replied, tensely, 'we're nearly back at the aerodrome. Alicia, I need you to fly this thing and land it; I can't do it from here, I can't reach the controls properly, and Jimmy could wake up at any time.'

'Sure, yeah, okay,' Alicia said, slowly turning back to face forwards and placing her hands back on the controls. She felt dazed and confused.

'Alicia, do you have control?' Graymond asked.

'Yeah — yeah, I've got this. I have control,' Alicia replied. She stabilised the aircraft and brought the balance ball back into the middle of the turn coordinator.

'D'you see the runway up ahead?' Graymond asked. 'We need to start the descent.'

Alicia looked earnestly out of the window and spotted the runway, a strip of dark coloured tarmac in the middle of green. She glanced at the GPS; they had four miles to run. She started to descend and called the control tower. There were no other aircraft in the circuit and permission was given for a straight-in approach, if they wanted it. Alicia accepted and continued the descent. Three miles to run. She started her pre-landing checks, switched on the fuel pump and set the fuel mixture to rich.

'Gray, you're not strapped in,' she said with concern.

'I'll be fine, just don't screw up the landing,' Graymond replied.

Alicia put the flaps down in stages, which allowed for a greater descent at a slower speed, and informed the tower that she was on final approach with less than two miles to run. She was cleared to land and, as the Cherokee glided onto the runway she gently pulled the stick back as they touched down. It was a textbook landing and the tower gave taxy instructions to the apron. As they approached, Alicia caught sight of four police cars, parked haphazardly, with flashing blue lights and uniformed police.

'Oh crap,' Graymond said under his breath.

'I think you'll find they're not here for you, Gray.'

'What makes you so sure?'

'Trust me on this one.'

A marshal stepped out in front of the police cars and signalled for Alicia to bring the Cherokee to a full stop. As they approached the group of law enforcement officers, Alicia stepped gently on the brakes. She switched off the comms box and cut the fuel mixture, shutting down the aircraft. The engine died and the police officers ran toward the Cherokee shouting instructions. At that moment, Jimmy opened his eyes and appeared to regain consciousness. He looked around in bewilderment.

'What's going on? Where are we?' he said. He tried to move but he was firmly secured to the seat with the duct tape and no amount of wriggling would set him free. He looked from the approaching police officers to Alicia and back again.

'I've arranged a ride home for you,' Alicia said sweetly. 'Your new home that is; a cosy cell in a Jamaican prison.'

'What?' Jimmy said in a low voice. 'I'm not going anywhere with the police. You've got nothing on me, Alicia.'

'Sorry Jimmy — spoiler alert,' Alicia undid the top three buttons of her shirt to reveal a small microphone and a wire, 'I think I have plenty on you, but don't worry, the police aren't here about that.'

'What are they here for then?' Jimmy asked, a frightened look coming into his eyes. An unsmiling officer stepped up to the Cherokee and knocked firmly on the passenger door.

'Sam Leeburne, open the door please, and step out of the aircraft immediately.'

'What is this?' Jimmy said to Alicia.

'Sam Leeburne, open the door now,' the officer said again.

'Do I look like I can open the door?' Jimmy shouted angrily, struggling against the duct tape. The officer leaned over the wing and peered through the aircraft window at him.

'Just a moment, officer.' A voice came from the back seat. Graymond reached for the door handle beside Jimmy, opened the door and pushed it towards the police officer who stepped up onto the wing of the aircraft. He looked taken aback to see Jimmy taped to the seat. Jimmy glanced defiantly at the police officer before turning his head to look at the man who sat behind him. For the first time in seventeen years their eyes met. It was the first time since Graymond had cradled Jimmy's head in his hands, shaking at the sight of his best friend, wounded and bleeding. He recalled the hopelessness and despair with which he had tried to save him, the desperate way he had dragged him out of the Cessna onto the tarmac, a trail of blood behind them.

As Graymond looked steadily into the cold, remorseless eyes of Jimmy Keyes, his feelings of hatred and anger were deadened by the knowledge that the past could not be undone. From the first moment that he had seen Jimmy's posthumous photographs on the clinic database, he had been through in his mind what he would say and do when they met. The anger had gained momentum during the flight from London; he wanted to inflict as much pain as he could on the man he had once called a friend, but who had ruthlessly betrayed him; he wanted to see him suffer bitterly, he wanted to hear him cry out in agony and beg for forgiveness. He wanted to pay him back for the seventeen years of his life that had been lost, wasted, destroyed, and that could never be reclaimed.

In that moment, however, Graymond knew it wasn't the way. The past was behind him and could never be changed, but he had a future, and Jimmy could never take that from him.

'You finally found me,' Jimmy said coldly, his steely gaze fixed steadily on Graymond.

'Looks that way,' Graymond replied calmly. 'What happened to you Jimmy? Was it all really worth it?'

Jimmy shrugged. His conscience had died many years before, and along with it the knowledge of right and wrong, and the ability to feel joy and happiness.

'I guess we'll never know,' he replied with the emotion of a dead man. 'Is that it, Gray? Is that all you're gonna say after all this time?'

'I've got nothing to say to you, Jimmy.' Graymond said, looking away. He nodded at the officer who had been signalling to one of his men to pass him a knife to cut Jimmy free from the duct tape.

'I see you've already got him in custody,' he remarked, looking at Graymond and Alicia. He cut the tape and turned Jimmy around in his seat, roughly pulling his arms behind him and attaching a pair of hand cuffs.

'Get out,' the officer barked.

'What are the cuffs for?' Jimmy asked sullenly, as he stepped down off the wing onto the ground, assisted by two other officers.

'Let's see,' the first police officer pretended to refer to his notebook, 'we'll start with possession of illegal substances…'

'What? Where?' Jimmy snapped.

'Cocaine. Found in your beach house this afternoon.'

'I don't know anything about that; I've been set up.'

'We'll discuss that at the police station, shall we Mr. Leeburne?'

'I hope you had a warrant to search my property,' Jimmy said furiously.

'We had a report from a concerned resident of a disturbance and suspicious activity at your beach house. When we went inside to check things out, guess what? We found the cocaine in full view, just sitting right there on your kitchen work surface.'

'But — how?' Jimmy looked round at Alicia as the police led him away. 'You set me up,' he shouted over his shoulder, 'you'll be sorry.'

'I doubt that very much,' Alicia said to Graymond, rubbing her neck, 'he'll soon find he's got other problems a lot bigger than me.'

'Such as?' Graymond asked from the back seat.

'Sharing a cell with a bunch of inmates who know he's responsible for a ruthless drug trafficking ring. He also put a large number of locals out of business after buying up half the bars and clubs in Negril. He's wanted for tax evasion from his earnings, most of which are stashed in off-shore accounts on other Caribbean Islands. And then there's the shocking way he treats his employees: everyone from the young assistant at his water-sports business to the head waiter at The Leeburne Room. I suspect the worst thing for Jimmy though, will be the fact that he's an arrogant, rich, white boy. The authorities have been wanting something on him for ages, and now they've seized their chance, they won't be going easy on him.'

As the last of the police cars drove away, the marshal signalled for Alicia to taxy to the parking spot between the Cessna 152 and the Piper Warrior. She checked the area in front of the aircraft near the propeller was clear before restarting the engine. Nodding an acknowledgement to the marshal, she taxied slowly across the apron and onto the grass where she lined up the Cherokee neatly between the two aircraft, cut the fuel mixture and removed the key. They sat in silence for a few minutes before Alicia removed her headset, unfastened her safety harness and turned in her seat to Graymond. Her neck was sore and she had to turn her whole body to face him.

'So tell me Gray, how on earth did you end up in Jamaica, hidden underneath a cover on the backseat of a small aircraft?'

'It's a long story,' Graymond replied, 'but I guess the short version is that I didn't see why you should be having all the fun out here while I was stuck in cold, rainy England.'

'I'm glad you're here,' Alicia said smiling.

'I am too,' Graymond replied, 'but I think we've done enough flying for today.'

'I'm not sure you and flying are ever a good combination,' Alicia said laughing as they climbed out of the aircraft. They handed the key to Mack and walked back to the motel, side by side.

CHAPTER THIRTY-SEVEN

Dinner that evening was at Alpen's Beach Shack at a table over-looking the beach and the sea beyond. As Graymond and Alicia tucked into plates of jerk chicken with rice, plantains and vegetables, Denzel the barman appeared by the table to announce that dinner and drinks were 'on de house'. Glancing at Graymond, Alicia asked if they might have something non-alcoholic that evening. No problem, Denzel informed them, he was renowned for the best virgin cocktails on the island. He winked at Alicia.

'What's that all about?' Graymond asked with intrigue.

'Denzel and I had a mutual problem that needed taking care of; we formed a joint task force, which I think we can agree was quite successful.'

'Jimmy Keyes?'

Alicia nodded. She explained to Graymond that after Denzel had told her about Jimmy — or Sam, as he had reincarnated himself — and his involvement with drug trafficking, tax evasion, threatening local businesses and being an asshole in general, she had suggested a way that they might finally be able to take him down. At first, Denzel had been reluctant to come onboard; Sam was a problem that had bothered the locals, including the police authorities, for a long time, but he had always meticulously covered his tracks and been one step ahead of anyone looking to expose him. When Alicia explained that she would need a police escort for him when she arrived back at the aerodrome after their flight, Denzel was listening. It took little to convince him when Alicia described what she had in mind.

While she had Sam Leeburne safely out of the way, Denzel's man Vincent let himself into Sam's property through the security gate, the four digit security code having been provided to him courtesy of Alicia, who had memorised it from the night she accompanied Sam to his beach house. After letting himself in through the balcony door, Vincent then switched off Sam's intruder alarm with another security code which had again been noted by Alicia. Vincent was an ex-con. He'd been inside a few times, mostly for drugs-related offences and petty theft. Vincent had contacts and it therefore took no more than a quick telephone call to a brother who fixed him up with a few bags of cocaine, which Vincent planted in Sam's kitchen.

Once the cocaine had been planted, Vincent's girl gave a quick anonymous call to the police, posing as the concerned resident reporting a disturbance at Sam's house, giving the police the opportunity they needed to check out the property. The cocaine was all they needed to bring Sam in for questioning and provided a useful opening to explore the other avenues of the questionable business dealings he was involved with. In return for the assistance provided by Denzel and his associates, Alicia had spoken to a travel journalist contact and Alpen's Beach Shack was in line to receive a very favourable review in a prestigious travel magazine, with special reference to Denzel's infamous cocktails.

'The anonymous phone call to the police didn't work out so well for him this time, did it?' Graymond observed. 'So what will happen to him?'

'The Jamaican authorities have him in custody for now,' Alicia replied, 'and once I've got his recorded confession to one of my contacts in the CID back home, they'll be wanting to speak to him too, on the subject of conspiracy to murder and art theft, amongst other things — that's if he survives the Jamaican prison, of course.' She grinned. 'But anyway Gray, you still haven't answered my burning question: how did you get to be in the back of the Cherokee?'

Graymond took a moment to consider his reply. He took a bite of his chicken and chewed slowly, savouring the spices and flavours of the traditional Jamaican cuisine.

'You know Alicia, after seventeen years of the monotony of prison food, I'll always be thankful for dinners as good as this.' He finished his mouthful and put down his fork. 'The answer to your question lies in the database of archived records belonging to The

Cosmetic Artistry Clinic. I was almost at the point of giving up when I found a medical record under the name of Sam Leeburne. Sam was a patient who had received skin grafts for extensive burns to his body. He had also undergone a radical facial reconstruction. In addition, the name rang a bell: it was the name of the man you told me you had met out here. As alarming as those things were, nothing could prepare me for the worst shock of all: the before photograph was of my old friend Jimmy Keyes. There was no mistaking it.

'What I didn't understand was that all the dates of the surgery were *after* his death. It didn't make any sense to begin with; how could anyone have surgery when they were already dead? I had seen him covered in blood and fighting for his life that night at the airfield; his body was found in the aircraft wreckage and he was positively identified by his dental records. I didn't have answers to those questions at that time, but I knew that somehow, he had pulled off a pretty clever trick and had become Sam Leeburne. To make matters worse, you had suddenly disappeared off the grid and I was worried something had happened to you.'

'Sorry about that,' Alicia said apologetically, 'I really should have made more of an effort to contact you after I lost my cell phone.'

'Don't worry,' Graymond replied, 'I still would have come anyway.'

'How did you get your passport sorted so quickly? I thought it was going to take weeks for the Probation Service to grant you permission for foreign travel.'

'Yeah, about that,' Graymond shifted uncomfortably in his seat.

'Gray,' Alicia said slowly, 'how did you get here?'

'While I was in prison, I made a good friend. He was in for a whole bunch of stuff, but his specialty was forgery; passports, driving licences, official documents, anything you wanted. I knew it was risky, but I didn't have a choice. He worked half the night and set me up with a passport, along with a respectable background story and records, if the authorities did any digging.'

'You're kidding, right?' Alicia asked incredulously.

'Afraid not,' Graymond replied, 'I'm actually Mark Harvan, a businessman taking a winter water-sports vacation. Things were pretty relaxed with security and customs because I got two of my pilots to fly me here in one of the Gulfstreams and we flew into a private strip rather than one of the bigger airports on the island. The pilots were more than happy to take one of the jets for a little transatlantic test-flight, and what better place to come than a tropical island for a couple of days. I've promised them they'll be back with their families for Christmas and they're getting holiday bonus pay, so they're not complaining.'

'How did you know about my flight with Jimmy?' Alicia asked.

'As soon as we landed, I took a cab to your motel in Negril, but you weren't there and I still couldn't reach you on your cell. The motel desk clerk thought you'd mentioned something about taking a flight from the aerodrome this afternoon, so I headed over there as fast as I could. Mack, the guy in the hut, told me you'd booked out the Cherokee from four p.m. to take a friend flying. I wasn't sure whether to confront you and Jimmy there and then or to get in the back of the aircraft, hide under the cover and come along for the ride.'

'I can't believe you were in the back the whole time,' Alicia laughed.

'I think I nearly died of heat stroke under that cover,' Graymond smiled, 'and I'm sorry I didn't rescue you sooner, before Jimmy got his hands round your neck.'

'Gray, you were right on cue, it's only a few bruises,' Alicia said, putting a hand to the red marks on her neck.

Denzel was back at the table with another round of fresh drinks, the cocktail glasses decorated with a dazzling array of coloured umbrellas and fruit garnishes. He hugged Alicia, shook Graymond's hand warmly, thanked them for everything, and promised them a warm welcome and more drinks on the house the next time they were on the island. The steel drum band returned to the stage after a short break and began a lively medley of Christmas carols. Graymond and Alicia clinked glasses and drank to the future, starting from that moment on.

Later that night, they strolled along the beach, hand-in-hand, admiring the moon and the stars in the dark night sky; their light seemed more resplendent on tropical shores than at home. The palm trees sashayed gently in the warm breeze and occasionally a wave crept up onto the soft sand in front of them as they walked. Graymond breathed in the clear night air, taking in every moment of the feeling of freedom, as he had promised himself he would, on the first day he left prison. He glanced at Alicia.

'So you finally got your story,' he said, 'the final chapter of the first case you ever worked on.'

Alicia stopped and turned to look up at him.

'Yes, I got my story,' she replied. Her eyes studied his face. 'But you should know that even if I never got to write that last chapter, it wouldn't change anything anymore.'

'So, you're saying…' Graymond spoke cautiously, still not daring to believe that he would hear the words from Alicia that he had dreamed of hearing since the night of their first meeting.

'I'm saying that the way I feel about you Gray, is different to how I've ever felt about anyone before. If I never got that story, I'd still want you as much as I do now, and nothing will ever change that, if you feel the same.'

Graymond gazed at Alicia for a long moment before replying.

'You know I want you, Alicia. I've always wanted you, ever since you walked into my life and ruined my Persian rug that very first night.'

He kissed her. He had intended it to be gentle and playful, slowly working up to something more intense, but he couldn't hold back his emotions any longer. It was as if the floodgates of his feelings had opened and there was no stopping them. He kissed her deeply and passionately, and she responded with an energy which only fuelled his desire even more.

He pulled back briefly.

'Don't stop Gray,' Alicia murmured, her eyes still closed and her lips parted.

'I'm only just getting started,' he whispered. The night was warm and the beach was deserted. He pulled her closer to him and kissed her again.

CHAPTER THIRTY-EIGHT

It was still early and not yet light on Christmas Eve morning when the Gulfstream touched down on the runway at Blackdeane Airfield. They had cleared UK customs without a hitch at a larger airport twenty minutes earlier before becoming airborne once more for the short flight to Blackdeane. There was a thin mist covering the ground and a pre-dawn hush over the airfield as Graymond and Alicia carried their cases down the steps of the private jet, thanked the pilots and made their way past the clubhouse to Graymond's truck, parked where he had left it two days previously. They drove back to his house in silence. Alicia had been in touch with her contact in the CID, to inform him of the recorded confession she had obtained from Jimmy Keyes and which she would deliver to him as soon as possible.

Following their discussion, he had called back soon after to inform her that the Art and Antiques Unit of the Metropolitan Police was liaising with the Jamaican authorities to arrange for the return of Desert Town from Jimmy's beach house. The Unit had a man in the Caribbean who had already been to the house to inspect the artwork and who had confirmed that it was indeed the original, painted by Kleid Kaufman in 1905. In addition, the stolen art team were onboard to renew their efforts to trace the other six stolen paintings.

From another source, Alicia had also learned that Landon Davidson had been taken into police custody where he had confessed to the murder of his mother, Dora Davidson. The toxicology report from the post mortem had revealed high levels of diazepam and the muscle relaxant agent rocuronium in her bloodstream. The medical examiner had found a puncture wound in her left arm, confirming that the rocuronium had been injected just prior to her death. Initially, Roy and Landon Davidson, and Kevin Mason had appeared to have solid alibis confirming that they were attending an event at the Blackdeane Golf Club that evening. Security footage, however, showed Landon leaving the club in Kevin's car, returning forty-five minutes later. Despite wearing a baseball cap, his face was picked up by a traffic camera, enabling the police to make a positive ID. The time he was away from the golf club matched the time of death.

'Why d'you think he killed her?' Alicia asked Graymond.

'She probably had a pretty good idea that he was involved with it all somehow,' Graymond shrugged. 'She was utterly convinced of my innocence the whole time I was in prison and now I know why. Maybe she knew where he was on the night of the murders, or became suspicious of how he got the money to fund his airline training. And then there was his trip to Jamaica, a complete incongruity with his usual holidays which were always taken in a caravan in Great Yarmouth with a couple of old school friends. She must've known all that time, but never confronted him with it. Perhaps she was afraid to know the truth and wanted to protect him as he was her son.'

'What do you think she was going to tell us?'

'I guess that's something we'll never know,' Graymond replied. 'Perhaps Landon never knew either, but he realised that whatever it was could potentially expose him as a murderer. He must've been within earshot of our conversation for some time on the day that we visited his mother. He already knew that we'd been asking questions; he'd been watching me since the day I got out of prison. On the first night, when I was walking by the airfield on my way home, I had a feeling that I wasn't alone. He was there then, in the undergrowth, having followed me from his parents' cottage where I'd stopped to pick up my house keys.'

Graymond pulled up outside the wrought iron gates to his house and they opened slowly.

'I'll grab your mail,' Alicia said, jumping out of the truck and stepping over to the mailbox, set into the wall. When she climbed back in with a bundle of post, she looked pale.

'Alicia, what the hell's wrong?' Graymond asked as he accelerated through the gates and up the driveway. Alicia didn't reply, but continued staring down at the main picture on the front of a local newspaper that she had retrieved from Graymond's mailbox.

'It was him,' she said quietly. She was looking at a picture of a man being escorted to a police car, flanked by two uniformed police officers. He was wearing a navy baseball cap pulled down low over his face, which was turned slightly away from the cameras in an attempt to remain unidentified. It was the same face that had haunted her dreams at night and her thoughts by day. Strangely, the face had a look of utter relief, almost resignation. The first time she had seen this look, it had been relief in the knowledge that he had successfully framed another man for a murder that he had committed. But this time, Alicia knew it was relief that he would no longer have to live in fear; fear that the truth, which had been buried for seventeen years, would one day be revealed. It was the face of Landon Davidson.

Graymond was looking inquisitively at the picture.

'Landon?' he asked, confused.

'Yeah, he wore a navy baseball cap in the courtroom throughout your trial. He had it pulled down low over his eyes, like in this picture. It's why I didn't recognise him when we met him a few days ago. When I caught a glimpse of his face in the courtroom on the day you were convicted; it was that same look.' She pointed to the photograph.

They got out of the truck, unloaded their luggage and went inside, Alicia still staring down at Landon's half obscured face.

'There's one more thing that still puzzles me,' Alicia said thoughtfully.

'Tell me,' Graymond replied putting his arms around her and kissing her on the forehead.

'What did Landon do with his painting? It's the only one that was never accounted for. Do you think he sold it?'

Graymond smiled before replying.

'No, I don't think so, but I'm pretty confident I know where it is now.'

'Where?' Alicia asked in surprise.

'Remember in the Davidsons' living room there was a large aerial photograph hanging above the mantlepiece in a cheap frame?'

'Yes?'

'It was the only thing that had changed in that room for seventeen years. I'll bet you anything that the aerial photograph is concealing something underneath.'

'Landon's stolen painting?'

'Exactly. I think it's been hanging on the wall in the Davidsons' cottage all this time; a painting worth millions of dollars. I guess Landon didn't know what else to do with it, and so he hid it practically in plain sight. To everyone else, it was just a framed aerial photograph, but Landon knew its true value.'

'I think that about wraps up my sensational news story,' Alicia smiled suddenly at Graymond and hugged him tightly. Graymond held her close to him before pulling back a little.

'Alicia, why don't you take a shower while I fix us some breakfast? And then we'd better go Christmas tree shopping; it is Christmas Day tomorrow, after all!'

Alicia kissed Graymond on the cheek before she disappeared upstairs, leaving Graymond alone in the kitchen. As he filled the coffee machine, he picked up the newspaper. The headlines were full of Landon's arrest and he was quickly bored; he turned over the next few pages which contained the usual media reports of the world in 2016. He was almost up to speed with the twenty-first century, he thought to himself proudly. He turned another page; it was the announcements page listing births, deaths, marriages, engagements and other appointments. He was about to move on, when something caught his eye. It was one sentence, under the heading "Text for the Day". It was from the Bible, in the book of Amos, chapter five verse twenty-four. It read: "But let justice roll on like a river, righteousness like a never-failing stream!". They were the same words he had read that day in the prison library. And Graymond knew, seventeen years later, that justice had finally been done.

Printed in Great Britain
by Amazon